MAN FACING WEST

MAN FACING WEST

DON GAYTON

thistledown press

Thistledown Press Ltd.
633 Main Street
Saskatoon, Saskatchewan, S7H 0J8
www.thistledownpress.com

Library and Archives Canada Cataloguing in Publication

Gayton, Don, 1946-
Man facing west / Don Gayton.
ISBN 978-1-897235-79-9

1. Gayton, Don, 1946-. 2. Ecologists--Canada--Biography. 3. Authors,
Canadian (English)--20th century--Biography. 4. War--Moral and
ethical aspects. 5. Pacifists--Canada--Biography. I. Title.

QH31.G32A3 2010   C818'.603   C2010-905542-X

Cover photograph: stock.xchng.com
Cover and book design by Jackie Forrie
Printed and bound in Canada

Mixed Sources
Cert no. SW-COC-001271
© 1996 FSC
FSC

 Canada Council   Conseil des Arts
for the Arts   du Canada

 SASKATCHEWAN
ARTS BOARD

 Canadian   Patrimoine
Heritage   canadien

Thistledown Press gratefully acknowledges the financial assistance of the Canada
Council for the Arts, the Saskatchewan Arts Board, and the Government of Canada
through the Canada Book Fund for its publishing program.

ACKNOWLEDGMENTS

I would like to thank the staff at Thistledown for their editorial professionalism; Seán Virgo for his passionate attention to the content of this book; and my wife, Judy, who is both partner in this voyage and exquisitely sensitive to dangling participles.

CONTENTS

Prologue

THE CONFERENCE AUDITORIUM WAS NEARLY FULL, a cross-section of Alberta hands-on types; range managers, agronomists, biologists, and some oilpatch people. They had all listened politely to the morning's upbeat presentations on land and resource stewardship and, now with the dissenting view of an ecologist, I was taking the podium. Are we, I asked, overspending our natural capital? Of course we are, I answered rhetorically, but we don't like to be reminded of it. I went on to list carbon dioxide increase, the loss of wild salmon stocks, the accumulation of toxins in our rivers and bodies. I described the accelerating loss of natural habitats, the decrease in soil productivity, the slow winking out of old-growth forests. The list goes on and on, and we all know that list, most of us only too well. So, I told the Alberta audience, we are in the curious position of knowing the answer in detail, but not wanting to ask the question.

As I built my case, I saw the audience's looks of growing apprehension. I felt a wave of déjà vu, transporting me back to undergraduate Botany class, circa 1969, when I gave an uninvited speech on toxic defoliants being used by the US Army in Vietnam. Even though separated by fifty years and an international border, the looks of consternation I saw in the Calgary auditorium were identical to those of my fellow students in that long-ago Botany class. The crafted speech I was giving now, on tar sands and petroleum overdependence, strangely mirrored my own youthful sentences on the aerial spraying of those distant jungles. During both talks I felt the same sense of turning on a select guild that had reluctantly accepted me. I was the mole, the disruptive heretic. But as I plowed on through my Calgary speech, I sensed another identical feeling from 1969, that these were things that needed to be said, and rudeness be damned.

That fifty-year journey, from Vietnam forward, forms a large portion of this narrative. Personal passions tend to telescope into each other over time. In my case, resistance to an unjust war transformed into a passion for rural development and then morphed again into an all-consuming bond to natural landscapes. Each new passion retained a strong flavour of its predecessor. If I were to assign a compass bearing to those telescoping passions, they would point mostly to the dry western half of this continent.

This is a roughly chronological work, but is neither memoir nor autobiography. Various voices and styles are interwoven. I believe the true and ancestral home of information — be it about politics, development or ecology — is in story, so that form is honoured here. And often, stories about others illuminate far better than a narrative about oneself.

This book is an attempt to capture my three enduring passions momentarily on its pages, and hold them up to the light. It can be thought of as literary catch and release, for which you do not need a license.

Flag Day

THE WOLF DEN WAS A CONVERTED garage at the back of a suburban home in our neighbourhood. The Den's ceremonial campfire was made of real pine branches nailed together to form a kind of small tepee. Our Cubmaster, Mr. Kirby, had stapled red cellophane around the inside of the tepee and put a light fixture in it, so when we had Circle, we Cubs were bathed in a reddish glow. At Circle we learned the mysteries of Webelos, and then we worked in the Den on projects having to do with outdoor lore, like building birdhouses from pre-cut plywood kits. Somehow, the woodcraft did not correspond very well with what I watched my father do on family camping trips.

When one of us finished a project, Mr. Kirby, who had a buzz cut and worked in aerospace, would award a little cloth badge during our ceremony, which our moms could then sew onto the sleeves of the blue, scout uniforms. The badges were tipped in yellow, which matched the flashy, yellow scarves we wore around our necks. The scarf was held in place by a wonderful, brass wolf's-head ring. I was intrigued with the uniforms and caught up in the general excitement of the Wolf Den, but was poor at completing projects. As my fellow Cub Scouts accumulated badges all the way down to their elbows, mine petered out just below shoulder level.

Mr. Kirby's backyard served as our ceremonial ground. Every meeting, before we went into the Den, two senior Cubs would attach the American flag to the wooden flagpole in the centre of the yard, and we would recite the Pledge of Allegiance. Even though fifty years have passed, the events of one Saturday afternoon on that ceremonial ground still burn in my memory.

After our flag-raising and Pledge ceremony, the Cubmaster was called into the house unexpectedly, so a dozen unsupervised Cubs milled around the yard, with the usual adolescent pushing and shoving. The knot of tangled boys eventually bumped up against the flagpole, which was about twelve feet high. "Dare anyone to climb it and touch the top," someone said, probably one of the older Cubs. I was quite deficient in Projects but pretty physical, so here was a way to gain some unofficial standing in the Pack. I stepped up and spit on my hands. Grabbing the pole as high up as I could, I began to shinny up. My high-top sneakers gave me pretty good purchase on the pole, and soon I was working my way past the flag, which flapped and fluttered in my face. Suddenly, there was a sharp report, like a gunshot, followed by the sound of splitting wood. Wrapped in red, white, and blue, I experienced a brief, exhilarating moment of free flight, and then landed heavily on the ground.

When I came to, I opened my eyes to bright, California sunlight, mingled with the stars of the flag and the vivid electric stripes of shock. The entire Cub Pack was staring down at me, frozen and open-mouthed. An unearthly, horrified silence prevailed. I had just broken the fundamental vow of every American — to never, ever let our flag touch the ground.

Pack meeting was cancelled, and we were told to wait in the Wolf Den while the damage was repaired, and Mr. Kirby consulted with the Regional Cub Council. I sat by myself while my fellow Cubs conversed among themselves in whispers. A tectonic shift had occurred, and I was alone on a new continent. George Washington, Patrick Henry, and Iwo Jima were now on a distant shore.

We were called to assembly in front of the repaired flagpole, lining up in our usual formation. Mr. Kirby called me forward. He was red-faced and angry. Using his wife's sewing scissors, he methodically removed the few pathetic badges from my uniform, and drummed me forever out of Pasadena Cub Scout Troop #32.

Yosemite Landscapes

THE BACK OF THE STATION WAGON was filled, right to the roof liner, with our standard family camping inventory; tent, cots, sleeping bags, cookware, fishing rods. The 1954 Chevrolet Woody was just the right size for the four of us, the dog, and the gear. I worked like a dervish to help finish the unpacking, so I could be free to race around and explore the campground. I had my genuine Davy Crockett coonskin cap on, which gave me a boost of outdoor energy. First, we laid out and staked down the big canvas tent and, as always, I volunteered to crawl into the flattened structure and erect the wooden centrepole. In those few seconds of pitch darkness, I inhaled the signature odours of western camping: waterproofed canvas; dry pine needles; and crushed ants. My father had built a nifty plywood box with drawers to hold our cooking utensils and dry food; one side of the box was hinged, and it dropped down to become a tiny kitchen counter. At suppertime the two-burner Coleman folding stove would come out, and then later, Dad would perform the holy of camping holies, the lighting of the Coleman lantern. The lantern had its own custom-built box too, with separate compartments for the felt-lined funnel, the white gas container, and the fragile asbestos mantles.

This trip was to the Yosemite Valley, and as I began my campground exploration, I caught glimpses of towering mountains and sweeping rock faces through the pines. Children have little basis for separating the ordinary from the extraordinary, so I took the breathtaking geology of El Capitan and Half Dome for granted. After all, we had already been to Carlsbad Caverns and the Redwoods, and trips to the Grand Canyon and Hoover Dam were in the works, so vacation landscapes of high drama were a given for me. And besides, I was far more interested in finding chipmunks for the dog to chase, and picking out the best fishing spot.

It was not until I was much older that I began to realize the significance of the Yosemite landscapes. Ansel Adams memorialized them in his black and white photographs, which I first saw in his 1979 book, *Yosemite and the Range of Light*. But, it took a chance bookstore encounter with a forgotten 19th-century American landscape painter to show me the real emotive power of Yosemite.

Albert Bierstadt (1830–1902) trained as an artist in Europe, became a member of the Hudson River School of painters, and eventually fell in love with the landscapes of the West. Like Adams, he visited Yosemite over and over, painting it in every conceivable light and mood. Many of his canvases were huge, to match the landscapes he worked with. Sky is always a major element in a Bierstadt painting; glowing, burnished shades of light emanate from the clouds. In his evening paintings, the light springs from the very air itself. Such was his preoccupation with light and sky that Bierstadt was often referred to as a "luminist" painter. In his Yosemite canvases, the valley bottom of the Tuolumne River is peaceful, almost pastoral; in many of the paintings, a five-point buck deer poses regally in the middle ground, guarding his doe and fawn. But then the paintings sweep upward to looming thunderheads and wild, towering cliffs. That duality, of pastoral peace juxtaposed against forbidding, danger-filled wilderness, is a constant in Bierstadt paintings and, indeed, in our collective notions of nature itself. We *do* like the view from either side of Eden's wall.

Yosemite and its Canadian counterpart, Banff, are the national cradles of wilderness, the places to which we attach a diverse string of adjectives: dramatic, pristine, dangerous, eternal, spiritual.

Never having returned to Yosemite, I can only vaguely recall its landscapes, except for a very specific one at Lake Tenaya, where my sister and I ventured out on the water on an old log raft we found. The wind came up suddenly and pinned us against a rock wall on the far side of the lake, and we had to be rescued. *That* image I remember with brilliant clarity. But in spite of my casual childhood reaction to Yosemite, faint images of that mountain valley surely must have accreted in my memory, laying part of the foundation for a profound adult fascination with natural landscapes and ecosystems.

Most people define themselves through jobs and achievements. I look to landscape. As they range from verdant to arid, youthful to ancient, honoured to mistreated, so do I. Forbidding cliffs and pastoral valleys are all mirrored within me. With each new place, I imagine how I might live there, and how I would adapt myself to the locale. I have turned our western Manifest Destiny tradition on its head; instead of remaking the landscape, I let it remake me. That is why I bonded immediately with Albert Bierstadt; he too let landscapes transport him, and he did not stop at the boundaries of conventional, perceived reality. As magnificent as Ansel Adams' Yosemite photographs might be, I am far more moved by the romantic paintings of Bierstadt.

Our perceptions of nature are bound by culture, and thus by time. In Bierstadt's era, nature was seen as a place for spiritual fulfillment, but it was also seen as an unlimited supplier of resources. We still seek spirituality in nature but the space in which to do that shrinks apace. As for the cornucopia, we know better now. In fact we now talk openly about nature going the way of the free-ranging bison that Bierstadt loved to paint. Somehow we have gone from nature as bountiful provider to the end of nature, without ever contemplating a sustainable balance in between.

As an ecologist, I connect to Bierstadt on another level. Historical ecosystem states and processes are a useful guide to the management of ecosystems in the present and the future. Early paintings, writings, and photographs are a treasure trove of ecological information. To utilize Bierstadt's paintings as sources of historical ecology, I have to reluctantly shift from romantic appreciation to rational dissection, carefully filtering out the visual culture of both the era and the painter. Right away I see two elements that are verified by other Western observers of the time; very open landscapes, and superabundant wild game. This helps to confirm the state of Western wilderness in the mid-19th century. It was still very open and flush with forage from the periodic burns that First Nations applied to the landscape, but elk, deer, antelope, and bison numbers had ballooned to unprecedented levels. First Nations populations, who relied on these animals as their main protein source, had been decimated by European diseases. So, the hunting pressure that normally kept ungulate herds in check, was effectively eliminated by smallpox. Thus, early settlers not only totally disrupted the ecology of the West, they totally misinterpreted it.

The fuzzy frame of my childhood memories of Yosemite has now been overpainted by the vivid landscapes of Albert Bierstadt. I am indebted to that gentle and prolific painter, but in my travels now, I shy away from the iconic places like Yosemite. I don't want the landscapes to do all the work,

commanding my attention by their sheer grandeur. I prefer
the humbler places that demand something of me before a
connection is made. That might be why I came to specialize
in grasslands, the most challenging of natural landscapes
to bond to. I have been known to throw myself down onto
them and roll around like a dog, for the sheer animal joy of
it. And stick my face deep into grassland badger dens, sniffing
carefully to see if the den is presently occupied. And I can
identify fifty or sixty grasses by sight, a skill that is in very
minimal demand, but one that makes me happy.

In the end I value Bierstadt's work more for its romance
than its ecology. It is curious how that landscape romance
folds inward on itself. A good portion of Bierstadt's creativity
was directed at marketing his paintings to Easterners thirsty
for images of the newly (to them) discovered West. So he
gave them statuesque trees, illuminated clouds, and impossible mountains, all carefully arranged to maximize depth of
perspective and aesthetic appeal. But an idealized landscape
is still a landscape, with its origins somewhere or some place
in the earth's time, and not in the human mind.

One of Albert Bierstadt's more famous paintings is set in
the shortgrass prairies near the foot of the Colorado Rockies.
The hazy blue mountains loom above the prairie. A surveyor's
covered wagon stands to one side. There are no trees, no middle
ground, and no way to judge distance. The lone surveyor, his
back to us, stands gaping, completely thunderstruck by the vast
distances and the solitude. I can see myself in that canvas, over
to one side where the vegetation is a little thicker. I would be
the one down on my belly, naming the grasses.

DESTINATION DUNGENESS

HUNTING WAS NOT A PARTICULAR PASSION for my father, or even a hobby. He simply saw it as part of what he did as a man. In the early fall he would bring home ducks, quail, and pheasant, and then in late fall, he and my grandfather would head off for two weeks to hunt deer in Utah. It was an odd contrast, living in a California suburb but eating venison all winter. When I was still too young to go on the hunting trips, I got to participate in a small way by sitting beside Dad at his neatly organized workbench, absorbing every step in the elaborate process of reloading ammunition for his deer and target rifles. My job was to run the little press that popped the spent primer from used shell casings. Dad would then install a new primer, add a carefully measured load of powder from a calibrated dispenser, and then with another press, seat the shiny new copper-jacketed bullet into the casing. Then I would put the finished cartridges into hardwood blocks that Dad had drilled forty holes into, so each cartridge had its own numbered place. Above his workbench was a shelf of National Rifleman's Association magazines and ballistics manuals. He would occasionally consult these, and then make calculations or take notes. He had no need for lined paper, and always printed, in a spare and precise hand that he learned in drafting.

In fact I never saw a single example of his cursive writing, except for his completely illegible signature.

In the off-season Dad would go out to the dry, scrubby hillsides east of the Los Angeles Basin to shoot gophers with his heavy target rifle. I got to come along as a spotter. We would lay down on the ground in front of a grassy hillside, he with the big .22-250, which he referred to as his "varmint gun," and me with a powerful wide-angle spotting scope. I would scan the hillside, looking for furry heads peeking up from burrows. We mentally gridded the hillside into quadrants, so when I found a gopher, I called out the coordinates so he could find it with his rifle scope, which had a much narrower field of vision. When he squeezed off the shot, I was able to confirm the kill, which meant a gopher a hundred metres away suddenly evaporated into very small body parts. Dad didn't miss very often. I think he did make brief mention of how destructive gophers were, and how cattle might break their legs by stepping in their holes, but mainly it was a lot of fun.

The telescope on Dad's varmint gun contained a delicate set of crosshairs, which broke during one gopher expedition. Dad had read somewhere (probably in an NRA publication) that the silk of the black widow spider was a durable and extremely fine material for telescope crosshairs. He consulted with me, since I was the neighbourhood expert on all things to do with spiders, lizards, and snakes. I located a big spider underneath the back porch, with a shiny black abdomen the size of a grape. Grasping it carefully with a pair of chopsticks, and with Dad supervising, I dabbed her spinneret across the two axes of the crosshair mount. It worked perfectly, and that particular rifle took on a kind of iconic value for me after that, since it was now somehow doubly lethal.

As soon as I was twelve we began to bird hunt together. I got to use a beautiful Browning 16-gauge Dad had hopefully bought for my mother. She was too influenced by the books of

Ernest Thompson Seton and Charles G.D. Roberts to ever shoot a quail, so I got the shotgun by default. Dad's style of hunting was conscientious and methodical, and it always involved a lot of walking. It was during those times that we developed a very strong father-son bond, which made it all the more painful when the relationship was subsequently torn apart.

My early reading was all from my father's library, and mostly about war, sailing ships, and hunting. I read all twelve of C.S. Forester's novels about Horatio Hornblower, the plucky eighteenth-century English naval commander who was plagued with self-doubt but always showed fortitude in battle.

Guns, military history, and Republican politics were all major themes in our household, as they were in the country itself at the time. One of our summer trips was to Tombstone, Arizona, where we watched a re-enactment of the gunfight at OK Corral. I memorized all the principals in that confrontation, and knew what kind of pistols they carried. I even wrote down some of the epitaphs from Tombstone's graveyard:

Here Lies Lester Moore

Five shots from a .44

No Les, No More.

But there was also a persistent minor theme, again both in the household and in the country, of the importance of the individual conscience, of a healthy mistrust of government, and of patriotic dissent.

My mother and father were from different religious backgrounds and couldn't agree on a church for my sister and me. So we were sent off on a kind of bizarre religious shopping tour, trying out Sunday Schools of various denominations. These were formal, starchy affairs and my sister and I were subjects of some curiosity, as we were sized up by the veterans of each new Sunday School. For my part, I had no idea whether I had the right stuff to be a Lutheran or a Presbyterian, or any denomination, for that matter.

The religious tour continued in school, where once a week women of the various denominations would arrive to drive their contingents off to church for an afternoon of bible study. The ladies had to park their cars on the other side of the street from the school, because of the Separation of Church and State. I happened to be in a Christian Scientist phase, and was fortunate to be the only one. The vivacious Miss Gustafson would come for me in her shiny Packard convertible, which was exactly the same colour as cooked lima beans. Instead of going to church, we would clandestinely drive to an ice cream parlour. I would slump down in the front seat of the Packard and hide from the other religions while she went in to get us each a double-scoop ice cream cone. She always got peach melba; I was partial to rocky road. We would then drive around town with the top down, licking our ice cream cones, while she quizzed me casually about Solomon and the Ten Commandments. To this day, I'm very partial to Miss Gustafson's style of religion.

In the end, the family quietly gave up on church. In some odd way, the works of Henry David Thoreau, John Muir, Rachel Carson, and others came to be a substitute for religion in the household. It was an odd compromise, this reverence for the outdoors passing for spirituality, but it satisfied my mother's transcendentalist view of nature, and my father's passion for it as the matrix for hunting and fishing. They both arrived at the secular sublime, but from different starting points. I embraced those authors too, right along with C.S. Forester and Thor Heyerdahl. Embedded within those works on nature was the importance of the individual conscience, made explicit in Thoreau's famous essay "Civil Disobedience".

On Saturday afternoons, my sister and I were allowed to walk downtown to the matinee showing at the movie theatre. These were always festive occasions. Usually it was a movie, but sometimes it was two manic hours of cartoons. Our friends and classmates would all be there, and we enjoyed entire afternoons of popcorn and mayhem. But there was always a nagging anxiety to my Saturdays. The US Army Recruiting Office was on the same block as the movie theatre, and bright yellow footprints were painted on the sidewalk in front of the office. The footprints started out following an ordinary straight line, but then veered off precipitously into the doorway of the Recruiting Office. The footprints were disturbing; I knew they had something to do with me, and my future. One day, on a whim, I might make a casual change in the direction of my own footsteps, and my life would be different forever.

Every Saturday afternoon I slowed down when I reached the yellow footprints. My sister would go on ahead, anxious to meet her friends. The feet were bigger than mine, but narrow and elegant, like those of a dancer. As I lingered in front of the Recruiting Office windows, I could see exciting posters of guns, aircraft carriers and cool uniforms. A couple of muscular fellows in buzz cuts and neatly pressed khaki watched me from their side of the window. These were the officers that could turn dandies, wimps, and small-heeled lounge lizards into real, serious men. That was their talent, and they were just waiting to exercise it. They also probably knew how to calibrate bombsights, drive tanks, and fly jets. Eventually I would turn my attention back to the Saturday matinee, but with a nagging sense of guilt. Even though I had no idea where or what boot camp was, I had this sense that I should be there, instead of watching Road Runner cartoons.

My other favourite Saturday activity was going to the local war-surplus store. World War II was only a decade past, and the dimly lit building was piled with every conceivable military item. You could look at leather flight jackets, empty shell casings big enough to stick your arm in, bayonets, badges, survival knives and of course, pistols and rifles. The store had a unique smell to it, composed of gun grease, water-proofing compound, and must. Since I couldn't collect guns like my dad, I bought knives. I had a machete, a Bowie knife, a WWI bayonet, and a switchblade. Switchblades were techni-cally illegal, and the front-loading kind were hard to find. But the hinged ones were available. If I asked to look at one, the guy at the counter would correct me by saying, "no, that's not a switchblade, it's a folding knife, son." It was easy to disable the locking spring that held the blade in the closed position, so you could then pop it open with a practised flick of the wrist, and envision yourself as a passionately doomed teenage gang member in the alleys of Brooklyn.

Nature was still available to me as a suburban California kid in the 1950s, albeit in small doses. Vacant lots and brushy hillsides awaited the next uptick in housing demand to go under the bulldozer but, in the meantime, they were my playgrounds. I searched for bird's nests, watched the ground for the nearly invisible trap door spider burrows, and stalked jackrabbits, but mostly I focussed on snakes and lizards. At one time I had half a dozen different cages in my bedroom, each housing a different reptile I had caught. Elegant bull snake, stubby rubber boa, smelly garter snake, fragile alligator lizard. My friend David and I split the cost of a lovely, five-foot-long indigo snake we bought from a pet store. David owned the front half and I owned the back. Each of us would keep it for two weeks, and then trade off. Walking the three blocks through the neighbourhood to David's house with a shiny, blue-black snake draped around my neck was pure adolescent heaven.

I kept a journal, which I called my Reptile Record. In it, I tracked what I saw, what I missed, and what I caught, what I brought home, what they ate, and what they wouldn't eat. My mother was very patient.

The family camping trips continued, as did my dad's hunting and fishing trips. The pull of the outdoors was strong in him, and eventually it drove him out of southern California. I came home from school one day to see a For Sale sign in our front yard, and a month later we were settled in a rural area of Washington State, along the Strait of Juan de Fuca. Dungeness was the name of the place, not a town really, just a collection of small farms and dairies, and a general store. Dad traded off a lucrative southern California engineering job to sell insurance on commission up and down the Olympic Peninsula, in exchange for the privilege of devoting every spare moment to hunting and fishing. The nearby Dungeness River was famous for its steelhead run, and my mother soon joined the local sorority of steelhead widows. I have to grudgingly admire a man who makes a major career decision on account of a fish.

Even though it was deficient in snakes and lizards, I embraced the Olympic rainshadow ecosystem of Douglas fir and cedar, and went on to discover the joys of tideflats and driftwood. As I walked the beaches, I could look across the Strait to the foreign and magical skyline of Victoria, which would elongate vertically in summer heat mirages. I visualized it as full of exotic minarets and towers, even though I was pretty sure it was just an ordinary town. I could not have imagined then how important Canada would be to my future.

Renegade Letterman

IN THE EARLY 1960S OUR FAMILY moved to Seattle. The public high school I entered drew from a convoluted mix of Jewish, Scandinavian, Black, Italian, and Asian neighbourhoods. Kids from each of these groups all shared the shock of discovering that their own community's lifestyle was just one of many. Two-thirds of my football team were black kids, and on the playing field and in the locker room, those of us with white skin experienced minority for the first time. It was all jokey and self-conscious of course, but we honkies did get the rattiest lockers, and were last in line to get into the showers after practice.

To get to school I had to take a city bus downtown and then transfer to another bus. I lied to my parents about how long the trip took, so in the afternoons, I could get off in various parts of the downtown, explore for half an hour, and then catch the bus home. Third Avenue, where the bus stopped, was all fancy shoe stores and department stores. But, like a lot of port towns, things got seedier — and more interesting — the closer you got to the waterfront. Second and First Avenues housed an eclectic mix of pawnshops, taverns, war surplus, used bookstores, cheap hotels, and marine supply houses. Certain news stands, I found, would tolerate furtive scanning of men's magazines. Groups of sailors pitched and rolled up and down the sidewalks of First Avenue, making the best of shore leave.

Sometimes, I made my bus transfer on Jackson Street, which was the black commercial district, and spent my half hour experiencing its unique pulse and vibrancy. Nobody seemed to mind the presence of a gangly and pimpled white kid.

In my junior year, I made the varsity football team, mainly because I had been playing football for more than half my life. Being on the varsity team meant that you received a Letter. The Letter was a big cloth F, about ten inches high, which stood for Franklin High School. The Letter was designed to be sewn onto expensive Letter Jackets, which your proud parents would buy for you. The jackets were an absolutely gorgeous. Kelly green with real leather sleeves and black piping. They really marked you out in the school hallways, and at the Drive-in. Some of my teammates rarely took them off. The Letter had a little football stitched into the centre of the F which, along with your size and attitude, also set you apart from the second-tier guys who had lettered in say, tennis or golf. When you got a Letter, you were automatically a member of the Letterman's Club. There was an induction ceremony, where you swore to uphold the school's grand tradition, and to neither smoke nor drink. At my swearing-in ceremony I looked around to my green-jacketed peers, some of whom I had pulled underage beer and cigarettes with, for some sign. If not a belly laugh, at least a nudge or wink. But the fleshy, testosterone-laced Letterman cadre stood at serious attention, faces forward, making no acknowledgment whatsoever.

So I took the Letter, out of solidarity with my teammates, and gave it to a statuesque Korean girl who I desperately admired. Even though I thought the jacket was classy, I never asked my parents to buy one for me, which they would have done willingly. Something, some little voice in my head, said no. And I didn't attend the Letterman's Club meetings. That pissed a lot of people off, but it seemed like the only way I could deal with the hypocrisy. I was becoming comfortable being an outsider.

Our football coach was, of course, white — this was 1963 — but the team's real identity revolved around the soft-spoken, black assistant coach, Brennan King. Brennan had time for everyone, even us grunts in the interior line. Brennan could play the unctuous assistant coach role when he needed to but, during the games, when we were in tough, the head coach would become red-faced and apoplectic and Brennan would calmly take over, calling in the plays and substitutions. He and the black kids on the team were part of the emerging dominance of black athletes in football, and everyone knew it, except perhaps the head coach.

After the last game of my senior year, when I took off my shoulder pads for the last time ever, Brennan invited the twelve graduating players, some white, some black, some Asian, to a black-owned steak house on Jackson Street. Everyone wore their letter jackets (except me) as we filed into the darkened, nightclub atmosphere and stood, awkward and self-conscious, not knowing what to expect. Every patron in the entire restaurant stood up and applauded us. We ate like kings and listened to live jazz, paid for from Brennan's own teacher's salary. I have never felt so honoured.

Football and literature made an atypical combination, but it suited me well. A renegade high school journalism teacher brought me back into Thoreau, as well as introducing me to John Milton and Eugene Victor Debs. Mr. Wettleson also attracted other student misfits, who naturally bonded together. We callow seventeen-year-old dissidents were not even sure what we were dissing against, but we sought each other out. At lunchtime we gathered in a deserted stairway on the upper floor of the old school building to sing the songs of Peter, Paul and Mary, and Bob Dylan. We sang "The Times They Are a Changin'", over and over; it was as though the repetition made us stronger. I was personally convinced that Bob Dylan and Joan Baez would soon get married.

Mr. Wettleson pretty well let us write what we wanted in the weekly school newspaper, but we started our own underground newspaper anyway, just to test the limits. We scrounged an old Gestetner printer, and painfully typed out our editorial outbursts, youthful introspections, and first attempts at poetry onto the master stencil, then cranked the pages out one by one. One of the editorials was entitled, "What is the Difference Between a Bow Tie and a Beard", in reference to the ties our martinet vice-principal wore, and the beards we boys were unsuccessfully trying to grow. We were bitterly disappointed that the school authorities didn't censor us or shut us down, and we ran out of steam after five issues. I think Mr. Wettleson was deeply hurt by our breakaway newspaper, because he really wanted to move the school newspaper beyond the endless reporting on pep rallies, football games, and student elections. We had abandoned him, and I think he never forgave us for it. But the underground newspaper did give us a tantalizing first taste of direct action.

John F. Kennedy's assassination hit like a giant meteor, shattering the very small universe of Franklin High School. Because we were members of the 1963 varsity football team, we had been asked to wear suits and ties to school that day, and each of us had been given a red rose to wear in our lapels. When I got the news I stumbled outside into bright November sunshine to cry and wonder alone, and slowly crush the red rose between my fingers. I started reading newspapers in the wake of the assassination, and have done so ever since.

In some strange way, the killing of the president simply reinforced our belief that the times *did* have to change. It is interesting to look back across the span of decades to the Kennedy legacy. In many respects he was simply a handsome, but ambiguous, vessel through which an optimistic generation channelled their expectations. Although I accept the official lone gunman theory of the assassination, it was still a fundamental conspiracy, in a metaphorical sense, against youth, beauty, and change.

Shortly after my eighteenth birthday I drove my Vespa scooter down to Seattle's King County Courthouse on First Avenue for the mandatory registration in the military draft. When they asked me if I was healthy, I hesitated for a split second, but youthful pride won out. As a football player and shotputter, of course I was disgustingly healthy. I had a slight sense of foreboding in the Draft Board office, but I felt certain there were thousands of experiences just waiting for me, and I couldn't be bothered questioning this one. After all, I was just registering, right? On that day, the courthouse was simply a big, grey building; just a few years later I would be viewing it in a very different light.

During my senior year, my father took a job working overseas, and my mother went with him, so they arranged for a young couple to live in our house and look after me. This turned out to be a great arrangement, since the well-meaning couple had no idea what the acceptable parametres were for an eighteen-year-old, and I had a separate entrance. We were cordial, but I arranged my lifestyle to suit myself. After a few false starts, I learned how to manage this unprecedented freedom. A desire to be different, always there in the background, was now a strong motivation. It was never clear to me if I had some internal drive to set myself apart, or whether I was just growing more confident in my own skin.

After school, I would go to sports practice, come home and nap for an hour, eat, and then read until the wee hours. Ambrose Bierce, Bertrand Russell, Lafcadio Hearn, Thomas Mann, Hermann Hesse; it was an eclectic lot of authors, but all interesting. Like many young men, I also fell under the sway of the Russians; Dostoevsky, Gorky, Bashevis Singer, Tolstoy, Lermontov. Modern Languages Press in Moscow was publishing well-bound, inexpensive English versions of the Russian novels, but the translations were awkward and sometimes terrible. My career aspiration had recently switched from oceanography to linguistics, and I actually wrote to Modern Languages Press offering my services as an editor of their English translations. I wonder if that letter is on file somewhere in Washington, DC.

In the spring of my senior year I came to school one day without socks on. The motive, as I recall, was probably less political than a lack of clean socks, but shock and awe rippled through the hallways and, by lunchtime, I was hauled in front of the vice-principal and kicked out of school for three days. Upon my return, I had to see the school counsellor, who informed me that an official letter about my crime had been sent to my parents overseas. She went on to say that such flagrant behaviour could mitigate against me in the future. The clear implication was that universities would think twice about an applicant who chose not to wear socks on a spring day. Most of the lecture was lost on me, since I was quite proud of my vocabulary, and was mortified by not knowing what "mitigate" meant.

I was pretty sure that my parents wouldn't take the offense too seriously, but I still had to wait a nervous two weeks to get a letter back from them. I was relieved when they wrote that they had gotten a good laugh upon reading the counsellor's letter.

Here was a small, but classic, 1960s lesson — the imposition of overwhelming authority in the service of trivial and arbitrary infractions not only lends itself to parody, it often contains the seed of its own demise. To that officious high school guidance counsellor I offer a belated comment, the same one delivered to Officer Krupke of *West Side Story*: krup you.

Bowling with Tito

DAD LOOKED AT THE LITTLE CRANES on the dock, and then looked down at the massive Caterpillar D8 deep in the ship's hold. He was silent for a long time. The cranes and their thin cables were designed for moving pallets of lumber or sacks of flour, not for deadlifting an eighteen-ton bulldozer. So, in his best, newly minted Serbo-Croatian, my dad tried to explain the problem, but the local dock workers would not listen to his concerns. I suspected national pride might be involved. The Pula dockworkers went ahead and shackled up the D8, but dad insisted that everyone stay well away from the crane and the ship's hold once the lift started. A lot of preparatory yelling and shouting ensued, and finally the crane operator tightened the slack and the lift began. So far, everything about Yugoslavia was exciting for me, and this was no different. Dad had found a safe spot on the ship's bridge, so I could watch everything.

The crane's diesel engine growled and bit down hard. Deep down in the hold, the great yellow machine began to stir. A hush fell over the ship and the dock. As the D8 started to inch upward, hundreds of cases of promotional Coca-Cola bottles, which had been stacked right up against it, began tumbling and falling underneath the enormous machine. When the tractor was three feet off the bottom of the ship's hold, the cable's wire strands began to pop and fly apart. We watched in silent horror as my father's engineering analysis played out, as if in slow motion. The last of the strands finally snapped and the entire cable exploded into frenzied, black spaghetti. The D8 crashed back down into the bottom of the freighter's hold, shattering untold numbers of Coca-Cola bottles.

Thanks to the cushioning effect of that carbonated icon of American consumer culture, the D8 did not proceed to the bottom of northern Yugoslavia's deepwater port.

The tractor and a bunch of other products were bound for a trade fair in Zagreb. These fairs have a long history in Europe, dating back to the era of medieval city-states. But this was the era of Cold War, and national governments had muscled into trade fairs, providing exhibition buildings for domestic manufacturers and adding their respective layers of thick patriotic gore on top. My dad worked the trade-fair circuit for the American government; they liked him because he was a good fixer, and a good foreman. He did trade fairs from Irkutsk to Kyoto, pulling together local work crews to construct exhibition buildings and move exhibits in. Buckminster Fuller geodesic domes were brand new and popular as exhibition buildings, and Dad had managed to build one on the Zagreb fairgrounds, mainly through sign language and hands-on example. Dad's stint in Yugoslavia came up just as I graduated from high school, and I got to sign on as his unpaid assistant.

Twelve hours after the cable failure, working under generator lights, Dad and the dockworkers had moved two cranes together to work in tandem, reinstalled heavier cables, and gotten the D8 out of the hold and onto a railroad flatcar for its trip to Zagreb. But the Caterpillar ordeal was not quite over.

Yugoslavian trains were narrow-gauge, and the massive Cat hung over the edges of its flatcar for a couple of feet on each side, like a fat man on a narrow chair. The train had barely left the dock when we realized the Cat would smash every railroad sign along the route. So Dad and I joined a taxi squad of train workers, and together we removed and reinstalled every single railroad sign between Pula and Zagreb. He and I were finding more and more areas of disagreement, but we both thrived on action. The trainmen were intrigued with us, these two grimy Yankees who wielded wrenches and shovels. Our little crew soon got into a rhythm though, piling off the train every few kilometres to remove a sign, let the D8 through, and then replace the sign. Both of us reeked of sweat and the particular odour of spilled Coca-Cola. A bottle of something called Slivovitz soon appeared, and each completed sign removal/replacement was celebrated with a glass. I was amazed at how a drink so vile could be produced by a fruit so innocent as a plum.

The D8 finally did arrive at the Zagreb Trade Fair grounds, as did the remaining cases of Coke and, in a subsequent shipment, a single ten-pin bowling lane. My sophomoric concerns about American cultural and economic imperialism were drowned in the general excitement of getting the exhibition ready for the start of the month-long fair.

Opening day was a big event, with huge crowds, and the flags of dozens of countries flying everywhere. I had already snuck into most of the Pavilions, so I focussed on building up my *znachki* collection. *Znachki* was the polyglot term used to describe the gaudy lapel pins and buttons that the various exhibitor countries gave away. By the time the fair opened, I had a double handful of them. The clear winner, in terms of design and flashiness, was the Red Chinese lapel pin. One of those would get you at least three other pins in trade.

When President Josep Tito's delegation arrived for the opening day of the fair, a kind of electric tremor ran through

DON GAYTON

the crowd. This country builder, this Nazi resistance fighter, this lion-of-the-Balkans, turned out to be a short, portly, and balding man, who was dwarfed by his beautiful, raven-haired, fourth wife, Jovanka. My dad had the privilege of being part of the entourage, and I managed to stick close by it, looking as official as my eighteen years, ill-fitting suit, and bad acne would allow.

One of the first stops that Tito made was to the heavy equipment display. His government was embarking on a major road-building initiative, so a number of countries had sent graders, cats, and dumptrucks to the fair. The big yellow D8, still smelling faintly of Coca-Cola, was parked alongside the Russian entry, which was painted forest green. At a signal, both machines started up, revved their engines, and clanked around. For a moment it looked as if the two operators might take each other on in a nightmarish, Cold War, industrial wrestling match. Tito watched appreciatively, no doubt planning how he could incite the two combatants into a bidding war for his country's business. Eventually he had seen enough, and moved on. The crowd followed.

The next exhibit was the single AMF bowling lane with an automated pin-setter, which was housed in a raised, glassed-in building so everyone could watch this newfangled, capitalist invention. Tito enquired about the exhibit, and was invited in to try out the bowling lane. Without a second's hesitation he agreed, and was escorted inside. The large crowd immediately circled the building and watched as the AMF representative explained the workings of the pin-setting machine to Tito's interpreter. Tito kept nodding in response but, even from a distance, you could tell he was impatient. Finally, the AMF man handed him the big, black, American bowling ball. Tito hefted it appreciatively, and smiled to the crowd outside.

At that moment, the man must have made an instantaneous political assessment, which would have gone something like this. "I am Josip Broz Tito, president of Yugoslavia. These people outside are my people. I ask a lot from them, in terms of sacrifice, in terms of tolerance. This bowling lane is American technology, which I am interested in, but not beholden to. I know how to play both Russia and America. I must meet this bowling lane on its own terms, and I must, above all, make a strike."

Holding the ball in the five-pin manner, without putting his fingers in the holes, portly Josip Broz Tito cast his steely, resistance-fighter gaze on the ten pins at the other end, bent down, and with two, quick, sliding steps, released the big ball. It rolled slowly and unerringly down the lane, past the upturned faces of that now-forgotten nation, and executed a perfect strike.

The Springfield Reckoning

AFTER A YEAR OF TRAVEL AND study in Europe, I returned to the States to continue my schooling at Antioch, a small, liberal-arts college in rural Ohio. My route to this college was circuitous. While I was still in high school, an artistic young woman that I admired greatly and managed to date once or twice, told me she had been accepted to Reed College. Reed was a well-known, West Coast, liberal-arts school. My infatuation was such that I immediately applied there too, but they rejected me. Someone told me, "if you can't get into Reed, go to Antioch." So in my dejected state, that was what I did. Antioch was a freewheeling kind of place, with many students from the big cities in the East, lots of opportunity for self-directed courses, and a work-study program that helped keep liberal flights of fancy grounded in workday reality.

Michael Doktor was one of the first people I met at Antioch. He was a true sixties pied piper, introducing me to marijuana, an obscure guitarist named John Fahey, and the power of the press. Doktor was a printer, in the classic sense of the word. He designed typefaces and had an ancient, hand-driven printing press in his dormitory room. A lot of people at the college were turning on to drugs at the time, and small-town Ohio was a pretty safe place to do it, except when federal narcotics agents came to town. But Doktor somehow had contacts within the local police department, and he received advance notice of the narcotics agents' visits. Michael was a rare combination of 'good old boy', political animal, hippie, and master craftsman. He found ways of relating to everyone, even cops, whom the rest of us disliked instinctively. Perhaps the local cops confided in Doktor because they believed they had things under control and didn't like being pushed around by the feds. At any rate, well in advance of the federal agents' arrival, small, beautifully crafted handbills in an elegant font would magically appear around campus, announcing:

NARCS ARRIVING.

COOL IT

APRIL 20-24.

Antioch attracted poets as well as undercover agents. Once the celebrated poet, Allen Ginsberg, came to the campus to give a reading. He embodied much of what the Sixties was about for me — defiance, creativity, sexuality. I got to the reading venue an hour early, with my treasured early edition copy of *Howl* in hand. But it turned out America's poet laureate was in his Zen phase. He didn't read a single poem, but, instead, chanted Buddhist prayers for an entire hour.

When a new chapter of the Students for a Democratic Society held a meeting on campus, I decided to attend. The SDS kids had a sense of urgency and earnestness about them, and they talked a lot about the war in Vietnam. After a couple of meetings, we decided to take action. Holding a demonstration in our liberal-minded little college town would mean absolutely nothing, so we got some money together to rent a school bus to take us up to the City of Springfield, to hold our demonstration there. We decided to picket in front of Springfield's county courthouse, where the local draft board had their office. We had signs, and a few banners; it seemed like a civil and decent way to register a protest against the

War. We had chosen a Saturday, and a few other students from the area joined us. This was to be my very first citizen protest demonstration, which I knew to be a respected and time-honoured component of my country's tradition of political activism. Like every other American, I knew that the Boston Tea Party was a defining event in the life of our country; we were a nation forged from a potent mixture of political independence and dissent.

Three hours later, a frightened and humiliated group boarded the school bus back to Yellow Springs. Small groups spoke in whispers to each other, and one woman sobbed quietly. Even the local SDS leader, normally an outspoken militant, was silent. The good people of Springfield had unleashed a ferocious animosity toward our demonstration, our position, and our looks. They yelled obscenities, and they spat. They leaned into our faces and taunted us. They blared their car horns. Even the women displayed vicious, suppurating rage.

As the school bus trundled along the back roads of Ohio's heartland on its return to our liberal Antioch ghetto, I contemplated the massive fault line I had discovered, one that zigzagged the length and breadth of America. I also understood, for the first time, the terrible paradox of honouring the commitment and patriotism of individual soldiers, while questioning the motives of those who safely and comfortably send them off to war.

While in Europe, I had developed a routine of weekend hitchhike explorations, and I continued them in Ohio. The rural southern part of the state still looked like Currier and Ives engravings. The neatly organized farms, the scattered communities with their courthouses and churches, and the groves of maple, hickory, and beech, all looked as if they would continue unchanged into eternity. To grow up in this classically pastoral milieu, I reasoned, could easily make one believe in the essential rightness of every American intention.

The Dirty Thirties were nearly forgotten in places like southern Ohio, but the gritty and subversive romance of that era appealed to me. The classic activity of that era was "hopping a freight" to look for a job, or to just look at the country. A buddy and I, pumped full of Pete Seeger and Bob Dylan lyrics, decided to try it one weekend. After jumping into a coal car and getting filthy, we found an empty boxcar with both doors open. We scrambled into it and hid in the shadows until the train started moving. Then we sat down in the middle of the car and leaned our backs against each other, to watch the rural landscapes and small towns roll slowly by. I had only a vague notion of where we were headed, but the destination didn't matter. We channelled the hoboes and gandy dancers of the Great Depression, who would have sat just like us, secure in lasting friendships, not eating or drinking, and approaching a Zen-like state, nourished by the endlessly passing landscape. Since my buddy and I were both aspiring poets, we described what we saw to each other, as rural Ohio slowly spooled through the cinematic frames of opposing boxcar doors. America had literally turned its back to the railroad, so we looked right out on to intimate and unpretentious backyards, porch swings and clotheslines. I knew hopping a freight was already a heritage activity, and we had luckily squeezed through a southern Ohio time warp to be able to do it. I wished the day, and the friendship, would go on forever.

Some of my longer hitchhiking trips reached down into Kentucky and southern Indiana, which seemed exquisitely foreign to me, a west coast kid. There was a lot of anger on the roads. A knife collector who wouldn't let me out of the car until he had described his entire collection and what each implement could do to a man. Another who hated hippies with a passion. I guessed his need for company trumped his hatred.

A black guy, recently returned from Nam, whose driving was as impetuous as his talk, gave me a long ride. Disconnected in-country war experiences and anger poured out of him. At one point he reached down, still furiously driving, and pulled the shoe and sock off to show me his right foot. Three toes had been blown off by a land mine.

During my time at Antioch, I began reading and thinking about conscientious objection. Right from the start there was a problem, because conscientious objection was traditionally under the cloak of an organized religion, and I had no ecclesiastical leg to stand on. The prospect was new and somewhat frightening, but there was also something clean and almost heroic about it. There was simply no way of having a rational discussion about conscientious objection with my dad. My grandfather and I had always gotten on well, so I decided to seek his counsel.

We three Gaytons were linked by the same first name, so my grandfather, Donald the First, was always Pop to me. The tallest of three tall men, Pop had a booming voice and an easygoing manner. He didn't see action in World War I but, shortly after enlistment, he was promoted to drill sergeant and spent the balance of his military service training new troops of the 26th Infantry Regiment at the Plattsburgh base in upstate New York. After the war, he made a career as a travelling salesman for Peter Cooper, a venerable New York company that made animal glues. Animal glue always struck me as something from another century, and it probably was.

During one of his sales trips to Ohio, Pop and I got together for a day to catch up on family news. I seized on this opportunity to get his reading on conscientious objection. I brought it up casually, as if I'd never heard of the idea before. "Conscientious objectors?" he said, and thought for a moment. "Yeah, we had 'em at Plattsburgh. "Conchies", they were called. We just shot them."

I'm not sure how well I disguised my shock, but I quickly changed the subject. I now had a visceral sense of the gravity of the issue, and just how completely alone I would be in exploring it.

Chicken Rites

At a speech given at 2AM at the University of Michigan, presidential candidate John F. Kennedy offered a challenge to the student audience. How many would be willing to serve their country and the cause of peace by working in the Third World? The response was enthusiastic. Four months later, in March of 1961, President Kennedy created the Peace Corps. This was the beginning of a brief and interesting era in American foreign relations, one suffused with enthusiasm, sincerity and refreshing naïveté. The era would be eventually crushed by the Vietnam War.

In the mid-sixties, the Peace Corps began recruiting agricultural volunteers to work in Colombia, South America. I was an aimless twenty-year-old with some agricultural background and an admirer of Kennedy, so I joined up. They sent me first to a university in New Mexico, where I was to be trained in the arts of small farming projects and nutritional improvement for the *campesinos* of Colombia. At the training centre I was joined by about fifty other young folks and, together, we were taught such useful information as how to peel tomatoes, the differences between English sheep breeds, the origins of the rebellion of Cuauhtemoc in 1642, and Spanish phrases such as, "give me a seat on the balcony, with a view of the third violinist".

Some of the trainees were a bit older than I, and politically astute. There was no formal mentoring, but I gained a lot from these individuals, and still hold them in great respect. Vietnam was, of course, a major issue. President Lyndon Johnson had functionally declared war in 1965, by committing US troops to ground offensives in south Vietnam. Officially, and in most of the media, the American involvement was being treated as a short-term, surgical insertion, not really a war at all. My colleagues, along with a significant fraction of the youth of the country, weren't buying that story. But several of the trainees voiced strong support. Midway through the training, a group of us asked permission to hold a debate on Vietnam, and permission was grudgingly granted. I don't remember many of the particulars of the debate, other than the intense emotions. The "pro" advocates tended to be from the rural South and Midwest, whereas we "antis" on the other side of the political fault line generally hailed from cities on either coast.

After three months of training, we were sent in pairs out to small villages in Mexico, for a week. The Peace Corps administration had designed this week as a kind of acid test, figuring it was far cheaper to put us in rural Mexico for a few days than it was to send us all the way to Colombia to experience the realities of Third World rural life. The administrators were right; about ten of our group took one look at the Mexican outhouses, the pigs wandering up and down the village streets, and the flies, and simply went home, never to be seen again.

My partner and I, on the other hand, had a great time. We both loved Mexican food, and we were fed by a different family each day. Montezuma did take his revenge, however. Between meals, we walked about the tiny village of Ocoyotepec with Spanish-English dictionaries in one hand, and rolls of toilet paper in the other.

After Mexico, I returned to the university for a few more weeks of final training in the mysteries of small farming extension, and soon found myself, along with about forty others, on a flight to Bogota. The airplane, a Boeing 707, was painted bright frog-green, and the stewardesses handed out dozens of those little bottles of liquor for free. I remember looking down on impossibly dense jungle as we crossed the coast and headed inland, but quickly turning my attention back to the slightly hysterical euphoria inside the airplane. By the time we arrived at the Bogota airport, most of us were drunk. Several people hesitated about leaving the aircraft, preferring the stale and boozy air of the 707 to the vast unknowns that awaited them in Colombia.

The next morning we were marshalled into a conference room where a Peace Corps official stood in front of a huge, wall-sized map of Colombia. An official gave us an inspirational lecture on improving the nutritional plane of Colombian *campesinos* by extending knowledge on small farming projects. Then he gestured to the map behind him, stepped aside, and said, "Ladies and gentlemen, please find your assignments." The entire group, which was now down to about thirty-five, rushed up to the map to find brightly coloured little pins with name tags attached, stuck into various towns and villages. There was much shouting and laughter as people found their assignments in villages near Bogota, others near Medellin, and still others near the coastal cities of Cartagena or Barranquilla. I didn't see my name anywhere. Most of the population centres of Colombia are ranged along the central spine of the Andes mountains, so I scanned the various *cordilleras*, looking in vain for a pin with the name Gayton attached. The crowd in front of the map finally thinned out, so I started over with a methodical search of the country, first the llanos to the east, then the Andes again, then the Caribbean coast, and on to the Pacific Coast, without finding my name. Finally, in a remote corner of jungle, way up near the Colombia/Panama border, several inches from any other pins and far off of the national road network, I found my name.

The village underneath my pin was called Riosucio. Other than rivers, and lots of them, there was nothing else on that part of the map. Riosucio. Dirty river, I repeated to myself over and over, as I stumbled away from the map, feeling completely and absolutely alone. Was this some kind of a cruel joke?

I had been somewhat of a troublemaker in the Peace Corps training program, and wondered if that was coming back to haunt me. During the training, I had triggered a kind of slave revolt by refusing to take a test administered by the program's psychologist, a kind of defanged vampire who wandered amongst us, taking notes. The test was a big hurdle, midway through the training program. It was called the MMPI, the Minnesota Multiphasic Personality Inventory, which asked questions like "do you step on, or over cracks in the sidewalk", and "how often do you have feelings of hatred towards your mother". Half an hour into the exam I stood up, tore my test paper in half, dropped it on the psychologist's desk, and walked out. If this psychobabble idiocy was to be part of the selection process, I wanted no part of the Peace Corps. To my enduring surprise and relief, a dozen people got up and followed me out. Shortly after that, the psychologist quietly disappeared, and the test was never mentioned again. But no doubt the action was held against me. And I also kept trying to talk Spanish in language class, when we were supposed to be studying the preterite subjunctive.

Perhaps that was why they were sending me to Riosucio. Well, to hell with them, I thought, I'll bet Riosucio is actually a fine town, and I'll fill it with so many Small Farming and Gardening projects that the residents won't know what hit them.

Two days later, after a fourteen hour bus ride, I was on the docks of the grubby Caribbean port town of Turbo, where an impatient regional Peace Corps supervisor handed over a leaky 14-foot aluminum boat, a twenty-five horsepower Johnson outboard motor, and a waterproof map. To get to Riosucio, he explained to me, I simply had to cross a shallow saltwater bay, called the Golfo de Urabá, find the main channel of the Atrato river, and ascend the river for about four hours, and *bingo*, I'd be there. Amazingly enough, I did just that, because I was twenty years old and mortality had not yet entered my mind.

The three thousand souls that made up the town of Riosucio, mainly ex-gold mining slaves from West Africa, a few mestizos, fewer Indians, and a couple of Palestinian merchants, conducted their lives on a narrow strip of land between the Atrato River on one side and a dark, tree-filled swamp on the other. So the town was about two kilometres long and about five houses wide. The heat and humidity were amazing, and the people were very tolerant of my fractured Spanish. I soon learned that there was no Spanish equivalent to my first name. My middle name is Vince, so I introduced myself as Vicente.

Riosucio had no roads. All travel was by canoe, or by the occasional motorized launch that travelled up and down the Atrato, picking up bananas and the dried skins of small local crocodiles. There was no phone and no doctor, but they did have the marconi, or the telegraph office. As time went on in Riosucio, I would receive occasional marconigramas as they were called, from Peace Corps headquarters in Bogota. They always came on crisp, yellow half-sheets of paper and would say things like "Monthly report overdue. Stop. Break down extension activities by half-hour time blocks. Stop. Refer pages 79 to 92 Peace Corps Administrative Manual. Stop." This was my first introduction to the vast gulf between bureaucracy and reality. What was being requested of me bore absolutely no relation whatsoever to the fiercely exciting field work I was engaged in. As a result, I have remained an uncomfortable thorn in the side of every bureaucracy I have been attached to since.

I did write letters to my father occasionally, trusting the grimy-handed banana-boat captain to post them once he got to Turbo. They were chippy letters. I flaunted my opposition to the Vietnam War, and I flaunted the risks to my health and safety in this remote village, for no good reason.

Riosucio was a fascinating little universe. I threw myself into my Small Farming and Gardening projects, with the enthusiastic assent of the mayor, the town councillors, the policeman, the priest, and the schoolteachers. A public demonstration of raised-bed gardening, right near the mayor's office, was my first project. There was a small sawmill in town and lots of reject slab wood was available, so I built a bed, filled it with a mixture of muck soil and sawdust, and planted it with a combination of Beefsteak and Early Girl tomato seeds taken from my Peace Corps Small Farming and Gardening Projects kit. Everyone in town thought this was a capital idea, and greatly admired the young gringo's expertise. The young gringo, for his part, was quite pumped up by this, and barely noticed the fact that the local population was actually extremely healthy and well-fed already, having a steady diet of fresh fish from the river and fresh fruits from the surrounding jungles, as well as daily exercise paddling their graceful dugout canoes. In fact, the young gringo somehow failed to notice that most of the men had physiques similar to Muhammad Ali in his prime. Now, the young gringo did actually notice that all the houses were on stilts, but just assumed that this was done for reasons of ventilation and cooling.

The next small farming project was chickens. At great cost and expense, I imported two dozen Rhode Island Red chickens, the first-ever chickens to set foot in Riosucio. I carefully raised them in a pen until they were old enough to be placed with two or three of my more-progressive small farmers and gardeners.

About that time, I began to notice a change in Riosucio's weather. By noon, huge clouds would build up and, around one o'clock, it would rain so hard that if I happened to be on the river with my boat, I would have to head to shore to avoid being swamped. If I took shelter inside a building, the pelting of raindrops on the tin roof was sheer punishment to the ears.

The rain episodes grew heavier and longer. I began to get concerned about my Small Farming and Gardening projects. The Rhode Island Reds glared at me as I made my daily rounds, and I had to drill special drainage holes in my raised-bed garden. Then, one fine, bright morning, disaster struck.

Overnight, the river had risen dramatically, and the whole town was suddenly flooded with three feet of water. I was horrified, and sloshed over to my raised bed garden. The corner posts were still visible, but the inside was a slowly swirling, foul black soup of sawdust and dead tomato plants. I sloshed back to the Mayor's office, and in my best and most official Spanish, demanded an explanation. "*Que horror, don Vicente,*" said Don Efrain, the mayor. "This has never before happened in the history of our fine community. Such a calamity must be the act of an angry and vindictive God, but I'm sure that if we all pray mightily, the waters will go back down in twenty-eight to thirty-three days."

As I left the mayor's office, I noticed a few small, spidery walkways had been erected above the water, using the same slab wood from the sawmill. Over the next few days this makeshift network expanded, first connecting the bar, then the Palestinian merchant's store, then the houses of the more prominent families, then the mayor's office, and so on. I never actually saw anyone erect them, they just appeared, and they were always just high enough out of the water that someone in a canoe could just pass underneath if they bent over. The narrow and tricky walkway leading out of the pub was the source of community amusement, since the patrons leaving that establishment were not always successful in negotiating it.

The hubbub over Riosucio's flood settled down quickly, so quickly in fact, that the young gringo began to get suspicious. After some quiet investigation, he discovered that it floods every year in Riosucio, always has and always will, at least until they dam the Atrato. If it weren't for the flooding, and the subsequent soil deposition, that narrow strip of land Riosucio sits on would cease to exist. The event and its aftermath taught me two fundamental extension lessons. The first one is: do your homework. Seek out and value local knowledge. Understand local climate, soils, biota, and life-ways before you recommend changes to local practice, or technological whizbangs from your Third World Development Kit. The second extension lesson I learned was that when you are trying to help a polite group of people who really don't need your help and actually know quite a bit more about their world than you do, the simplest, most economical, way for this polite group of people to handle you is to indulge all of your overseas development fantasies, knowing that you will go away soon.

So the whole town had played an elaborate joke on me, and everyone knew it. And I had no choice but to work my way slowly up and down the narrow boardwalks while people laughed uncontrollably, and I had to grin and bear it. There I was, the gigantic blond gringo idiot, balanced on a boardwalk, undergoing a humiliating rite of passage, and an entire Colombian village was helping me get through it.

Nacianceno, one of the promising young farmers that I had entrusted some Rhode Island Reds to, felt sorry for me and invited me to his shack for a beer one afternoon. A few neighbours, who were networked to Nacianceno's house by the boardwalks, came over too, and we all sat on the porch, talked, drank beer, and watched the swollen, but placid, Atrato river slide by between the houses. In the midst of our conversation, one of my prized Rhode Island Reds appeared on the porch, in some distress. The whole group fell quiet, watching the sickly bird, which was a far cry from the proud, majestic animals pictured in my Peace Corps manual. Its feathers were ruffled and dull, its wings dragged, and it seemed to be gasping, like it was trying to say something. My first thought was to grab the bird, take it back to my office, and check to see if its symptoms matched any of the ones listed in my manual, but I resisted the impulse. The bird seemed to get over its gasping spasm momentarily, and took several more wobbly steps towards us. Then it stopped, spun around, threw its head up in the air, gasped once more, and with a theatrical gesture worthy of early vaudeville, fell face down on the porch with a thud. Nacianceno began to laugh but instantly clapped his hand over his mouth and looked sheepishly at me.

I knew this was my final lesson. My rite of passage was almost over and I could now begin to learn real extension. I put my beer down and began to laugh. Relieved, Nacianceno and his neighbours joined in. I laughed until my stomach hurt and tears rolled down my cheeks. Then, just to make sure things were perfectly clear, I stood up, and with a theatrical gesture of my own, swept the dying chicken off the porch with my boot, allowing it to meet its maker, or more likely a local crocodile, on the millennial waters of the Atrato River.

The First Ever Mass in La Balsa

The helicopter circled Riosucio a few times to announce its presence, then touched down on the packed dirt of the town square. Father Leoncio Palaverde, whose outstanding traits were mildness and persistence, knew it was for him. He heard the excited hubbub outside the church as the town's children surged toward the square. The more sedate adults were close behind, and Father Leoncio hurried to join them, his small leather bag in hand. It would not do to keep the American *militares* waiting, so he walked quickly, establishing his position ahead of the adults, but behind the jostling mass of children.

Father Leoncio had never seen a helicopter up close before, and he was surprised at how small and fragile it looked. A large man stood in front of the plastic bubble of the machine's cockpit and surveyed the approaching crowd. He wore green fatigues and dark glasses, and a pistol was strapped to his waist. Father Leoncio hesitated. He had asked Vicente, the Peace Corps volunteer, to arrange this trip for him, since the *militares* were his fellow countrymen. It was indeed a wonderful opportunity for the faith, since the compound of the *militares* was near La Balsa, a tiny Indian settlement on the remote Pacific coast, a place with no priest, no church, no roads, no marconi, nothing. Vicente had grudgingly arranged the trip with the *militares*, but refused to come along, citing political differences. That left Father Leoncio to manage on his own. The crowd of adults gently pushed him forward.

He had been the priest in Riosucio for three years, his first posting since leaving the seminary in Madrid. His student dreams of spirituality and progress had been tempered by the town's huge, rat-infested tin church, the brawling African and Mestizo population, and the infernal jungle heat. As a consequence, Father Leoncio felt attracted to the remote Indian villages of his vast parish, where religion, he imagined, could be clear, bright, and new. He had no trouble convincing the bishop in Medellin of his plan to perform a Mass in La Balsa.

The helicopter trip was a frightening rush over treetops in the fragile cage of plastic and metal and, in less than an hour, Father Leoncio was sitting in the gleaming new compound of the gringos, eating strange food by himself while the pilot and the other *militares* sat at a separate table. They were polite, he noted, but basically they ignored him. Mayor Don Efrain had already been out to the compound, and had come back to Riosucio with two cartons of Marlboros, plus the information that the gringos were scouting a location for a second Panama Canal. To Father Leoncio this seemed plausible enough, but his friend Vicente was scornful and told him, "Don't let them sell you a cat for a rabbit." Vicente was forever collecting quaint figures of the local speech and trying them out in conversation.

After supper, Father Leoncio took his cup of weak American coffee and went out onto the white sand beach. The village of La Balsa was visible across the small bay, against a background of mangroves. He marvelled at the huge, empty expanse of water beyond the bay. The setting sun had turned a flaming ruby colour, and wisps of it seemed to float off the main body as it slid into the vast calmness of the Pacific Ocean.

Father Leoncio did not sleep well; after three years in a hammock, the cot the Americans offered him seemed totally unsuitable. He rose early and slipped outside.

A brisk walk on the sand around the edge of the bay soon brought him up in front of La Balsa. Several canoes of black, shiny wood were pulled up on the beach. They seemed exceedingly narrow and fragile. The settlement itself consisted of nine houses — large, circular buildings with raised floors, no walls and conical, thatched roofs. He walked slowly by them, taking in every detail, even noticing the rows of hammocks slung inside. The precision and symmetry of the houses amazed him. As he passed the last dwelling a small woman emerged, stopping when she saw Father Leoncio. Terrified, she quickly disappeared into the jungle behind. The priest panicked too, quickly adjusting his footsteps away from La Balsa. His face burned with a curious shame.

Beyond the bay, the beach narrowed to a mere strip between mangrove and ocean. He was pleased to be on the beach, which would continue unbroken all the way to the foot of Chile. Father Leoncio stopped walking to admire a hardy coconut that had taken root in the sand. From the top of the coconut a bright-green seedling emerged. The father looked around once more to the reassuring purity of mangrove, beach and ocean. Then, carefully, he folded his cassock and knelt in the fine white sand to begin the first ever Mass in La Balsa.

Humboldt and Bonpland

I AM ABOUT TO VIOLATE ALEXANDER'S private journals by reading them, something I never thought I would do. He had a dozen of them custom made before we sailed from Europe. Their coverings are his own design, made of fine leather, with a series of folding flaps and buckles so that, when the journal is closed, it is nearly waterproof and will even float for some time. I remember asking him about that, back in those heady days before we left the Continent. Alexander replied glibly, "Well, my dear man, the Casiquiare is said to be a very placid river, but there is always the remote chance that our craft will be swamped and, in such an eventuality, I would want to make every effort to save my written records."

If our craft were to be swamped! Swampings happen to us daily, on some hidden snag, or in a vicious rapid. A. actually used that term, placid, to describe the Casiquiare, as if it were the River Seine. The real Rio Casiquiare, this fecund and terrifying river, this dark passage into America incognita, has all the placidity of a sleeping jaguar. Even when we're not actually in the water, trying to set the boat right after a swamping, the daily rains and humidity conspire to nearly drown us anyway.

I still remember the great honour I felt when Alexander chose me for his second Venezuela expedition. The great Baron Alexander von Humboldt, the encyclopedic naturalist, the dean of European science, the mapper of the Orinoco, and the namer of ocean currents, could have snapped his fingers and a hundred eminent natural scientists would have rushed to join him. But he selected me, Henri Bonpland, an obscure Parisian botanist specializing in tropical palms.

We had met briefly at the Academy Bienale in Paris in 1798, he the magnetic speaker, I the admiring neophyte. I shall never deny the profound first impression that the man himself made on me, with his fine head and noble bearing, but the great surprise of my life was to find out that in the course of our very brief meeting, that I had somehow made an impression on him. I still remember the day his letter of invitation arrived at my tiny laboratory in the third arrondissement — I was the luckiest man in all of Europe. I remember thinking how this would be my chance to participate in some small way in the greatest scientific adventure of the modern era, the exploration and cataloguing of the New World. Finally, I would be able to quit studying the desiccated second-hand specimens of others in favour of fresh, living palms of my own.

Such were my innocent dreams, as I stood in my dusty laboratory, letter in hand. Dreams coloured in no small way by the passionate attraction I had for A. But that old Henri Bonpland is no longer; the person I am now (who am I now?) rejects all exploration as violence, rape, and travesty.

Now, to the journals. A. was obliged to go to Caracas to meet the new Governor, and I agreed to stay on at our Casiquiare encampment to look after things in his absence. My ruse of hiding his journals worked very well. I reassured him that they were definitely in camp, but had simply been misplaced when we unloaded cargo from our last venture up the Casiquiare. A. was even touched when I told him I would locate them in his absence. God knows he has already forgotten the journals several times on this expedition. Many is the time when he would set off before sunrise, in high scientific dudgeon, armed with sextant, harquebus and vivarium, but would forget his journal — the object of this infernal exercise — if I weren't there to remind him.

Going to such great lengths to read the journals of another man seems childish, on the face of it. But I know for a fact there's more in these journals than just scientific observations. A. has said more than once that he would abandon science immediately if it meant that he could not also be a poet, and an aesthete. Imagine, the great scientist von Humboldt, the lion of Venezuela, the cataloguer of the New World, the savant of the atmospheres, conqueror of Mount Chimborazo, and compiler of the Cosmos, as a fragile and sensitive poet! But his idea of poetry is so hermetic and secret; he saves none of that sensitivity for me, and none for this terrible, leech-infested existence we lead together. So, I need to do this just once, to hold A.'s written mirror up to myself, even though nothing he could possibly write can stop this slow grinding inside my head, or deter me from my chosen course.

The journal I hold is Number Eight, his current one. The numbers are burnt into the leather cover like brands — eight journals to cover four years. He had twelve of them made, so if time is measured by completed journals — oh damn, A. would have some elegant explanation of how percentages or ratios or some such could be applied to solve this problem, and then, in the end, never provide me with a direct answer. The hell with the man. I'm opening Number Eight.

∽

On the Rio Casiquiare, November 4, 1801

Temperature at 6AM, thirty-two degrees Celsius. Humidity already up to eighty percent. Afternoon rains started punctually at two o'clock, forcing us to leave the Casiquiare's main channel and take shelter under the jungle overhang. I think the boat would have swamped again had we not done this. Added another point to my Hot Equatorial Jungle isotherm. Environment for palms, lianas, Orchids &c. very stable, which likely accounts for the high speciation and diversity of those species here. Henri shows absolutely no interest, a fact which gives me great concern. After so many years sharing our lives together, he has, over the last few weeks, become a profound stranger.

Los Pantanales, near the Rio Casiquiare,
November 6, 1801

Spent the day investigating *Mycophorus horridus*, the freshwater electric eel. The Spanish naturalist, Mutis, had previously reported on the natives' accounts of this beast, but there are no first-hand or scientific accounts of the eel's unique talents. Our guides Scipio and Cesar led us on horseback to a series of interconnected ponds out on the savanna, where they said the eel could reliably be encountered. We tried several ponds to no avail; all of our efforts to capture an eel went for naught. Using a hook and line was of course out of the question. We tried bow and arrow, but as soon as Scipio or Cesar were able to shoot an eel as it came near the surface, its cohorts would seize and devour it.

There seemed no feasible way to determine the extent of the beast's electrical power short of an actual encounter. I hit on the stratagem of driving a spare horse into the pond, which we did, with some effort. After its first contact with the eels, the animal became wild-eyed and agitated, but its agitation seemed only to attract more eels, and soon the water around the horse seethed with these dark, sinuous creatures. The horse screamed piteously, but it was soon over. As it was pulled under by the eels, the horse's legs still thrashed, but I am convinced the animal was already dead and the thrashing was due only to galvanic action of the eels on the horse's morbid nervous system.

During this exercise, which consumed the whole morning, Henri stayed at a distance, under a scrubby patch of trees, not participating in any way. He appeared extremely agitated after the event. I regretted exposing him to this, but nonetheless could not hide my elation. I had proven my hypothesis about the purpose of the eel's galvanic powers: they frequented these shallow, muddy waters in search of wading quadrupeds like the coatimundi or the capybara, which enter these shallow water bodies to drink or graze. The first shock serves to simultaneously disorient the animal, and to alert other eels, which immediately join the foray, adding their voltage to the lethal exercise. In light of the horse episode, I judge these animals to be extremely successful in capturing terrestrial prey.

November 7, 1801 Casiquiare Encampment

I am beginning to sense that the eel experiment was a turning point in our relationship. Poor Henri! Only he would consider the life of a broken-down horse when I stand at the brink of another great breakthrough. Another small component fitted into Cosmos, this Encyclopedia of the Universe, this life work.

So, A. has at least privately acknowledged some of my anguish; I expected no less of him. As far as the physical pain though — the heat, the humidity, the leeches — he just ignores it, and expects others to do the same. It is as if he wills the unpleasantness away from himself and from other people. Acknowledging pain and privation is not part of his Prussian character.

In spite of A's surprising acknowledgment of my pain, I shall no longer participate. Not in European intellectual salons, not in crazed scientific expeditions, not in the life of the mind nor even life on the Casiquiare.

My only redemption is with Xochil, who comes to our encampment only at night, and provides me with silent comfort at crucial times. I know that she knows some French, and she knows that I know some Piaroa, but we choose not to communicate in words. It's better this way. Silence allows us to preserve the powerful innocence of our first times together, those nights when I brought her silently to my tent, after everyone else was asleep. This way, she still has her world in the village, and I have my life of deconstruction, of de-Europe-anization, of de-botanization. Our lives overlap in a narrow, yet perfect fashion. She provides me with something that A. refuses to give, except in these damned journals. Xochil is like a palm; she just is. When we're together, we don't concern ourselves with taxonomy, shades of meaning, and the endless process of definition. Nor do we perform experiments on each others' souls.

I am about to throw away science, not so as to embrace the life of the local Piaroa, but to wipe the slate free of all cultures, to begin the reassessment of the jungle, its flora — and myself — from that perspective. No more Linnaean categorization, full of phyla and genera and taxa. No more analytical study of local cultures. No more analogies and similarities; everything must be new and naked, as befits this New World. I am not "going native", I am turning away from all culture. Not toward Cosmos, but to Nova.

November 15, 1801. Upper Casiquiare, three days boat travel from the Encampment.

Today, Henri committed a surprising, even shocking act, an unprecedented gesture whose import I cannot fathom. We were exploring a stagnant side channel of the Casiquiare, looking for the Victoria water lilies that Mutis claimed he found, but never brought any specimens back as proof. Mutis describes the lily pads as being up to a metre across which, if true, would certainly cause a great stir back in Europe. Botanical gardens in a dozen countries would clamour for them. Henri did not want to go, but I insisted, wanting him to be the one to make the discovery and the collection if there was to be one. He had certainly earned the right. Henri was sitting in front of me in the boat, and Cesar and Scipio were poling, since there was no detectable current in this side channel. Henri was obviously restless, as he fidgeted and twisted about in his seat. Then, suddenly, as if by some strange, otherworldy impulse, he reached down into the cargo boxes at his feet, withdrew his prized, brass plant vasculum, which he had carried for years, and flung it away. It sank like a stone into the black water. Scipio stopped poling immediately and turned to me with a look of perplexity and amazement but, with a firm gesture, I commanded him to continue poling. I knew from recent experience that interfering with Henri in one of his agitated mental states could only make matters worse.

What would possess this man — this Henri Bonpland who has literally defined the palm family for science — to so casually throw away the very symbol of his profession? What crazed impulse? How could he be so cavalier? Yet, somehow, in some inexplicable way, acts like these are part of Henri's mysterious attraction. His feelings are so close to the surface of his skin; emotional luminosity, I'll call it.

I am also professionally indebted to Henri — my discovery of the source of curare, which enhanced my reputation considerably — was purely as a result of his work. I must repay that debt somehow.

Yes, that event on the Upper Casiquiare was a kind of turning point for me. Just at that moment I suddenly and clearly understood I would no longer be bound by the vasculum, symbol of the most subtle of servitudes, this rankest of all the scientific corruptions. With my vasculum, I have spent years removing the plant from its habitat, its associations, its sustenance, then finally, its life. I drain it of colour, blood, and nuance. Then, when I am in a museum or laboratory, under artificial light, I empty the shiny and unnatural brass cylinder of my vasculum and, with textbooks, formalin, and various dissecting instruments, I propose to define the plant, to describe it. Pah! This is why I committed the vasculum to the bottom of the Casiquiare, the way one would throw away a rotten fruit, or some shoddy, broken thing.

~

November 16, 1801. Sleepless in tent.

Xochil has come to camp again. I am fully aware of Henri's clandestine relationship with this rather striking woman from the Piaroa village nearby. She is totally unsuited to Henri's emotional sensitivity and scientific talents, yet there is a certain mystery about her; she walks as if she were the possessor of some primitive body of unknown wisdom. I am all in favour of the rights and the essential dignity of these local people but, nonetheless, it pains me to see Henri sharing his intimacy so casually, throwing away such great intellect and sensitivity. He deserves far, far more than Xochil can ever give him.

Henri hides the relationship with the native woman from me, an indication that it embarrasses him. She comes to his tent after dark, as she does tonight, treading silently on bare feet like a jaguar. She will steal away again, probably after Henri goes to sleep. I can usually tell when Henri has spent the previous night with Xochil; the woman's presence somehow calms him. Those are times when I feel a kind of barbaric urge to slap Henri, an impulse that must come from some unevolved and reptilian part of my brain.

It is my damnable restraint, my accursed scientific persona that prevents me from comforting Henri myself, from telling him my feelings about him, from helping him through his personal crisis. So he winds up confiding in Xochil instead, and she comforts him in some strange, almost diabolical way, without words.

November 20. Sleepless again

Xochil has come again tonight. Am I actually jealous of her? Am I displaying this base emotion, which I have always categorically rejected? Both Henri and I accept the virtues of universal love, so why do my eyes narrow and my jaws clench whenever I hear those soft footfalls passing by my tent? Is she providing comfort to him right now, while I swelter alone in the closeness of this canvas, entering the detritus of my day?

Hah. A. does not realize that Xochil means nothing to me. Everything and nothing. He does not understand that no one else can participate in my solitary process of deculturation. Even if I were willing and able to explain the process to Xochil, she is so immediate, that she would reject it. And of course A. is a vessel so overloaded with science and culture that he would be unable to comprehend the very premise of abandoning them.

There does remain the unresolved problem of the palms though. What do I do about the palms? The diversity of their various forms is dazzling — every day I discover new frond and stem patterns. With each new pattern comes the realization that I have been born to the palms, that I have been chosen to unravel their mysteries. A. says their arching and concatenated geometries have literally captured certain mathematicians and held them spellbound. Of course, he would not see any irony in mathematicians being swept away by elegance.

The palms are the one part of my existence, the one corner of science that has not been soiled, or trampled, or rotted away. Their forms and taxonomies hang in front of my vision, like a brilliant tapestry laid over a barren landscape. I myself did not discover how the plams started from a single progenitor and then speciated, each branch heading toward a separate and unique destiny — no. I did not discover that fact. The palms themselves simply and graciously allowed me to understand it.

So now, as a last gesture to the palms before I turn away from science, I shall publish a final paper on their taxonomy, one that is full of conscious errors of both fact and hypothesis, so that all my previous work, my oeuvre, can become discredited and consequently ignored. The palms may thus regain some brief peace before the coming scientific onslaught, some momentary freedom from the inexorable, crushing fate of European collection, taxonomy, science. No one will see my latest work, so it will take decades for others to find the progenitor, the ur-palm, which I myself have located, right here along the fetid Casiquiare. I already have a name for it, *Coccothrinax bonplandii*, but the world will never, ever, hear that name uttered.

I am finished with description, done with classification, done with Xochil, and A. is forever lost to me. I will leave the encampment before he returns, to live my life like the palm does, directly, automatically. I will no longer analyze the jungle. I will embrace it but, first, I must make my own entry into A.'s Journal Number Eight:

My Dear Alexander,

You will not have consulted your journal, and thus discovered this letter, until perhaps days after your return to our encampment, concerned as you would be about my unexplained disappearance. After days of frenzied and fruitless search, you would perhaps give yourself an hour in your tent to reflect, to try to put this strange event into some cultural or scientific context. That is when you would open the fateful Journal Number Eight, and read this note.

First of all, I am safe. I have taken enough provisions, I made a copy of the map that you have worked so assiduously on, and I have certainly learned many survival skills in our years of travel together, not the least of which is to ignore privation, of many and varied kinds. As difficult as our years together have been here in the Americas, at least I have never had to share your company with anyone else. Whether it was our victorious ascent of Mount Chimborazo to claim the world altitude record, or the discovery of curare, or the mapping of your famous Casiquiare Canal whose waters run both ways, or the hundred other accomplishments, we have done them as solitary companions. But when this expedition is over you will return to Europe and to tumultuous acclaim, and your companionship will no longer be shared by just one companion, but by dozens of eminent scientists, poets and heads of state. I could not bear this.

Yes, I have read your journals, and I know you are concerned about "my present mental state". Your concern is genuinely touching, but it does nothing to bridge the gulf that now separates us. I stand now far offshore from the continent of science, and equidistant from the landmass of culture.

The legacy of our relationship is one of contradiction. You were the one I was prepared to give myself completely to, and yet you were also the one who showed me, by example, how to create a part of my soul that is absolutely solitary and inviolate. Well my dear Alexander, not only have I created that solitary part, I have moved into it. This is the region of the soul's geography in which I now live. The beachhead I have established in this lonely country shall be my base camp for forgetting, for a reverse exploration, and for a shedding of science, of taxonomy, of culture.

I was attracted to you through our mutual love for science, yet now I am offended and repelled by that same science, as you saw with the electric eel incident at Los Pantanales. You demonstrated to me that analysis can never be separated from conquest, so I am formally abandoning analysis.

Please, do not blame yourself for this. Perhaps because you are such a powerful figure of science, I came to my conclusions sooner than I would have otherwise, but no matter, I would have come to them eventually, even if I had never met you, never even heard of your glorious name.

Goodbye, dear Alexander. My only regret is that, as fellow scientists, we were never able to explore the uncharted disciplines of love.

RED SQUARE AND COLTON COULEE

I FINALLY LEFT COLOMBIA — RELUCTANTLY — IN THE FALL
of 1968. I could definitely envision a more extended stay for
myself, and a kind of life doing agricultural extension in Third
World countries. But home concerns won out. I had visited
Washington D.C., shortly before joining the Peace Corps, and I
wanted to see more of it, so I chose to make my return there. DC
was an oddly prophetic choice, and a good reintroduction to
America, after a two-year absence. Race riots were in full swing,
anti-Vietnam protests were escalating, and a bitterly fought
presidential race was coming down to the wire. The sitting
Democratic president, Lyndon Johnson, architect of a major
escalation of the war, had seen the handwriting on the wall
and withdrew from the race. The Democratic star-candidate,
Robert Kennedy, had recently been assassinated. The moderate
Hubert Humphrey had narrowly beaten anti-war candidate
George McGovern in the Democratic primaries, and was going
head-to-head against the Republican hawk, Richard Nixon.
Third-party racial segregationist, George Wallace, was solid in
much of the South. His campaign symbol was a baseball bat,
and he handed them out at rallies.

I had heard about the phenomenon known as "reverse
culture shock" — a sense of alienation from one's own culture
after a period of absence from it — but what I experienced in
Washington, D.C. was something far more. Walking the city
at night was an eerie experience. Angry knots of people surged

up and down the streets, on missions of either protest or revenge. Storefronts and businesses were closed and boarded up. The night sky was lurid with the fires of abandoned, burning buildings. I had left America in the Peter, Paul and Mary era of peace and love, of innocent marijuana highs and "We Shall Overcome". I returned to a dissonant era of Altamont, of "drug-related" and of Picking up the Gun. It was a profound, radical transformation.

A lot of the sixties was about hair. My token acknowledgment of this, since beards were way too *fidelista* in Colombia, was to start one in my time in Washington D.C. It has been with me ever since.

I had two relatively aimless years of college behind me, but my time in Colombia had convinced me to become an agronomist. I figured that the simple expedient of producing more food was a way of dodging all the tricky, ethical questions of Third World development. So, after my stay in Washington D.C., I enrolled at Washington State University, in Pullman. In the common parlance, WSU was known as a cow college, one of the land-grant universities mandated to teach agriculture. Pullman sat in the centre of the magnificent Palouse Hills, probably the richest dryland agricultural area on the planet. The Palouse originated by being the prodigal eye of a millennial windstorm. Centuries of silt, lifted from the adjacent Columbia Basin, came to rest here, forming rolling and sensuous hills mantled in eight, ten, and even twelve feet of topsoil, which was then enhanced by the bunchgrass prairie that once covered the hills. Farmers could plant white club wheat (the primary grain used in pasta) in the late summer, harvest it the following spring, immediately put in a crop of peas, and then go right back to white club after the pea harvest. Everything was farmed; giant tractors and Cats pulled gangs of cultivators right over the hilltops and through the gullies.

I began to settle in to Pullman, a heartland community of wealthy, politically conservative farmers surrounding a university enclave.

I found a place to live at the School of Agriculture's sheep research barns, at the far end of campus. The room was a tiny apartment above the lambing pens, which I got for free in exchange for a certain amount of work during lambing and shearing seasons. The barn was a twenty-minute walk from the main part of campus where my classes were, and a forty-minute walk to the nearest grocery store, but the arrangement suited me fine. I was angry — about Vietnam, about American overdevelopment, about our treatment of the Third World. The isolation of the sheep barns helped me feed that solitary anger, and the smugness of the town and the University fed it as well. I got a big sheet of posterboard and made a sign, A FAST TO PROTEST THE WAR IN VIETNAM, and spent a solitary and foodless day in front of the University's Administration Building. Nobody harassed me — this wasn't like Springfield — nor did anyone acknowledge or speak to me, except for one African exchange student, who subsequently became a friend.

In my Introductory Botany class, I asked for time to present a talk on Agent Orange, the incredibly toxic defoliant that was being used to wipe whole swaths of Vietnamese jungle. The professor and the entire class were completely dumbfounded by my guerilla lecture. Any factual information I might have conveyed to them was completely overshadowed by the blazing irrationality of my action — this total stranger getting up to talk politics in the middle of a section on photosynthesis and the Krebs cycle. As I spoke, I was acutely aware of the absolute mystification of my audience, farm kids whose closest brush with politics was probably discussing wheat prices around the supper table. They had a dim idea what I was talking about, but absolutely no idea at all why I was talking about it. I was a terrible public speaker at the time, so on top of the strangeness of the moment, my delivery was abysmal. Midway through the talk, my vision began to blur, sweat beaded on my face and hands, and my heart felt like a runaway locomotive. That talk was so terrible it was a wake-up call: if I was to become an advocate, and influence hearts and minds, I could get no worse than my Agent Orange talk, but I damn well had to get better.

A rumour circulated through the university's tiny anti-war community, that a professor in the Agronomy Department had a contract with the US Army to study chemical defoliants. I volunteered to track the fellow down and confronted him. He was a good ole boy, like a lot of the aggie profs were, and he defused me easily and adroitly by agreeing he had done a contract with the Army, but that it had nothing to do with defoliants. Then he went on to ask me about myself, my classes, and my plans. My middling courage had been used up in simply finding and confronting the fellow, and I remember a feeling of great relief when I decided this pleasant weed scientist wasn't a war criminal. (As I reflect on the encounter, he could have been absolutely complicit, and simply played me.)

I got another part-time job, this one with the university's Soils Department, collecting water samples from the creeks around Pullman. My job was to drive a weekly sampling route in a big, four-wheel drive Chevrolet Suburban belonging to the department. In the process, I got to know all the winding back roads and lanes of the Palouse, as I filled my

sample bottles in the various creeks. These creeks ran brown
not just in the spring, but year around, as tons of precious
topsoil — together with their human cargo of fertilizer and
pesticides — eroded off the steep and overtilled fields. I was
furious about the erosion, and why the university would
simply monitor it instead of filing lawsuits, but driving the
Suburban was great fun. I'd never had much of a chance to
drive, and there were all those miles of unexplored back roads.

If not comfort, at least I found routine in Pullman. The
long walks to campus and the relative solitude of the sheep
barns gave me plenty of time to think. My boss, Jack, the
corpulent head sheepman, lived with his family nearby.
Periodically he would come down to the barns to talk to his
illicit lover on a pay phone that was inexplicably located right
outside my apartment door. So I had to listen to his mournful
conversations, lifted directly from the absolutely lowest grade
of cowboy hurtin' songs.

Otherwise, things were quiet at the sheep barns, except at
shearing time, when I had to miss classes to help out. My job
was to climb down into a long, Bemis gunny sack attached to
a platform. When a shearer finished a fleece, he threw it up
to the guy on the platform, who then dropped it down to me
so I could pack it tightly into the gunny sack with my boots.
The sacker job was a hot, sweaty one, the bottom rung of the
sheep-shearing hierarchy. Bloody fleeces and detached sheep
ticks rained down on me all day, but when it was over, my
leather work boots and cowboy belt were completely saturated
with lanolin, and soft as calfskin.

The local Quaker group invited the pacifist Ammon
Hennacy to speak. I walked in for the evening lecture, not
knowing anything about the man, but intrigued by the
name. Meeting this elderly gentleman, dressed in neatly-

pressed work clothes and sporting a shock of white hair, was a revelation. Here was a guy who refused to fight in two world wars, who worked tirelessly for the poor all his life, who hitchhiked through all of America, who picketed courthouses protesting capital punishment, who did time in jail for his beliefs. He was unassuming and charismatic at the same time. He cycled in and out of religion through the course of his life, which was not surprising, but his core beliefs — pacifism and social justice — never changed. Reading up on Hennacy later on, I ran across an anecdote reflecting his persistence. During a lengthy picket in front of a Phoenix courthouse, the presiding judge passed him every morning and they would acknowledge each other. One morning the judge asked, "Well, Ammon, have you changed the world yet?" To which Ammon replied, "No, but the world hasn't changed me."

Ammon's philosophy should have been the revelation, showing me the righteous and single-minded path of conscientious objection. Instead, he plunged me deeper into quandaries I was already wrestling with. Would I oppose all wars? If I was a young man in 1941, would I have signed up? How useful is it to be a martyr in jail? Can I match the commitment of Hennacy, who went to jail for refusing the draft in World War I, or of Tom Hayden, and others, who were jailed for refusing to go to Vietnam? Where is the line between single-minded determination and a kind of Don Quixote lunacy? Everything of course, was about me, and Ammon passed in and out of my life like a comet that you can't quite turn your head fast enough to see. Here was a guy who had actually lived through World War I, the Dirty Thirties, and World War II, and fought meaningful fights all his life, yet I ignored him. Years later, I discovered that Ammon Hennacy died just a few months after that lecture he gave in Pullman.

On my water sampling route, I took note of the many elegant old farmhouses tucked away in the coulees of the Palouse. Most of them were empty, as the owners had moved into new homes in Pullman's subdivisions. Some had been boarded up and used as granaries. In Colton Coulee, a few miles from town, one house in particular stood out; a two-story, square house with a steep, gabled roof and a big front porch. Surrounding it was the voluptuous monotony of Palouse wheatfields. The house was painted classic white with dark-green trim, and had leaded glass along the tops of the windows. Two big cottonwoods graced the front yard, and an American elm held court in the back. Discreet finials and gingerbread trim were tucked under the eaves of the porch. It was definitely a farmer's house, but from a time when farming was approached with more romance. I inquired in town and found that the house had been built by George Latah, one of the county's pioneer farmers, and was currently owned by his grandson. William Latah, one of the leading lights of the local John Birch Society, still farmed the land but lived in town.

It was spring, and the idea of living in the country, in that house, had taken a powerful hold on me. I trimmed my beard, put on decent clothes, and hiked up to the wealthy subdivision where Latah lived. I knocked on the door of his sprawling split-level, which had no hint of either architecture or humanity, and boldly offered to live in his farmhouse for the summer, in exchange for looking after the place. The fellow sized me up for a long moment, weighing the potential disadvantages — being accused by his fellow John Birchers of harbouring hippies — and the advantage of free upkeep. "Eighty bucks a month," he said. I did a quick mental calculation: that was eighty bucks more than I was paying at the sheep barns, but I wouldn't have that faint reek of sheep manure in my clothing, I would no longer have to listen to Jack's agonized telephone parodies, and I would have temporary possession of a veritable country estate. I agreed and we shook on it.

I went back to campus to gather up my belongings and visit a few friends. University classes were over for the summer. I crossed through the university's main quadrangle, which had become known as Red Square because of the number of protest rallies we had held there. It was nearly deserted now, which made the memory of those rallies and marches seem unreal. There was a definite split in the campus community, between those who left for the summer, and those who stayed on, and my friends were from the diehard, year-round community. They were virtually catatonic, reading comic books or sleeping off hangovers on front lawns. I left in righteous disgust. The great sixties mandala of radical change was pointing me towards the country.

It didn't take me long to move my few possessions. My friend, Richard, was going away for the summer and left me in charge of his motorcycle, a BSA 650 Lightning. It was a huge and stately machine, and I felt like I was driving the Queen Mary as I navigated the gravel roads between Pullman and Colton Coulee. I settled in, planted a small garden, and read textbooks. Buckman and Brady's *Nature and Properties of Soils*, and Cobley's *Botany of Tropical Crops*. Sometimes I just sat in the high-ceilinged living room of the house that belonged to a John Birch wheat farmer, in an overstuffed chair rescued from Pullman's dump, listened to The Flying Burrito Brothers, and watched the late afternoon sun work its shifting magic on the leaded-glass windows. The ancient timbers of the house creaked as they slowly expanded with the sun's heat, and the fine blowdirt on the windowsills gave off the smell of holy parchment. They were sixties moments, but they were not to last.

I was out weeding the garden and generally enjoying the sunshine, when the quiet morning was abruptly shattered by the whine of a powerful engine. Seconds later, a herbicide spray plane roared into view, valves wide open. I made a dash for the house, but not before I was coated with a fine mist of 2,4-D. The garden would be gone by nightfall, I figured, and the elms would take a major hit. William Latah was obviously regretting his decision, and ordered the spray plane pilot to douse me.

The summer became punctuated by these ugly incidents. A Caterpillar D9, towing forty feet of cultivator came next, lumbering down a strip of summerfallow behind the house, and tearing up a big chunk of the backyard as it passed by. Next a truck pulled up into the yard, and two of William's men unloaded fertilizer bags. I went over to look, and as soon as I got close, I caught the ammoniac flare in my nostrils — urea. At forty-six percent nitrogen, the bags were like green explosives, which Latah would use to carpet-bomb the Palouse Hills into agronomic submission.

William's John Birch associates and the neighbours in his pastel subdivision had obviously discovered that he was harbouring a communist-hippie-incubus in his house at Colton Coulee, and they were putting pressure on him. At the end of the month, William himself showed up in a brand-new diesel half-ton with dulies on the back. I came to the door with my eighty bucks in hand.

"I don't want your goddamn money," he said. "Just get your stuff and clear out by tomorrow."

I began to protest, but William turned and stomped off the porch. By the time I caught up with him, he was already in the half-ton, and had started the big Cummins. He rolled the window down halfway, and spoke.

"I need this land, and I'm tearing the house down."

I went into town and borrowed a van to move my stuff out of the house but, as I did so, I could not get a vision out of my head — the big D9, splintering wood, and crashing elms. Sacrificing a patrimony for one more acre of land. I closed and locked the house in my mind. I got to know many other roads that snake out into the Palouse Hills, but I was never to take the Colton Coulee road again.

The Crusade of Fierceness

I GOT TO KNOW MARCUS BECAUSE I pushed him into a chair. I first noticed him sitting alone at a bar downtown, hunched over a beer. He was a big man, and his long, black locks encircled his beer mug, like ragged curtains. There were a couple of worn paperbacks on his table, swelling unevenly as they absorbed beer sweat. At the time, Marcus Johnston was currently somewhere between disenfranchised farmworker, rising poet, and jaded sessional lecturer but, as a first-year agronomy student, I knew nothing of such midpassage crises. People at the bar simply told me he ate literature for breakfast, and had found evidence that Edgar Allen Poe was a plagiarist. Periodically, he would stop reading to write in a tattered notebook. Once, I saw him take a wad of paper napkins from the dispenser on the table, reach under his baggy sweater, and carefully wipe each armpit.

I began to frequent the bar when he did. I wanted to finally meet someone who was passionate about something that had nothing to do with money or politics. The latest word was that his major professor was also the editor of the *Poe Newsletter*, and his doctoral thesis was on the rocks. I also found out that he lived not far from me, with a woman named Joy. In the process of circling Marcus, I discovered that the bar was actually a pleasant place to read in the afternoons. The muffled click of the pool table, the subdued conversation, and the Janis Joplin were a nice change from the penitentiary-quiet of the university library.

Marcus was a member of the English Department, which seemed to have a cult of fierceness about it. A couple of the profs drove Harleys and wore leathers. One grad student had an MG with a big German shepherd permanently installed in the back seat, and another was a bowhunter who drove a Jeep and dressed in camos. Marcus, who walked everywhere and affected nothing more than long hair and his ratty sweater, was publicly acknowledged as the fiercest of them all, but I don't think he even gave it a second thought.

The afternoon in question Marcus was at the back of the bar, as usual. I was sitting with Mano and Pano, who never tired of teaching me elegant and swashbuckling Greek curses. They would first discuss amongst themselves, in Greek, the nuances of each particular curse, so my attention tended to wander. I could see Marcus at the back, hunched over a book. Suddenly I was fed up with the two brothers' endless linguistic scatology. I picked up my beer, walked over, and sat down at Marcus' table. A noticeable hush fell over the bar. I watched the man's consciousness being dragged up from some yawning poetic depth towards the surface, like a monstruous hooked coelocanth. The great, bearded jaws moved, and the dark, angry eyes flickered behind his reading glasses. Then he engaged each bushy eyebrow separately, like a pilot testing his engines.

It seemed time for me to say something.

"So, I hear you like literature."

The jaws clicked behind the dense, black beard, his eyes focussed in my general direction, and Marcus leaned forward.

"*Literature!*" he yelled, directly into my face. "Did you say litera-chure, or litera-teur, or lit-ri-cher" his voice swelled, "or just bloody goddamn books!" and he slammed his hand down on the swollen paperbacks. Again, I was conscious of a hushed silence in the rest of the bar. Even Mano and Pano had stopped their Hellenic obscenities to watch.

"Hey, I was just asking," I said lamely, "I've never really met a poet before."

"Just asking, just asking, just asking." It became a chant, getting steadily louder, and then he stood up. I heard the sound of swivelling bar stools behind me.

Marcus' leonine head shook, the jaws clicked some more, and then he spoke. "Listen, you wet-nose punk, I can give you a lesson in literature, but you're going to get it outside, in the street."

The whole bar was now completely quiet. Even the jukebox had stopped. I noodled around in my chair like Buster Keaton, and finally looked up at Marcus, who glowered over me, his clenched fists on the table. I figured there was about a one percent chance that this was some kind of theatrical postgraduate macho fraud thing, and all the other ninety-nine options included bloody noses and pavement rash. In desperation, I seized the one percent, reached up, put all my fingertips against Marcus' breastbone, and pushed him backward. He fell down heavily into his chair, the paperback books took on more beer, and the chair legs screeched against the floor. Then, from within that awful interval between detonation and annihilation, I said, "What do you know about the poet James Agee?"

Marcus studied me calmly, and then began to chuckle. The chuckle turned into a laugh, and then he threw his head back, sprawled in his chair, and engaged in what I could best describe as an extended bout of Olympian laughter. The muted and pleasant sounds of a college-town bar gradually started up again.

Marcus and I became fast friends, and I was initiated into passion for the abstract. It was exhilarating. He was a big fan of James Agee, and we started a mission dedicated to raising the reputation of the gifted, but tortured, American poet and journalist who chronicled the lives of southern sharecroppers during the Depression years of the 1930's. I called it our crusade of fierceness.

I became welcome at Marcus' home, although his wife, Joy, a sculptor, would grow silent whenever we opened the fridge for more beers. I got invited on Marcus' weekend magical mystery tours of the countryside around Pullman, together with Holman, a William Blake scholar, and his practical wife Annie. Holman also rode above the macho cult in the English Department, because he had thick glasses, incredible erudition, and immense height. These tours usually involved first finding an out-of-the-way lake or river, followed by finding an out-of-the-way bar. The express purpose for the out-of-the-way body of water was to skinny-dip, but I never actually saw Marcus and Holman do it. Joy and Annie would toss their clothes off and skip magnificently to the water, but Marcus and Holman would stay rooted on the blanket, drinking beer, making sandwiches, and slathering on metaphors. I was mightily torn between the literary fireworks on the blanket and the flash of hips and breasts in the water.

Marcus was a hometown boy and knew a lot of people in the neighbourhood around the university. These people became targets for our Agee crusade. We would warm each other up by quoting passages from *Permit Me Voyage* or *Let us Now Praise Famous Men*. Then Marcus would hit upon the name of some friend or colleague and we would descend upon the unsuspecting soul, books in hand, to offer unsolicited readings and commentary. This system worked well until we visited Brian. Brian had been a fellow grad student with Marcus but dropped out after his marriage fell apart. It was late afternoon when we arrived at his small apartment. Brian had gone macrobiotic and was cooking brown rice in a glass pot on a gas stove. He listened to us in silence, watching the pot as the water slowly diminished and the bed of rice expanded.

"All over Alabama the lights are out," Marcus read, paying homage to Agee's magnificent repeating coda, but I could see something was happening with Marcus' old colleague. Some profound and personal watershed was being crossed as Marcus read and the rice cooked. Brian studied the pot intently. His flushed face was level with the pot of rice, and he was making minute adjustments to the stove's burner-control knob. I could see a vein throbbing in his neck. Just as Marcus launched into Agee's brilliant description of the dirt-poor Gudger family, Brian shut off the gas with a flourish, and whirled around to face us. Marcus stopped reading, puzzled. Brian leaned toward Marcus and, in a forced and venomous whisper, said, "Marcus, I don't want to hear one more word from you or this James-bloody-Agee, and both of you people please get the hell out of my house right now."

I went off to work at an agricultural research station that summer. When I came back to school in the fall, I saw Marcus occasionally, but things had changed, in some subtle way. I began to realize that a passion for the abstract can be not only painful, but fleeting as well.

FIGHT OR PLANT

WE SEVEN, ALL YOUNG MEN, ALL strangers, sat on a bench. Waiting. The windowless room had a door at each end, and was completely bare, except for the bench. From time to time someone would fling a hopeless wisecrack against the overwhelming tension in the room. The seven of us had nothing in common, except age, gender, and vulnerability. It was 1969, and we had all received military-induction notices, ordering us to report to Fairchild Air Force Base, west of Spokane, Washington. The seven of us were given physicals, the first step in the military draft induction process. It had been a strange morning, as we were inspected, poked, prodded, and shuffled from one anonymous room to another. All morning, we had been processed as a group, but that was about to change, and I was the only one who knew it.

To help pass the time, I tried to remember some of the words to Arlo Guthrie's "Alice's Restaurant", which was popular at the time. I started singing it, softly, and the guy next to me chimed in, and soon we were all in ragtag male chorus. The meandering song was about Guthrie's experience at a draft physical; like us, he was subjected to "injections, inspections, detections and neglections". Each contributed the verse they could remember from the song, but we all chimed in at the refrain, "You can get anything you want (excepting Alice) at Alice's Restaurant". Then someone remembered Guthrie's verse about "sitting on the Group W bench," which was a kind of code for being in trouble with authority. Instantly, that was our anthem, and seven scared young men were momentarily in full unison as we waited for the next step in the process. Periodically, one of the enormous B-52 bombers headquartered at Fairchild would rumble down the runway towards takeoff, and the entire building would shake violently.

Eventually, a sergeant came in with a manila file folder in his hand. I knew the folder contained something I had written and handed over when I first arrived at Fairchild that morning. It was a single, onion-skin page containing statements I had labouriously typewritten, about pacifism, individual conscience, and war. I had already gone back to that ominous, grey building in Seattle and applied to the local draft board for conscientious objector status. They called me in for an interview, in which I spilled my ethical and moral guts for fifteen minutes while the chairman of the board signed a sheaf of draft-induction letters. Not surprisingly, my application was rejected. I appealed the decision to the state board and waited months for a hearing. Meanwhile, my induction notice had come in the mail. Some of my contemporaries had refused to participate in the physical or any part of the draft process, and I knew they were probably right. But here I was, trying to pick my way through the confused ground of conscience, obedience, honourable dissent, respect for the system but not for its outcomes, how much I was willing to sacrifice to oppose the war, and whether or not I was a pacifist or a coward. I compromised and went to the induction physical, but as a conscientious objector, handing over my inflammatory onionskin as I walked in.

The grim-faced seargent silently looked us over. Then he looked down at the manila folder, extended his hand, palm up, in the general direction of our bench, and began a slow, rhythmic wagging of his index finger. Seven faces watched in anticipation, six of them mystified. The index finger continued wagging in a long moment of almost-theatrical silence. Then the sergeant said one word: "Gayton."

The six strangers presumably went on to be soldiers, and I never saw them again. I went on to be a failed conscientious objector, a war resister, a belated draft dodger, and a passionate Canadian. But none of it came easily. Conscientious objection to war and pacifism had absolutely no part in my upbringing. My grandfather had been a drill sergeant in World War I. My dad was in the Reserve Officer Training Corps in university, and then worked as an engineer for Boeing Aircraft during World War II. They were both staunch Republicans. There was absolutely no common ground between what they experienced and what they stood for, and what I was attempting.

The sergeant ushered me into another windowless room, where I was questioned extensively by three men in civilian suits and short haircuts. They passed my onionskin to each other as if it were something unclean. At the end of the interview, they assured me I would be drafted as soon as my appeal to the state board was turned down. I spent the next few weeks in a kind of limbo, neither student, soldier, nor conscientious objector. My daily routine continued, but I felt like a ghost. Then, on December 1, 1969, US Congressman, Alexander Pirnie, randomly selected the first of 365 dated plastic balls from a large, glass bowl, thus inaugurating a draft lottery based on birthdate. My birthday ball did not come out of the bowl until after 350 others had. Five years of personal turmoil and moral anguish were suddenly flushed away; I had fallen through the cracks of war by way of pure, random chance.

Less than two years later, I had a degree in Agronomy and a soulmate, Judy. We talked a lot about our future in America. "Fight or plant", was a phrase we heard a lot during that period, meaning that the only two honourable choices left to us were to either fight the American military-industrial complex, or vote with your feet by leaving the consumer economy to live off the grid and off the land. Four of our contemporaries had recently been murdered in cold blood during a peaceful anti-war demonstration at Kent State University in Ohio. We decided to shift to planting, or at least to carry the antiwar fight to a rural area. I got a job as a hired man on a cattle ranch in Eastern Washington, and Judy followed me there soon after.

Hired Man

No creature likes going uphill, and cows wrote the book on it. The four of us pushed the herd all morning, towards their summer range on the Shingle Mountain allotment. We managed to get all four hundred across the river and up the steep road to the first bench. Cows, men, horses, and dogs were all exhausted, and an interspecies consensus arose: it was time to rest for a few minutes. Roy, Perry, and Fred stretched in their saddles, each in a particular way so as to relieve some chafe or muscle. I didn't understand why we didn't just dismount and stretch, but I was Roy's new hired man, the fallen-away hippie, and from outside the valley besides. So, I kept my mouth shut, took one foot out of the stirrup, and stretched as best I could.

I had reached a point where becoming a cowboy was inevitable. Like the descending pinball that eliminates possibilities with each bounce, my life finally dropped through the last hole, that of Roy LaGrange's ranch. I'd started working for Roy that winter. He was a settled and quiet man in his mid-sixties, living in the house he'd been born in. Ways of doing things were pretty well set in stone on his ranch. On the even years, his cows went up Shingle on the west side of the valley, and over east to the Balky Hill on the odd.

I called myself a cowboy but, really, I was a hired man, like most other cowboys. It is amazing how an entire lifestyle developed around the horseback part of ranch work, that you did for only four or five weeks a year. The rest of the job was pretty unromantic hired-man work, like cleaning out calf barns, changing sprinklers, and stacking hay.

The three adjoining ranches were a partnership of sorts, and they ran their cows together on the summer range. When Roy had work on his place that required more than the two of us, like dehorning or weaning calves, Perry and Fred would simply appear. And Roy and I would reciprocate. These men had some hidden way of communicating, and of keeping track. This was not done out of generosity. Somehow, close calculations of man-hour contributions were being made, even though I never heard them talk about it. They were probably continuing an arrangement their fathers had started. I called them the Confederates, but not to their faces, though they probably would not have been offended by the term.

The first of June was turnout on to the Forest Service mountain allotments. Most ranchers had long since switched to trucks and cattle liners, but not the Confederates. So here I was, on an actual cattle drive, unsure of whether it was a privilege, an anachronism, an environmental disaster, or all three.

We'd rested and it was time to get the cattle moving again. I was fascinated by Roy's two border collies, who did nothing but prowl around the ranch all day and who were now working like demons, in response to Roy's whistled signals. Slowly, the shifting, 400-cow amoeba began to make its way up Shingle Mountain road and I could see we were heading for trouble. The narrow Shingle Creek drainage had recently filled up with hippies and back-to-the-landers from the Coast, and they lived in yurts and teepees and domes. Some had bought parcels from broken-up ranches, and others just squatted in the wide spots between the road and the creek. They drove Volkswagen vans and raised biodynamic garlic;

they were my contemporaries. Now large parts of the herd were leaving the road and heading for their backyards. The cows desperately wanted to stop going uphill, get out of the heat, get a drink from the creek, find their calves, or just be cantankerous. The orderly cattle drive suddenly broke into a kinetic mayhem of shouting, dog-nipping, bawling, dust and cowshit. It was shock-and-awe, like the Hells Angels arriving at a church picnic. Obviously, no one had warned the hippies about the cattle drive. Garden beds were destroyed. Carefully husbanded dope plants crushed. Clotheslines full of tie-dye dragged to the ground. Mandalas and other New Age art objects knocked over and trampled. The Confederates stayed up on the road, eyes front, and sent me, the hippie apostate, to chase errant cows out of vegetarian garden plots belonging to stunned granola ranchers. One cow knocked over an awning and then splattered cowshit all across the front porch of a plywood Buckminster Fuller dome. It was horrendous. Here I was, ponytailed apprentice to the Western ranching community, wilfully destroying the sustainable lifestyles of my Aquarian brethren. I was dubious about both cultures, and a full member of neither. In that narrow American valley, there was precious little room for in-between.

After a hellish two hours of bovine destruction, we finally reached the cattle guard that marked the separation between private land and Forest Service land, and we all rested again, in the accustomed way. Barrel, the stodgy horse that Roy assigned to me when there was riding to do, broke wind again. Barrel had been farting all morning, giving one of the Confederates, Fred, an opportunity for vicious obscenities. I shifted one foot out of the stirrup to stretch again, wondering as I did so why my horse was the only one farting, when suddenly, with no warning or preamble, I was pitched face down into the dirt. I looked up to see my inverted saddle hanging loosely around Barrel's now deflated belly, and the empty stirrups flapping idly back and forth. Barrel was absolutely calm, as if nothing had happened. Roy and Perry looked away, not wanting to even contemplate the complete, abject humiliation attached to a grown man falling off a stationary horse, but not Fred. He went into gales of too-loud laughter, and then crowed about how much the boys back at the Legion would enjoy this story. I cursed silently as I righted my saddle and cinched it hard against Barrel's deflated flanks. Fred was a problem. He carried a pistol when he rode, which in itself was probably all right, but it was the way he carried it, ostentatiously, on his belt. And he referred to it a lot. A woman-hating bachelor, he was absolutely convinced of the total corrupt idiocy of everyone outside his very small circle of associates. In my mind, the very rankest of the Coast's shit-hippy doper-granola ranchers could not hold a candle to this guy.

We got the cattle moving again, for the last push from the cattle guard up to the open grasslands at the top of Shingle. I had a new respect for Barrel. Whatever the opposite of a hot-blooded horse was, he was it. A few weeks earlier, we'd been riding to check fences and Barrel had stepped right over a full-grown timber rattler. With each plod of Barrel's four big hooves, I expected to be launched into deep space, but he didn't notice the snake. Or noticed it and didn't give a damn. So I already knew Barrel was an equine Zen master of calmness and energy conservation, but now I had to add comic timing to his list of talents.

No more hippie houses complicated the drive, and the air was cooler now, so the cows were content to plod their way up the mountain road. The landscape of dense pine and fir thinned out, and then opened out into a broad plateau of grass. The older cows knew there was rest and forage ahead, so they picked up the pace. We let the herd fan out across their new summer home, and stopped for lunch next to an old windmill and water trough. I was beginning to wonder if we were going to eat in the saddle too, and was relieved when the Confederates dismounted.

I studied the old windmill as I ate my sandwich. This one was a classic Aermotor from the 1930s, with curved, metal vanes and a tail brake. It reminded me of the Tinkertoy windmills I'd built as a kid. The pump it had operated had been ripped out, and the watering trough was now fed by black plastic pipe that ran from a spring further up the hillside. But the windmill refused to die; its vanes still spun, tracking the constant and nuanced winds of Shingle Mountain. The disconnected pump's pushrod, cut off from meaningful labour, clattered uselessly up and down inside the wooden tower.

I asked the Confederates, and yes, their fathers had dug the well and put the windmill up in the Dirty Thirties, when the springs went dry. Fred was vocal about how he hated the windmill.

"Now's a good time to pull this old pecker down," he said.

"How come?" I asked. "It's not doing any harm." Fred ignored me. I asked questions all the time, as a way of maintaining a shred of independence, but not all of them got answered. The talk turned to how to actually do the job, and Fred had a ready answer.

"We'll tie all our lariats together and snug one end to the top of the tower. I've got a little swede saw in my saddlebag, and we can use it to cut partway through the legs. Then we can have one of the saddle horses pull it over for us, and lay it down in the direction we want." Fred had obviously thought this one out. "Who's going to climb the tower?" Perry asked. True to form, no one answered.

Thirty feet up, with a lariat tied to my belt loop, I could feel the subtle shifts and strains of the tower as it adjusted to the constantly-changing winds. The grasslands and ragged treeline of Shingle Mountain spread out below me. The cow herd had scattered, and every animal was head down in the luxuriant Idaho fescue. The situation felt faintly biblical; a sacrificial longhair hanging from a wooden structure. I stayed on the tower for a while, taking in the heart-rending beauty of the East Cascades landscape, and the ambiguity of my situation. I loved windmills; they were sustainable and Quixotic at the same time. They were part of my heritage as a westerner, vertical icons scattered across a dry and horizontal landscape. They spoke of a time before — and perhaps after — petrochemicals. The Confederates watched me from below. Would the hippie tie the lariat on, or not? They knew I was having a "moment", and even Fred shut up.

I did like working for Roy. We fed cows every morning in the winter, using a team of horses and a sled when the snow got deep. I cut the hay bales open and separated them into a dozen or so separate flakes. Then I kicked them off the sled into fresh snow, so the cows wouldn't waste so much. Roy was particular about the way he put up his alfalfa hay, crimping it and baling it at just the right moisture content. As a result, each flake was bright green and smelled as if it had been cut the day before. Day in and day out we fed, and my world became a tapestry of brown Herefords and green alfalfa, against a glittering background of white snow. Then in the spring we spent whole days in the hills, on horseback or in Roy's old Willys, fixing fence. I loved the work. The tools we used were straightforward and reliable: A bale cutter made from a section of sickle bar and a piece of an old shovel handle; fencing pliers you could use to either cut wire, splice wire, pull a staple or pound a staple; a heavy two-handled posthole digger; a wire reel; and a fence stretcher. I was trying ranch work on for size, and it felt good. Maybe I could do it for a lifetime.

We got along fairly well in this small community; Judy was good at making friends and the local ranching families tacitly accepted us, if not our politics. The fact that I knew how to work and wasn't an alcoholic or a wife beater all counted in my favour. The federal government instituted a 10% surcharge on phone bills to help pay for the Vietnam War, so each month we would go to the local telephone company office and pay our bill promptly, minus the ten percent. The ladies at the telephone company had never heard of such a thing, and were gravely concerned that we would be jailed for our forty-three-cent withholdings. These same ladies were central to the valley's informal communication network, so a political shockwave spread rapidly through the valley as people learned about our tax protest. Most were vehemently opposed, some were just pleased to have something new to gossip about, and the few supporters kept their mouths shut.

The Canadian border was not far from where we lived, and it seemed we were moving closer to it all the time, both politically and geographically. This job with Roy felt like a kind of swan song.

The last of the four lariats was now snugged around Barrel's saddle horn, and I stood in front of the horse, reins in hand. At Fred's sign I led him slowly forward until the lariats were taut. The first sign of collapse was the splintering noise of partly-sawn timbers. I looked back and Fred gave me another high sign, so I pulled on the reins again. Barrel strained, and then released as the quarter-sawn tower timbers screeched and finally surrendered. The whole fantastical windmill structure arced silently through the sky, then landed with an enormous crash, spewing dust into the air. The weight and momentum caused the wooden tower and the metal mill to collapse into themselves. The other horses shied and bucked, but Barrel never even looked around.

I went over to the shattered mill to look for a souvenir, perhaps a piece of the cast-iron gear housing, but it had broken into unrecognizable shards. I felt slightly sick, knowing I had participated in something I would live to regret. I walked back slowly to where the Confederates were waiting. They looked at me expectantly, since they knew this had been some kind of rite of passage.

I mounted Barrel and then spoke, not to them, but to the landscape in general. "I just learned something. Never pull down your own windmills."

No one asked for clarification.

GROUND TRUTH

THIS LATEST GADGET IN MY LIFE was called a planimeter. It came nestled in a velvet-lined box and was encrusted with dials, measuring scales, and various adjusting screws. My ancestors had given me a genetic weakness for scientific instruments like this one. I tried to tell George how this new piece of technology could save us days and days of tramping around, measuring reserve fields. George was hostile, though, and would not pay attention as I put the gorgeous little device on top of a brand-new aerial photograph and began to trace out a field.

"Actually, you can't help being wrong on your measurements," George said, "since you're using those damn photographs. And if that's Fred Poitras' field you are trying to measure, forget it. I know that field. It's a Texas quarter because Fred farms the road allowance, so there's 170 acres total. His field was 110 acres to start with, so you subtract that, then there's ten acres of sloughs and also that fifteen-acre pasture in the corner that his kids use for calf roping, and you subtract those, too. And you remember we told the contractor to leave five acres of bush around Fred's house. So you subtract those five and there you go, what's left over is thirty acres of bush, and that's how much the contractor must have cleared. It's just simple math, Gayton."

I ground my teeth quietly, and kept on tracing. A lavish prairie sunset spilled through the windows of the drab office, where George, Anwar, and I had gathered after a day's work.

My transition from an eastern-Washington cattle ranch to this agricultural extension office in rural Saskatchewan had been rapid. We had finally gotten our immigration papers, packed our two infant sons, a beagle dog, and all our belongings into a 1953 Chevrolet half-ton, and drove to Saskatchewan. It was like the Dirty Thirties, but in reverse, since I was coming to the prairies instead of leaving them. I did some graduate study in Saskatoon and then landed this job, working with First Nations farmers. Meanwhile, we did our best to maintain a pacifist home. My beloved Browning shotgun was kept hidden in the closet, out of sight of our young children. I went on clandestine duck hunts, carefully gutting and plucking the birds, then wrapping them in grocery store meat trays so the children wouldn't know I had shot them. No war toys of any kind were allowed in the house but, to our intense frustration, the two boys would use sticks as rifles and bananas as pistols.

Some of the native farmers George and I worked with were expanding their operations, and we hired contractors on their behalf to bulldoze and clear new farmland for them. In the old days when Indian Affairs was in charge of this work, some of the contractors had gotten away with murder by padding their acreage claims, knowing that no one would actually go out to walk the fields and check on them. Not any more. In the slow dance of learning to work with each other, George and I found total agreement on the sanctity of measuring these newly cleared fields and not paying the contractors a single nickel more than their due. Getting accurate acreage figures became like a mission: we would spend days tramping over the fertile chaos of roots and soil, measuring and remeasuring, working behind the big Cats as they sheared off aspen and jackpine. It took a lot of time, and a lot of approximation.

"Fred's field isn't a fair test of this system," I said finally, "because you already know that field. Once I figure this planimeter out, we can use it to take measurements of any field, right off these photographs. And it could even be a field you haven't seen before."

George snorted. He was serious, but there were permanent laugh wrinkles in the corners of his eyes. He lived for calculation, and good arguments. "And what about that estimate you made on Harold Keesekoot's field?" he asked, derisively. "I guess that little machine of yours doesn't know the difference between forty acres and 400."

He had me on that point. But there I was, the new kid, and George had forty years of reserve farming experience. I still couldn't mark off an acre if it fell on me, and George not only knew most of the fields we measured, but had actually farmed some of them on cropshare. He talked about them as though they were members of his family. The planimeter and the photographs were going to be my way of getting professional parity with George. But my maiden estimate, on Harold's land, was a wonderfully precise disaster, right out to the third decimal place.

George leaned back in his chair, stretched out his legs, and thumped his big cowboy boots down on the corner of my desk. I could tell, he was beginning to enjoy this. George, Anwar, and I had been together long enough to know that each put in a full day working with the farmers, and we had come to see these occasional sessions after work as a kind of payoff.

"Okay," I said, resuming the argument. "I admit I've got to do some fine tuning on my planimeter technique. But look, some of our walking estimates could be way off, and you know it."

George denied that statement as if he were under oath.

"What about when mud gets caked all over the measuring wheel, and makes it bigger," I countered. "That's going to throw our numbers out of whack. Or what about when we start walking towards a field corner that we can't see because there's a hill right in the middle of the field. There's no way we can guarantee we're walking in a straight line towards the corner."

George was not even listening; he had turned to Anwar and started talking about a farm loan the two of them were working on. I knew he would answer eventually; this was his way of letting me know that my arguments did not merit an immediate response.

Finally turning back to me, George pointed to the photographs on my desk by motioning with the toe of his big boot.

"I tell you those damn things are no good. How could some bloody airplane pilot from Edmonton know anything about this land? He'd be lost in five minutes if he ever came on the reserve. Let alone be able to walk across a half-section that's just been broke. And that machine," he said, more for Anwar's benefit than mine, "that machine of yours is nothing but a toy for grown-ups."

"Ah, now I see. You don't like all this technology because it makes things too easy."

George responded that my biggest problem was that I couldn't add figures in my head, a statement that had more than a grain of truth to it.

Getting accurate measurements on some of the newly broken fields had been a real challenge. Indian fields, because of complex hereditary ownership systems and because of an enduring respect for bush, were never square, or even rectangular. Instead they were complex serpentines, trapezoids, and irregular polygons. Reserves had none of the geometric, easily measured landscape of the white man's prairies. Indian farmers tended to stay clear of sloughs with good muskrat, worked their way around old sweat lodges, and kept their cultivators at a respectful distance from sacred ground. Once we were measuring on Little Black Bear, George's own reserve, and he took me aside to a narrow grove of aspen that wound through the field. There, in the bush, half-buried in aspen leaves, was the single gravestone of one of his relatives. I brushed the leaves aside; below the man's name was the date of his death in France — 1914 — and below that was inscribed a single word, one that spoke volumes: SAPPER. We went back to our work without comment, but I kept on mulling the gravestone over in my head. Underneath it lay the remains of a young man who had none of the rights of his fellow citizens, couldn't buy land, couldn't leave the Reserve without permission, and yet undertook war's most dangerous job — clearing land mines — in the service of his country.

Our standard way of measuring a field was to divide it into a series of blocks, rectangles, and triangles, then walk the perimetre of each one, pushing a measuring wheel in front of us. The wheel was made in Cederholm, Texas, and had a handle with a little counter on it. The wheel measured six feet six inches in circumference, and every revolution moved the counter ahead by one. Six-feet-six was a number of pure Anglo-Saxon mystery, since it related mathematically, by obscure multipliers, to the chain, and the chain to the acre. Rods and furlongs were separate.

I would puzzle over these curious, quirky units as we walked behind the wheel, wondering if they could be traced back to some ancient rites of mensuration at Stonehenge, or some other mysterious place. I could visualize hooded figures pacing off sacred distances in the dark of night, measuring barleycorns and knuckle joints. Torches would flare against carefully placed stone slabs. There would be chanting, and sometime around sunrise, a sheep or goat would be sacrificed. Forever after, farmers and fieldmen would pay secret homage by muttering about chains-to-acres and rods-to-furlongs. And here we were, deep into the twentieth century, still thinking it was all science. Meanwhile, George would be working and reworking numbers in his head, adding up the little blocks and rectangles and triangles. Half a quarter here, add two forties, subtract ten for the woodlot, call that borrow pit two acres, and so on. Sometimes the mosquitoes were fierce.

We were still measuring on foot, balancing George's direct-intuitive against my pseudorational, when someone told me that the whole region had been recorded in aerial photographs, and there was a device called a planimeter that one could use to measure land area right on the photograph. I persuaded head office to let me buy the measuring device and a set of photos.

A quick look at the manual revealed that you placed the planimeter right on top of the photograph, held the weighted base steady in one place, and slowly moved the jointed measuring arm, capturing sloughs and bluffs and fields. The central part of the machine had a set of tiny number wheels, like an odometer. As you moved along the edge of a field with the arm, the number wheels would spin, slow, or reverse direction obediently. When you had traced the field all the way back to your starting point, the final figures on the number wheels could be converted into acreage, again by an obscure formula. I had no idea what actually happened inside the little machine, but was naturally attracted to it.

George finally slid his boots off my desk and sprawled them across the floor of our cramped office. We all felt a bit like overfed housecats in the warm sunlight. Then, George came back at me with his big gun, his most trenchant criticism: photographs flatten out the hills that are so painfully evident to the farmer on his tractor. That to him was a most damnable fact, and he was eloquent about the three-dimensional nature of farmland. Anwar was obviously enjoying this, I had to admit I was too, as the whole argument began to slide into play. We made an odd trio, the quiet Egyptian, the older Indian farmer, and the young honky pseudorational. It was clear from the first day we started working together that any friendships would first be subject to performance; each one of us had something to prove. So far we had been doing well. We all managed to do some violence to nearly everyone's stereotype, and that was a help. Head office was a hundred kilometres away, and that was helpful, too.

George stood up to go.

"Look, Gayton," he said. "We're settling up with Holovaty and Sons tomorrow on that big clearing contract on Ministawin. You bring those damn photographs and that little machine of yours along."

I was surprised. Old Metro Holovaty was our toughest contractor, and the farmers told us he had taken Indian Affairs to the cleaners a couple of times. Whenever we negotiated with him, Metro was always flanked by his two mountainous sons, who were usually flanked in turn by their mountainous, rumbling D8 Caterpillar tractors. The Holovaty clan's idea of contract negotiation was to spread the maps and the contract out on the muddy treads of an idling D8, and then yell at us over the sound of the engine. They moved in an atmosphere of diesel, and the boys seemed to genuinely enjoy knocking trees over with their big machines.

··"Jeez, George," I said, genuinely surprised, "I didn't think I would ever convert you so easily."

George Belanger leaned over my desk and casually moved one of the weights holding down my stack of unrolled photographs. Instantly they re-rolled themselves into a tight little bundle. My precious planimeter was inside, along with several pencils, a notepad, and my calculator.

"Just bring 'em along, Gayton. Old Man Holovaty will be so impressed with your scientific stuff that he won't dare pad his acreage claim. You just baffle them with your bullshit and we'll use my numbers."

He left. Anwar smiled and shook two fingers quickly, like he had just burnt them. We listened to George's big boots echoing down the drab, green stairwell. He would be heading to Regina to spend the rest of the evening at the racetrack, working more numbers. Anwar stood up to go too, since there wasn't a lot left to say.

I stayed on, saying I had to make a few phone calls. When Anwar was gone, I went out to the confectionery and bought a big bag of taco chips, then came back to the planimeter instruction book. An hour later, I had it — ground truth. A fundamental that I had missed on my first reading.

Ground truth turned out to be a minor revelation, a good concept with some poetry to it. Find two specific landmarks on the ground that can also be seen in the photograph, and then measure the distance between them, once in the photograph, and once on the ground. Fix those two distances into a ratio, like an inch on the photograph equals a mile on the ground. Suddenly, two independent objects, the little quadrant of real earth and the photographic image of it, now have a bond and a fixed relation to one another, a benchmark, a *ground truth*.

Now I could verify my photographic artifacts, my representations of reality, in reality itself. And by inference, all the other parts of that artifact would bear the same ratio to the real world. The measure from the slough to the edge of the aspen bluff then, or from the grid road out to the working corrals, is meaningful. Those humble distances are a leg up into the universe.

I felt illuminated, and couldn't wait to tell George about ground truth. I could use analogies to explain it, like what a person says can be ground-truthed by what they do. Scientific theories can be ground-truthed by known facts. There was even a ground truth for what we were doing: the success of an agricultural extension program could be ground-truthed over the scratched formica of a beginning farmer's kitchen table.

I thought about how the next day at Ministawin might go. We had walked every inch of that clearing project, and Metro would get paid for exactly the amount that he had done. George would have the figures, and I would have the supporting hardware. I could show Metro the velvet-lined box, and perhaps mention ground truth. George might even buy in to the concept if he thought it could gain us an edge in negotiations with Metro.

Finally, I put the planimeter and manual back into the box, and closed up the office for the night. I did truly love extension, and was grateful for having stumbled onto the profession: the conveying of appropriate technical information; the honouring of experiential knowledge; the edge of social justice.; the delicious reciprocality; the Jeffersonian conviction of the value of rural people and rural life; the notion that if you are really proficient at extension, at providing people with not only good information, but good sources of information, you've successfully worked yourself out of a job.

VICTORIA PARK

IF HE SHAVED A FEW MINUTES off either side of noon, Breti could grab a bag lunch and coffee at the deli, and get a full hour in the Park. The five blocks over was a forced march, pushing the limits of sidewalk decency, but as he crossed Albert Street, he slowed down. Slowing down was essential: the whole park was a single city block, and if you approached it with too much speed or urban hype, you could miss the whole point.

He found a strategic, unoccupied tree trunk that was in partial sun, partial shade, and sat down facing the open centre. The Jesus people weren't singing today, that was good. They had been there several noon hours last week, and he was sure they were disturbing the normal pattern. Shelley, his new co-worker at the shop, complained about them too. She was loud and raucous and she loved the park. That was a good sign.

As he unwrapped his salmon on brown from Burtzyk's Deli, he chuckled, realizing he had unconsciously chosen a spot by the very criterion he was attempting to define and measure. "Subject James Breti selected partial sun, with sufficient dappled shade that sweat would not be a factor. And sufficient shade was present to minimize glare on the page as the subject took notes." That would be anecdotal evidence — real, but not quantifiable. It could eventually be laid alongside the main hypothesis, like a sprig of parsley.

This was Sector Four, with one of the higher insolation values, but Sector Five, the open area next to the Cenotaph, contained the central mystery. Women gathered there, in groups of two, three, and sometimes four. They settled down slowly, tucking and arranging as they did, perhaps taking off a sweater to expose arms and shoulders to the July sun. Once they were nicely settled, those in dresses would often slide hemlines up, carefully, until the first part of the thighs were exposed to the sun. Massive, old American elms encircled Sector Five, softening the vast and brassy light of July noon.

He had already proven the hypothesis numerically, but he knew he had to re-prove it, wear it, and even live in it. He had been wary of the hypothesis at first, since it was a blatantly obvious overlap of science and desire. There was the sensual attraction of the women, of the rich colours of the trees and flowerbeds and grass, of the sun, and of the gentleness of the noonday park. Yet, out of this same environment he had managed to forge a hard-edged hypothesis, a reduction of experience to mechanism. The park engaged him analytically and lyrically at the same time. His friend, Hannon, had sent him an essay by Albert Einstein that helped ease his doubts. Einstein described the process by which scientists make a hypothesis. First they selected certain facts from the plane of experience, and then stepped back into abstraction to create the hypothesis which, in turn, should explain and corre-spond to events in the plane of experience. The entire process is rational, said Einstein, except for the initial choosing of facts. That was where the intuition, passion, and the subcon-scious leak into the scientific method. The individual scien-tist's fundamental presuppositions — his "themata", Einstein called them — intervene at that crucial point. Breti was relieved when he read that. He had many themata. Some of them he was not even aware of yet.

It was Hannon that got him started in the Park. Hannon spent most of his time in the Rockies, climbing mountains with windswept and distant-sounding names. Once in a while he came down to Regina to visit Breti. Hannon lived in the mountains, but he also lived in a world of ideas and Socratic dialogue. The last time Hannon visited, Breti was depressed about his chances of ever going back to school. Hannon, who was older, had been a grad student, and even did a stint at the National Research Council, was sceptical.

"Jim Breti, all you can talk about are the projects you are going to do once you get into school. Why don't you see what you can do right now?"

"Right now I am working full time in a photography shop, in case you hadn't noticed."

"So, where is this law that says scientists can't work in photography shops?" Hannon responded. "Look, the last two visits I've made out here, all you can talk about is what you are going to do, not what you are doing. And besides, what is there about some second-rate university that is going to change your life?"

"That's not fair. You know as well as I do that that's where the equipment is, the libraries, the knowledgeable people, the time . . . I just can't do anything right now."

"Do you remember that play we read, Brecht's *Galileo*?"

"Sure."

"Do you remember when Galileo invites the official astronomers to look through his telescope, to prove some point he was making? The chief astronomer says, 'allow us the pleasure of a learned disputation first,' and the bastards never do look through the telescope, do they?

Breti nodded, wincing a little.

"What I want you to do, Jim, is to stop worrying about studying science. Why don't you just go out and do some science."

That conversation nagged for months, until the park idea alighted, like an unexpected butterfly on his arm.

Groups of people that had finished restaurant lunches and had a few minutes to spare were trickling into the park, strolling the pathways and talking. That meant his own lunch hour was passing too. He shifted his back against the tree and turned to his notes again. There was the problem of which discipline his research would fall into (Biology? Anthropology? Landscape Architecture?), and that it was totally without financial or functional importance. He reminded himself again that those were other people's problems, not his.

Turning to the worn notebook, Breti skimmed the hard-edged prose he was working on. Passive tense, elliptical grammar, emphasis on objects. Generic categories rather than individual identities. Hands-off. Brutally short. And the conclusions; negative and minimalist, almost as if they were written by a rival who was trying to destroy his hypothesis. There was a quote from the Galileo play that hit on this very point, and he had memorized it:

"Yes, we will question everything, and everything once again. And we shall advance not in seven-league boots, but at a snail's pace. And what we find today we shall strike from the record tomorrow . . . "

The recollection of that speech always gave Breti a warm tingle up his spine. He especially liked the way Galileo told his assistant that they would start their work on the existence of sunspots not by assuming they were clouds, which was within the realm of the possible, but by assuming they were fish tails. The null hypothesis. What a poetic way of stating it, Breti thought. He re-read the crucial Materials and Methods paragraph:

> Sectors were established using a combination of natural boundaries (internal walkways and sidewalks) and arbitrary divisions, to create seven of roughly equal size. Sector areas were further corrected to remove monuments and statuary. Insolation values were taken using a Weston P-18 hand-held visible radiation meter. Weekly observations were made at five random points in each sector at solar noon through July and August. All values for each sector were averaged and found to be significantly different to $p=0.05$ (see Table 1).

He had taken the classical approach; intuit the hypothesis, then state the opposite — the null hypothesis — then attempt to prove the null hypothesis wrong. The risks involved in proving oneself right, instead of proving oneself not wrong, were subtle but large, Breti knew.

He remembered the first time he took measurements in the park, with a borrowed meter and clipboard in hand. He soon found there was no way to work discreetly. But the people who noticed were friendly, sometimes curious. They assumed he was a city employee working on Dutch elm disease or something like that. Most of the time he would go along with the Dutch elm idea, which sounded like an interesting study in itself, but occasionally he would try to explain what he was really doing. The inevitable response to his explanation was — why? That was a good one.

What a crazed idea, he thought, with no conceivable practical application. Winding between seated groups of people at momentary rest, measuring sunlight. Winding in and out of art and science, practical and abstract, rigorous method and silly whim. If a research project reaches a certain standard of purity, does it risk decaying into frivolity? Am I breaching this hallowed separation in our culture, allowing the lyrical to infect the scientific? This tendency could be identified as a major psychological affliction. *Lyriosis. Scientia passionale.* He furrowed his brow and read on.

> Sector population gender counts, and insolation measurements were made on the same days, counting occurring between 1220 and 1250 hours, the period of maximum seated population. Totals and gender ratios for each sector were obtained and averaged. No corrections were made for movements before or after counting. Individuals seated on benches or other objects were counted; standing individuals were not.

He looked up to see how things were developing. The pattern was in full flower, brought on by bright, sunny skies and a light breeze. This was his first scientific hypothesis, almost like catching a first fish, and it was beautiful. The jump to the plane of abstraction was perfect, and re-entry into reality made hardly a ripple.

> The hypothesis that female individuals prefer areas of the park with higher insolation values was shown to be true. Female-to-male ratios were consistently higher in the Sectors with highest solar-flux density (Sectors 4, 5 and 7). Males showed a definite preference for shaded areas, with shaded park benches particularly sought after. As further proof of concept, the gender distribution pattern broke down on overcast days, with genders distributing randomly.

Individuals! They were men and women, working out careers, worried sick about the company's plans for downsizing, being whimsical for a moment in the park, thinking about a molar that should be pulled, wishing they had packed one more sandwich, and quite possibly falling in love, if only momentarily.

Men seemed to require benches, but the women sat on the ground with abandon, exposing bright pastels and skin to the pleasant ravages of grass and earth and sun. His experiment had proven one very mundane thing about women — they respond to summer in a more physical way than men do. He knew that was the mere tip of a gender iceberg, and that the rest of that iceberg belonged not in a scientific journal, but in a poem.

A bright pastel loomed over him, and he looked up. It was Shelley, and she was brushing bits of mown grass off her skirt. "Hey, guy, are you going back to work or not?"

In Residence

THE MAN WAS STANDING PERFECTLY STILL in the middle of the quiet residential street, facing the bright morning sunlight. Gary Jenkins stepped quietly out onto the balcony of his new second-floor apartment to get a closer look at this odd sight. The man's arms were outstretched, as if nailed to a crucifix. Jenkins put his age to be late fifties, but he was still fleshy and powerful. His clothes were ill-fitting, and his lanky, grey hair fell from underneath a greasy baseball cap. An old-fashioned paper grocery bag with jute handles lay on the pavement beside him. My god, Jenkins thought, here's a man standing in the middle of the street looking like he's being baptized, and he's not thirty feet from my balcony. Hurriedly, he stepped back into the apartment and locked the sliding glass door, shutting the disturbing image from his mind.

The apartment's living room was almost bare, but that would soon change, when all the equipment was set up. The new chesterfield was definitely a plus, and it had been a simple matter to browbeat the landlord into replacing the old one. The apartment would be just fine and the rent was a third of what he had been paying in Toronto. The city itself was another story; it had a kind of alien rawness about it. Even though it was sunny, there was a bitter edge in the wind, and it was only September. When the news of his Regina appointment came, his acquaintances regaled him with stories about the isolation, the winters, the lack of culture on the prairies, but Jenkins only gritted his teeth. A writer-in-residence appointment was a definite career step, an asset on grant applications, and almost a requirement for tenure. It was were nearly impossible to get one in Toronto.

His new apartment was in a downtown neighbourhood that was a mixture of old brick houses and newer apartments. These few blocks could almost pass for Toronto, he thought, so long as one didn't look too far down the wide, flat streets. But there was a strange air about the town, even in this neighbourhood. Men in overalls and women in scarves moved about on obscure errands. How they earned money and carried out their lives he had absolutely no idea. They all appeared slightly feverish, like the strange man in the street. It suddenly occurred to him that the behaviour of the man outside his balcony could be considered quite normal here.

Day One, he told himself, with eight months to go. Unpacking could wait until after he went out for some breakfast. He decided to walk, but to leave the building through the back, to avoid the man in the street. Passing through the basement parkade, he looked over fondly at his minivan, parked neatly against the far wall. It was the perfect vehicle for him, handling like a sports car while still allowing ample room for storage. The minivan reminded him of other, more pleasant expeditions — the reading at McGill, the Maniwaki Writers' Retreat, the Poetry Exchange at Cornell. The culture in those kinds of places would no doubt seem even more meaningful when he returned.

There was a restaurant a few blocks from his apartment. He had noticed it the night before as he arrived; the outdoor tables and Perrier umbrellas had caught his eye. Now, as he walked through the restaurant's deserted patio, he noticed the tables and chairs were brand new, and several umbrellas had blown over in the night. A mound of dry leaves spun in the corner.

The waitress had no croissants and did not know what a latte was. He ordered dry toast, and made allowances. Last night's Champagne Reception for Gary Jenkins, New Poet in Residence at the Public Library had been no different; the champagne was Baby Duck, and it was right out in the open. Instead of imported cheeses and crackers, there were perogies and something called *holubchi*. Jenkins was amused, and sipped a glass of the wretched local water. Prairie matrons and earnest young men with bad skin fawned over him, posing searching and awkward questions. Making an effort to mingle with the crowd, he'd overheard the words "Toronto, published" more than once, and had liked the sound of it. He could wear that mantle of "Toronto, published" quite nicely out here, along with the classic black turtleneck and dark silk jacket.

As he ate his toast, he began to plan the morning's unpacking. All the electronics were neatly stored inside the minivan: CD player, amplifier, and speakers; then there was the computer, printer, CD-ROM, and modem, and of course the monitor and stereo VCR. By setting it all up properly, I can create a complete interior environment, he thought. A few tropical plants and maybe a small, tasteful fish tank might add a subtle natural touch. Eight months' residence could be just that. I'll do the readings and classes and some polite edits of grubby manuscripts about farms and pretended urban life, or whatever it is these people find to write about. This residency is for my c.v. and does not include ethnic foods or assimilation or large, old men transfixed by September sunlight.

On his way back to the apartment he passed a huge, industrial-looking truck parked right on a neighbourhood street.

On the pavement near the back of the truck was a small pile of grain of some kind. No one else was on the street, so he quickly reached down and grabbed a handful, realizing intuitively that the hard, shapely kernels must be wheat. They were a deep-amber colour, and seemed almost translucent in the bright sunlight. The loop of a poem flickered momentarily, connecting grain and sunlight and transfixed men, but he quickly dropped the handful and walked on, hoping no one had seen him. The day would be a pleasant one, getting the apartment set up, making sure everything was properly wired and balanced. He could make his formal appearance at the library tomorrow.

I might as well bring up the first armload on my way back to the apartment, he thought, as he entered the steel self-locking door of the parkade. He liked the quiet atmosphere of the structure. Its clean, bare concrete was well-lit by fluorescent lights, and the cars were all newer models neatly arranged, as if in a showroom. The perfect, gunmetal blue of the minivan awaited him. He had put it through a carwash the night before, just as soon as he arrived. Everything worked together in the vehicle — the classic, swept front, the European radials, the high, boxy back, and the lightly tinted windows.

Jenkins came around to the back of the minivan and froze in the bright, respectful silence. His brain tried desperately to reject what his eyes showed him, this horrendous flaw in an otherwise-perfect image, this brutally missing rear window. Neatly, surgically excised, no broken glass, the job was absolutely, coolly professional. He didn't have to look any further, but he did (he was from Toronto). The cargo storage area was spotlessly empty. Like the slow-motion films of buildings being imploded, Jenkins felt his residency begin to crumble.

There was an Ace Hardware on the corner, full of shovels, garden seeds, and ghastly Ukrainian ceramics. Numbly, without speaking, he bought a roll of duct tape and some clear polyethylene. He knew he would have to stretch the poly tightly to avoid irritating flapping noises at highway speeds. A double layer of tape should prevent it from working loose in the wind. Doing a quick mental calculation, he decided he could make Winnipeg by late evening. That wheat poem could be his best, he knew, but he vowed to himself never to write it.

No Sex, No Supper

FIVE-YEAR-OLD JOE SLIPPED AND KNOCKED HIMSELF out on the marble floor of the cavernous station, just before the train arrived. Weeks of anticipation for our midwinter trip to Vancouver hung in the balance as we rushed to gather up his limp body. The rest of the kids huddled around us, wide-eyed as the seconds ticked down on the huge station clock. We could feel a goose egg beginning to form on the back of Joe's head.

I was about to go for the ambulance when Bork, who was travelling with us, yelled, "Wait! He's opening his eyes!" Judy held her hand in a Boy Scout salute in front of Joe's face and said, "How many fingers?" Joe said, "Two," in a groggy voice. As his piercing wails began to fill the great, vaulted dome of the Regina station, we grabbed our luggage and sprinted out to the waiting train.

Passenger train travel is supposed to be romantic; as a Canadian I know this to be a self-evident truth. Or, at least it is supposed to be about adventure. And if not adventure, then train travel at a minimum should expose some of the identifying fabric of our country, some of the heartland warp and woof. As we boarded our train, two conductors stood by in heated debate, something about overtime. They completely ignored us, providing a swatch of national cloth for me to file away and left us to load ourselves, our bags, and all the associated paraphernalia that four young children require, onto the train. The car we clambered on to was Car

163, not Car 212, as our tickets specified, so we established a temporary base camp on 163 while I went one direction and Bork, who was coming with us because he didn't drive, did not "do" airplanes, and needed our moral support even to get on a train, went the other, in search of Car 212. When we finally gathered in the appointed car, we found that our seats were occupied by a group of enthusiastic Tupperware ladies from Winnipeg. We compared tickets and, sure enough, ours were identical to the Tupperware ladies', right down to date, car number, and seat numbers.

At that moment there was a catastrophic bang followed by squeals of tortured metal, and the train shuddered into motion. Later on, I was to learn that these noises did not indicate catastrophe, and that there is simply no gentle way to start a train. At this point a conductor arrived, having finished his overtime discussion. Conductor Soames, as his nameplate advertised, was entirely encased in a blue uniform and an enormous, matching trainman's cap. Like a kind of aging, blue rooster, he surveyed the situation and demanded to know what the problem was. Judy held out our unpunched, virgin tickets for Conductor Soames to see. He then looked at the Tupperware ladies' tickets and confirmed that, yup, by gum, they did have the same date, same car and same seat numbers.

"Well, it doesn't matter," Conductor Soames said with an air of finality. "Try some of the other cars. Just find individual open seats wherever you can, and we'll get a group of seats for you when we add more cars in Calgary." With that, he extracted his shiny, silver punch tool, and reached for our tickets.

Like a pair of opposing magnets repelling each other, the further Conductor Soames' hand reached forward, the more

Judy's hand, and the tickets, drew back. Eventually, a kind of apogee was reached, when Conductor Soames' hand was fully extended, and Judy's was fully retracted. The conductor's eyes narrowed to slits behind his bifocals.

It was Judy who first broke the pregnant silence.

"When we get seven seats together, like we bought and paid for, then you'll get your tickets."

The rather stale air of this portion of Car Number 212 suddenly crackled with drama. Conductor Soames' demeanour shifted perceptibly from bored disinterest to judicial formality, and a muscle in his left cheek began to twitch.

"You are hereby in breach of Section 54," he declared. "It's against the law to be on this train without giving me your ticket to punch," he said, pulling himself up to his full height of about five-foot-five.

At this point the Tupperware ladies, who had been on the train since Winnipeg and had imbibed in preparation for the big sales convention in Vancouver, began to take an interest. It turned out that Car 212 was entirely full of Tupperware ladies. A boozy and slightly pugnacious ripple spread down the length of the car. These home-based entrepreneurs were not a group to stand by while a young mother was being bullied. All eyes turned to us to watch the response.

"Look, Conductor Soames," Judy said in an even tone, as if she had rehearsed it, "we bought these tickets a month ago with our own hard-earned money, so we can go to Vancouver and let my parents see their grandchildren. We kept our end of the bargain, but you didn't keep yours. When you give me seven seats together, you'll get these tickets."

By this time the train had cleared the city and was streaking through the early morning wheatfields of the Regina Plain. The situation in Car 212 had reached a kind of Saskatchewan standoff. As the sun rose, several Tupperware ladies at the far end of the car took the opportunity to do some morning calisthenics. Standing on the backs of their seats and holding on to the baggage racks overhead, they gyrated back and forth, singing at the tops of their lungs, "No sex, no supper, just Tupper Tupper Tupper." Other Tupperware ladies began to gather in the aisle around us, in a kind of impromptu support group. These were wives and mothers who hustled extra income for summer holidays and braces for the kids by selling plastic kitchenware out of their homes, and they were not to be messed with.

Outwardly, Conductor Soames remained the picture of calmness. He methodically put his silver punch tool into its leather holster, withdrew a two-way radio from a pocket of his uniform, and spoke into it. "Soames here. We have a Code Blue in Car 212. Radio ahead to Moose Jaw and tell them to have the Mounties meet the train."

The kids wanted to know what was going on, so Judy explained to them, in a voice loud enough for all the Tupperware ladies to hear, "Children, this bad man here wants to kick us off the train so we can't see Grandma and Grandpa." The younger ones began to cry and the older ones glared at Conductor Soames. Bork, the portly socialist, stood by dumbfounded, momentarily forgetting his fears of moving vehicles. I began to have visions of a full-blown donnybrook in Moose Jaw, followed by missed connections, police interrogation rooms, and distraught grandparents waiting anxiously. We had been saving for months for this winter escape to the fabled decadence and mildness of Vancouver, where we could swim again briefly in the warm embrace of family. So I nudged Judy with my elbow and whispered, "Give the guy our tickets — we'll figure out someplace to sit."

She said nothing. There was a titanium glint in her eyes.

The Tupperware support group became more vocal. "This same conductor has been obnoxious to us ever since we got on in Winnipeg," one of them said. "Yeah," said another, "the advertisements say rail travel is supposed to be fun, but this guy is about as much fun as a dead carp."

Conductor Soames decided on a strategic withdrawal. "We'll let the RCMP handle this when we get to Moose Jaw," he announced, and stalked out. Now all the kids wanted to know what would happen next, would we go to jail in Moose Jaw, and what about Grandma and Grandpa. Joe, whose bump on the head had not dented his curiosity, wanted to know if the Mountie would bring his horse onto the train.

The train was now rocketing along at full speed, and the village of Belle Plaine flashed by the windows. The click-clicks as we passed over track joints were now continuous, like a steady dribble of ball bearings dropped on steel plate. Car Number 212 swayed gently from side-to-side as it hurtled forward over the prairies. Bork was eating Gravol pills like they were Smarties, convinced we were headed for gruesome annihilation. Watching him, I could tell he was reassessing his need to see his brother in Vancouver, and could even be looking forward to being thrown off the train in Moose Jaw. The older kids dispersed to explore, and the Tupperware ladies gathered us into their friendly, pre-convention euphoria. One of them assured Judy she had the right stuff for a second career in home-based product sales. The moment gave me time to look around the train car. The décor lurched from the 1880s to the 1950s, from red plush upholstery to stainless steel. The windows hadn't been washed for some time, and the carpet was fraying. It was a pleasant enough space though, a kind of elongated, well-worn living room.

Outside, a fat summer sun seemed immensely pleased to be presiding over fields of spring wheat and canola, and in that moment, during the dying days of the southern passenger route, a flicker of Canadian romance may have actually passed through Car 212. In no time, though, we pulled up to the red brick station in Moose Jaw.

RCMP Corporal Hadikin ducked slightly as he came through the door of Car 212 and, after touching his meticulously gloved hand to the broad, flat brim of his hat, offered a cheery "Good Morning" to everyone in general. Several appreciative noises, including one or two wolf whistles, issued from the Tupperware crowd. Conductor Soames arrived and was about to explain the situation to Corporal Hadikin when a vivacious young Tupperperson, her face still flushed from doing X-rated callisthenics on the seat back, interrupted.

"Sergeant, this conductor has been absolutely icky to us ever since Winnipeg, and now he has decided to harass this poor family who's trying to get to Vancouver so the kids can see their grandparents, and it was completely the railroad company's fault that they don't have any seats, and this poor lady here is just trying to look after her family, and this conductor thinks he's bloody Napoleon or somebody and, hey! Wait a minute, don't I know you? Of course, you're Geoff Hadikin, Moose Jaw High, 1978! Go Warriors! Don't you remember me? I'm Christie Binford, I married Jim right after we graduated and then we moved to Winnipeg. Say, did you and the Fitzpatrick boys ever get caught for that combine joyride? Boy, I'll never forget that. The nerve you guys had, taking that brand-new Massey Self-Propelled right off the lot and driving it up Main Street at three in the morning! So, are you married yet?"

The Tupperware ladies, ourselves, Bork, and even Conductor Soames waited breathlessly for the response. RCMP Corporal Geoff Hadikin's cheeks had flushed to closely match the colour of his scarlet tunic. He opened his mouth a few times, but nothing came out. There was really nothing to say. At this point Ivan, our oldest child, came running back to us. "Mom, Dad, there's a bunch of ladies down at the other end that are going to the Bar Car for the whole entire day, and we can have their seats! Can I go with them to see the Bar Car?"

Conductor Soames silently surveyed the smoking ruins of what was supposed to be his triumphal defense of Section 54. His pension loomed. He thought about how much he hated passengers, how much he hated his job, and particularly how much he hated Moose Jaw. He did like the precise and satisfying ritual of putting the lozenge-shaped perforations on the smooth face of each ticket though. On impulse, he turned on his heel and stomped out of Car 212, without a word. The Tupperware ladies cheered wildly, and started doing their rude callisthenics again. For my part, I thought about my own self-appointed image as the family's resident radical activist, and how that image was now in need of re-evaluation.

The unfortunate RCMP Corporal Geoff Hadikin, for his part, thought hard about his chances for a dignified exit from the train. In the end, he just tipped his hat and said, "Have a safe journey," but his words were completely drowned out by the raucous chant of "no sex, no supper, just Tupper Tupper Tupper."

Gliding in the Pleistocene

Visitor has been with us for a whole season now, and he is still a mystery. Even to me, and I watch him a lot. We first saw him when the winter-dying trees had their new leaves, and we had just left a big kill. We were pushing into new country, keeping sunset off the throwing hand and sunrise off the other, which is what we've been doing ever since I can remember. When we first saw this solitary traveller, we naturally kept our distance, since you can't ever be too careful in these situations. As it turned out, we were headed in the same direction as he was. We kept him in sight for two days, drifting closer together all the time. They say that, on the third day, he joined us. If the truth is known, we actually joined him, but no one would admit to that.

I'm TooYoung. Not a man yet, but a good memory. I've made it my job to keep a record of things that happen to us. Keeping track is real easy for me though, so I gave myself a second job; I watch Visitor. He doesn't take part in the talk that goes on every evening around the campfire. Instead, he'll work on a spear, or maybe just stare into the flames. I think he doesn't even listen to the others and their endless discussions. I know he's interested in the before days, but he just doesn't talk about them. All the other adults sure do. They love trying to remember things. When did we last see the ice wall, who was firstborn after the sun went black, that sort of thing. I don't see how people can get such enjoyment from a simple case of collective bad memory. They could just ask me, TooYoung. BigMouth too, some of the adults call me, but I know our story better than anyone, right back to the Crossing. Instead, they root around in their memories, like warthogs in a mudhole.

Visitor never says much to anybody, but his face tells me stories. My guess is that his memories would be way more interesting than those from our band, and I know he would have all the details right.

I often wonder if old Visitor has a plan for his travelling. We've got no plan, I know that for a fact. Basically we just go in the direction of the winter sun, and look for game. Our band has some great hunters though. We can easily kill all we need, and more. It does seem strange that we are the only ones here, when the hunting is this good. Maybe the ice walls kept the Passage closed until now. Maybe there were bands here before, like the Others might have been, but we just missed their sign. For sure no one will ever miss our sign!

Nobody knows how old Visitor is. Old, for sure, but tough and stringy. Fast, too, when he wants to be. We don't know what band he comes from and, even if he told us, it probably wouldn't mean much. When you are on the move as much as we are, you mostly avoid other people. Visitor has this thing about tigers. He loves them, talks to them and probably dreams about hunting them. Really, they are horrible animals; fierce and sneaky at the same time. I think they hunt us more than we hunt them. Their howls are creepy, and the sight of those great fangs, even on a dead tiger, sends a feeling of winter up and down my spine.

Not long after Visitor joined us, an unnamed child was killed by a tiger. It was an awful loss, and everyone grieved around the fire. What made it worse was we could hear the bloody tiger moaning and howling in the distance. In the midst of our grieving, none of us noticed Visitor had left the campfire. When we woke the next morning he was back, and a huge tiger's head lay in the ashes of the fire, gory with dried blood. One fang was missing.

I don't think any of the adults will ever mix up the details of that story.

Cochrane sat patiently in the cockpit, waiting for launch. He felt a twinge of something like embarrassment. Gliding was part of his quest for a certain kind of experience, like when he lay down in a dream bed he had found on the prairie. The vague feeling of silliness he felt as he lay in that shallow, stone-lined pit was identical to what he was feeling now, waiting for the flight to begin. He had stayed a couple of hours in the dream bed, long enough to sense the deliberate pace of a midsummer prairie day. The wind moved gently through the grasses above him, an ant crawled labouriously across his arm, but nothing came to him. None of the dramatic visions the aboriginal elders talked about. Thinking back, he wondered if his dream-bed exercise failed because some part of his mind was busy preparing explanations for his colleagues at the museum.

This would be his first glider solo, but certainly no rite of passage because of all his extra hours and hours of training flights, far beyond the required minimum for his license. In between the training sessions, he rehearsed with virtual flights, thinking through takeoff, responding to turbulence, doing crosswind landings. He was so focussed on learning gliding that the mental training sessions were vivid and fully detailed. And lately he had been awakening in the morning sensing traces of dream flights.

Cochrane's colleagues feigned some interest, but he had already been pushed outside their circle because of his overkill hypothesis. His role at the museum had lately become wrapped in a bubble of scientific tension, and he retreated more and more into his own private paleontology. Stood at the foot of the Wisconsonian glacier. Walked the ice-free corridor. Touched the alien grasses. Watched the movements of mastodonts. He wondered if the museum's marvellous dioramas, which he passed every day on the way to his office, were pulling him into those half-known landscapes. The dioramas had been painted years ago by a local artist/naturalist. Cochrane had never met him, but sensed a kindred spirit who had found his own way of creating visions.

As Cochrane's weeks of flight training had become months, the other scientists became openly sarcastic. "Cochrane's finished his Master's in glider training. Now he's going for the Ph.D." That comment galled him, but he liked to do things methodically. Research, conceptualize, test; that was how he had built his hypothesis, and that was how he had learned soaring.

Heat accumulated under the Plexiglas bubble of the cockpit, and he began to sweat. Without the cooling effect of moving air, his stationary glider was quite an effective solar cooker.

The towline went taut, and finally he was moving, in that curious mechanical phase of every flight. All the incredible design of the glider meant little now; it was a mere captive, dragged forward by the powerful motor of the tow plane.

Out of the corner of his eye, Cochrane could see his runner trotting alongside, holding his wing level until the wind caught it, and then suddenly, he was airborne. He stayed low, just a few feet off the ground, to reduce the drag on the tow plane as it lumbered towards takeoff.

When he reached release altitude, Cochrane grasped the cable release lever and banged it down hard. He liked that movement, it was clean. No ambiguity there. The tow plane banked left and headed back to the airfield. Jack McFarlane, the burly, patient pilot for the Gliding Club, gave a wing wave as he passed.

The freed glider was instantly alive and responsive. Gliding was the most contrived of experiences, requiring tow planes, airfields, wing runners, and all sorts of specialized equipment. Yet the essence of the activity was something totally natural, even primordial. He was pleased. He made a few gentle turns as he watched the movements of a bit of red yarn taped to the outside of the cockpit. This was the glider pilot's simplest instrument; if you kept the yarn pointing directly to the rear of the fuselage, you knew the glider was not skidding sideways during a turn. Sun glinted off the long, white expanse of wing, and occasional pockets of air turbulence sent tremors up and down its sinuous length. Now that the tow plane was gone, the only sound was the steady whisper of air over the glider's skin, and his own heartbeat. Dr. John Cochrane, Provincial Paleontologist, specialist in the North American late Pleistocene, that shadowy period between the Ice Age and the present, was flying solo in a glider.

He watched the wing and mentally ran through the concept of aerodynamic lift, as the textbook explained it: airfoil, air pressure, laminar flow, washout. Physics intrigued him in the way it could tease out and identify all these separate components, when lift itself was such a single, glorious entity. Put a wing into the air, a rigid surface with a curved top that is skewed toward the leading edge, and it flies. That was the fundamental equation, in place since the time of the first pterodactyl.

He checked his watch; only twenty minutes of airtime had elapsed. Staying aloft for another two or three hours should be no problem. Shifting his body, he relaxed a bit, and banked the craft to get a good view of the ground. He could see a series of tiny, dry gullies wandering through the wheatfields, in a kind of dendritic pattern. Each time one gully joined another, the resulting channel cut a little deeper into the earth, and eventually they all came together to form a steep-sided main channel. Somewhere off in the hazy distance, he knew that main channel would join the broad valley of the Palliser. Cochrane was fascinated by aerial views of the earth. Before learning gliding, his only glimpses were during occasional commercial flights to conferences. He clung to those fleeting views of ground patterns, as some anonymous passenger jet thrust him into the air. Now, in the glider, he could savour the precious aerial perspective for hours.

He scanned the ground again. Evidence of that massive Wisconsonian glacier was right there, visible, even under the cover of grain crops. He reminded himself that it wasn't that long ago — ten centuries — that this land was entombed under ice. Low gravel ridges snaked through the soil below him, all angled southwest-northeast. End moraines, the geologists called them; the piles of rock that the expanding glacier pushed in front of it. But then, on one fine day, the ice stopped pushing and retreated, leaving those lines of half-buried rock. The poor fellow who actually farmed that land would understand the twist and warp of the morainal pattern far better than a geologist ever would.

He remembered the first digs he went on as a student, when he cursed the glaciers. They ground everything down and mixed age strata together. Doing paleontology on the Canadian prairies was like trying to separate scrambled eggs. When he had first discovered human artefacts and mastodont remains together, he automatically assumed it was simply glacial mixing of strata from different time periods. After all, paleontological doctrine stated that the end of the Pleistocene megafauna and the arrival of humans in the New World were two events separated by thousands of years. But then he went on to other prairie digs, where remains of superbison, saber-tooth and even the gargantuan short-faced bear were found among firepits and stone implements. The doctrine, which no one seemed to want to question, began to tatter and unravel for him.

Enough of this, Cochrane decided, and re-focussed on the present moment. Under his wings, prairie stretched comfortably to the horizon, and he was pleased to feel so tiny and insignificant above this vast expanse of earth. He was nearly free of manmade structures; the glider, in spite of its highly evolved aerodynamics and complex instrument panel, seemed more like a large, quiet animal.

He scanned the land in front of him for thermalling terrain. Thermals were the heart and soul of soaring. You couldn't see them, but they could be visualized as great pillows of sun-warmed air that occasionally broke free of the ground to float upward. If you were lucky enough to find one, you circled your glider in it and gained altitude along with the pillow.

Treed areas were good sources for thermals; their dark colours absorbed lots of sunlight and periodically all that energy would release as a mass of warm, buoyant air. But much of the region had been stripped of any trees; the soil was simply too good for that. Summerfallow fields provided some lift, so he started looking for them, hoping to keep his altitude until he reached the rough country of the Palliser Uplands, where there were not only trees but hills, which also generated thermals.

Two hours later, flushed and happy, Cochrane turned back toward the airfield. He'd caught the tail end of one thermal and regained some altitude. In a glider, altitude ruled, providing both distance, and time aloft. The bright glare of late afternoon was giving way to a classic prairie evening; the sun had finally relented, allowing the sky to settle into layers of faded rose and phosphorescent grey. The generous tapestry of wheat, summerfallow, pasture, and bushland lay in a great circle beneath him. Plumes of dust lingered along the grid roads, where he knew the evening swallows would be dancing with the midges. The glider balanced on the earth's azimuth, and time flowed toward a single point. It seemed to Cochrane the world was somehow poised, ready for some profound inversion. As it would with a child's origami figure, a gentle tug might produce some new shape, unexpected but perfect.

Visitor does amaze me sometimes. Here we are, approaching a bluff of trees one day, all tensed up like hyenas. We know something is in there. Everyone gets deadly serious except Visitor. He starts a little comedy routine. Does a quick mammoth dance for us, then pole-vaults on his spear a few times. Pretends the spear gets stuck in the ground, and makes a big to-do about getting it out. He really loves the moment before a hunt. So confident, so in control, the guy is able to joke around and loosen everyone up.

So we slip into the trees and the air is suddenly cool to my skin. The bugs are fierce, but soon we'll have mud to smear on. Visitor is in the lead. He's serious now, a bundle of concentrated energy. There are noises up ahead, probably mammoth. We move forward, crouching. The ground is soft and wet. In this dense growth you can never tell what you're up against until you're right on top of it. There is a steady cracking of branches. The ground shakes. Big, whatever it is. Visitor heads directly towards the noise, moving like a shadow.

There — we come into a small opening and two mammoth trumpet and crash away through the trees, with us right behind them. Visitor is already far in the lead, spear-arm cocked and legs churning. I am hustling over a fallen tree when I hear that soft "chunk" noise and look up to see Visitor's spear deep in the neck of the lead animal. It takes several more spears to bring the hairy beast down, but the hunt was really all over when Visitor made his spear throw. There is so little fuss when he hunts with us.

Mammoth is awful to move so we set up camp right there, bugs and all.

These swampy forest bluffs always remind me of our time in the Passage. Dark, wet and creepy. Only the Passage was way worse than the bluffs. Sometimes it was so narrow we could see both ice walls at the same time. They were alive, those walls, big grey monsters that rumbled and cracked all the time. Our camps were wretched. A few, green willow sticks for firewood and nothing but fish to eat. Water everywhere. No one got any sleep because of that relentless grinding noise. Our band always moves fast, but in the Passage, we were just a blur, we were that anxious to get through it.

I know all of us, secretly maybe, figured the ice walls would close up sometime, and crush us all. Or we would go all that way down the Passage and reach a dead end. I suppose we could have gone back to Old Crow, but we didn't like staying on there. Coming this far from the Crossing, no one wanted to stop halfway, with a whole unknown world just in front of our noses. Somehow we knew our destiny lay in the direction of the winter sun, and now you can see we were right.

Anyway, back to my story. We gorged on mammoth that night, but Visitor was disappointed. No tigers. We all like mammoth meat, but these big shaggy animals are no challenge for him. I think he killed the second one from sheer disappointment, because we surely didn't need it.

We stayed in that forest camp for two days. On the third morning the sun got really hot, and the gutpile smelled awful. The adults sat around pretending to relax and enjoy the rest, but none of them are any good at pretending. I could see black looks creeping into the faces of the men. Mothers fussed with little ones. Even my mother started in on me for talking too much. Everyone fidgeted. These feasts are supposed to be the reward for all our long treks and hard work. The adults talk about them all the time, and look forward to them, but none of us really enjoys them after the first day; we'd all rather be up and moving. I could tell Visitor was going crazy with the bugs and the smell, but he didn't let on. Didn't move a muscle in fact. He just sat there like a big old toad, watching everything and slowly running his fingers back and forth over his pouch.

We don't ask questions about pouches, but I know what Visitor keeps in his. The day after he killed that tiger, there was a fresh bloodstain on the pouch. I figured out that he collects fangs from his tiger kills, and keeps them for medicine.

Anyway, Visitor just sat, rubbing his pouch back and forth, back and forth. We were all just dying for an excuse to leave. I could have stood up and made a move to go, but I'm TooYoung, and it wouldn't have worked. So I didn't.

As we sat there, a shadow passed over us for just an instant. That did not fit, because the sky was bright and sunny. I looked up, but with all the trees and snags above us, I didn't get to see what it was. Visitor noticed too, but when I looked at him he just raised his eyebrows. There is a lot we still don't know about this country.

That forest place was getting oppressive. Finally, Visitor stood up. He did it just to stretch, but by the time he put his arms down, everyone was up, belongings in hand. He acted like he was surprised, but I know better.

A soft knock sounded on Cochrane's office door, and then a face appeared. It was Janet, one of the museum's new summer students. He closed the research journal he was reading, and threw it on top of a precarious stack of other journals.

"Come in, grab a chair," he said, trying to put her at ease. She was several months pregnant, and lowered herself into the chair slowly. There was a curious intensity about her that Cochrane remembered from the job interview. She was easily the best candidate for the position, but Cochrane was concerned about the pregnancy. The museum's personnel director had reassured him that she was a healthy and determined single mother-to-be, and that her pregnancy would not interfere with the job.

She paused, and composed herself. "Doctor Cochrane, I just got back from a farm call out at Hopewell. You have to see this one." She leaned back slightly, evidently finished with what she intended to say.

Cochrane smiled.

"You think so, eh," remembering all the wild goose chases he had been on, many of them inspired by overenthusiastic summer students: concretions thought to be prehistoric snakes, scoria thought to be dinosaur dung, horse skulls thought to be eohippus, and so on.

"No, this isn't what you are thinking, Doctor Cochrane. It's an effigy, and I know it's an important one."

She was slightly out of breath. At first he assumed it was because of the pregnancy, but now he realized it was not.

"A surface effigy? What does it look like?"

"We can't tell yet. I think we're seeing just a corner of it, and the rest is buried under dune sand. You need to see it."

"Well, I have this budget mess to deal with." He riffled through the official-looking documents in front of him. The museum's budget crisis had gone on for so long now that it seemed almost routine.

"You say it's near Hopewell, eh? That's not far out . . . "

He knew he would not be touching the documents that afternoon anyway, even if he did stay in.

"Okay. Look, I'm busy, or rather I should be busy, but maybe we can go out over the noon hour, and eat our lunches on the way. Why don't you bring the half-ton around to the back entrance just before noon, and I'll meet you there."

Janet left abruptly, leaving Cochrane to speculate. The Hopewell area was southeast of town, a belt of sandy land between the Uplands and the river. He knew it well, had even flown over it. The area was not known for any major finds, except for recent arrowheads that were exposed from wind erosion. Which it did fairly regularly. Farmers in the Hopewell area struggled on their poor soil, and were generally not very well off.

As Cochrane shuffled papers in a vain attempt to straighten out his desk, he mused about Janet. He was impressed with the way she was handling her summer job, taking phone calls from the public. A few of these calls were from cranks, about lost civilizations, flying saucer landing sites, things like that. The majority were more ordinary, a weathered cow's tibia thought to be from a dinosaur, and so on. Now and then, there was the odd call that really meant something, and it was up to Museum Extension, where Janet worked, to do preliminary site investigation, and then report to him. She sorted through the welter of summer calls, reassuring people, getting the necessary information, making judgment calls on whether a visit was necessary. This reclusive student was a different personality on the telephone, and her judgment seemed confident and sure-handed. It was as if she had been doing the job for years instead of weeks. He hoped for her sake that what they were going to see was a legitimate find.

Janet drove the museum truck right past the farmer's house and into the fields. The crops were blasting in the heat, and the bone-dry sand squealed under the pressure of the tires. The lane they followed headed up the side of a long, sand ridge. Probably an ancient dune field that had stabilized and settled. Over the centuries the blow sand would develop a bit of a profile, its surface would turn from white to light brown, and eventually some gullible farmer, like this one, would be fooled into thinking you could grow a crop on it, or at least qualify for subsidies. Then a combination of too much cultivation and a good strong windstorm would cause a blowout. As they came to the top of the narrow ridge, Cochrane saw all the usual elements of a farmsite discovery, the parked half-ton, a figure hunched over a shovel, and a scalloped breach in the windward side of the stabilized dune. He also saw that the farmer was smart enough to have put up some windbreak fence, so the whole hillside wouldn't blow away.

Janet introduced Cochrane to the farmer and they chatted briefly. She had only seen this guy once before, he thought, and yet they obviously felt comfortable around each other. The man talked excitedly, describing his find, but Cochrane listened with only half an ear. A cynical thought crossed his mind, that this fellow's interest in paleontology was actually an escape from the much grimmer business of farming a sandpile like this one. Cochrane was anxious to finish and get back to the office. He had opted out of a museum budget crisis for days now, without any real justification for doing so, and it was time to start dealing with the raft of urgent memoranda.

He walked over to the effigy, a U-shaped set of stones that had been partially exposed. The open end of the "U" ran back into the dune. The stones were resting on a paleosol, an ancient soil surface that had since been buried by moving sand. Whatever this thing was, it has been covered over for a while.

Janet's intuition was correct; he had seen lots of stone effigies — the strange and wonderful figures marked out with stones — but never one this old, and never of this particular shape. The find could indeed be significant. Janet and the farmer stood by, looking at him expectantly. Mentally, he ran through the official steps for an excavation: file a report, draft a budget, get Committee approval to proceed, then do all the preliminary surveying and staking. That would take weeks, even longer because of the budget crisis.

"All right, we'll dig a bit more, but two ground rules. We won't go any deeper than the tops of the stones, and when I say stop, we stop."

Cochrane turned back to the truck to get the shovels, but Janet already had them, and she solemnly passed them out. She was wearing a loose-fitting maternity blouse, probably homemade. As she bent over the stones in front of him, he saw her swelling, anticipatory breasts. A lacy, white support bra barely held them. Cochrane caught his breath, and his eyes swam. He quickly bent to his work, but an afterimage remained.

So, finally we break out of that murky forest camp, with its stink of dead mammoth, back into grassland and bright sunlight. Right away Visitor surprises us by taking off like a frightened antelope, in that funny crouching run of his. We can't see what he's after, but I know it would be some strange new animal. There's still a lot we don't know about this country. A couple of the young men take off after him, figuring to get in on the action. The Stallions, I call them, they're a few seasons older than me. I stay back. There is no way anybody is going to catch up with Visitor. The Stallions don't know that, but I do.

The rest of us walk on in Visitor's general direction until sundown, knowing that he will meet up with us when he finishes. We are into new country again, moving fast. Grass is such a pleasure to travel through, and it makes us feel big, important on the landscape. The forest bluffs are where we hunt, but the grass is where we live. It's safer, and there's fewer bugs, particularly if you stay up on the ridges.

Some days, like right after a rainstorm, you can see incredible distances, and it fills your head with possibilities.

The Stallions rejoin us about midday, all played out. Of course they never caught up with Visitor. The man himself returns after we make camp for the night. He's really fired up and excited. I figured a good chase like that might have loosened his tongue a bit, and it turns out that I'm right. He eats a little of the mammoth meat we brought along, and then stands up in front of the fire to begin his story. His lean, bony arms and legs reflect the firelight as they move, and his great shaggy head bobs and sways. Anybody who's dozing is quickly prodded awake, and we all become like a single watcher.

Two Man Bison, he says. None of us have ever seen these animals before. He tells us that he spotted them just after we left the bluff. He ran until he was in range, then dropped down on his belly to crawl, getting pretty close to them before they finally bolted. When they run, they are like the great winds, he says, and they take strides the length of two spears. He says they are the height of two men at the shoulder, and they make the ordinary bison look like mice.

Stepping back from the fire, Visitor shows how his encounter happened, making us the bison and him Visitor. He throws himself on the ground and crawls toward us. None of us are sure what a Two Man Bison is supposed to do, so we paw the ground and swing our heads low through imaginary grass as we watch him. Then he stands up in front of us and becomes Two Man Bison himself. Lowering his head toward us, he places his hands by his ears and makes a slow, outward sweeping motion. When his arms are fully extended, they move slowly upward, and then inward again. We all get very quiet.

I notice then that Visitor's tiger pouch is no longer around his waist. His spears are with him, of course, but that precious pouch is nowhere to be seen.

One of the Stallions breaks in and starts talking. He is not a wise person. He says anything that could run as fast as a Two Man Bison wouldn't be able to pay much attention to where it was going, and what if you could run a bunch of them right off a cliff or something. What an ignorant fellow. Visitor is quiet for a minute. Of course he wouldn't have anything to say about a poor idea like that, and he gets back to his story.

I'll always remember his words. He spoke passionately, and his dark eyes seemed to glow in the reflected firelight. I don't want to kill Two Man Bison, he says, I just want to quietly get close to one and jump on its big, shaggy back, scramble up onto its neck and hold onto those mighty horns, as my chosen beast takes off and builds up speed. I want to feel the wind in my hair, hear the crash of the hooves as they settle into a pattern of blurring, dizzying speed, share in the animal's blind anger, urge it on faster and faster, cover ten days' travel in an afternoon, see land we haven't seen, run down the grass, straddle the spines of mountains, cross rivers and plains, touch oceans, feel the sun burn on my skin and never, ever stop. Just keep crossing this new place forever, toward winter sunlight.

That's what he said.

Next morning we're off again. When the whole band moves as a group, we fan out and move in a staggered line, like geese migrating. We work back and forth, foraging, looking for signs, or just plain looking. Old folks and little kids walk straight on, keeping to the middle of the foraging line. I am working my area, not looking for anything in particular, when I see Visitor's pouch. It's not cached or anything, it's just lying there, like an old bone he'd thrown away. In fact, that's my suspicion, since he's not like some in our band who lose things all the time. I pick it up, and untie the thong wrapped around it. I figure it's safe enough to take a short look inside. Fangs, all right. Gruesome and sharp. I feel little earthquakes running along my backbone, and I wrap it back up in a hurry.

I work my way across the line until I meet up with Visitor. He takes a quick look at the pouch in my hand, then looks back to the horizon. I hold it out to him, and he looks down at it like it is rotten meat or something, and shakes his head. I am astounded, but I don't forget myself. I hold it to my chest, still looking at him, and he nods. This is really strange. It's like Visitor is going to change his medicine, and he now cares so little about his sabretooth vision that he throws the fangs away.

We walk on together, a little apart from the rest, me holding the pouch like it's food and I haven't eaten for months, and Visitor scanning the horizon. The grass is tall and rank, so thick in places that it tangles around our feet. Brightly coloured flowers poke up through the grass. This prairie seems so friendly, compared to the forest bluffs, which are always dark and smell rotten.

Then I see the Pelican.

We think Pelicans have lots of medicine. We're not sure what it is yet, but there is something special about them. This is really their country. At first all I can see is a white speck far off in the distance, above a bluff. I point it out to Visitor but, as soon as I do, I realize he's been watching it for a while, and I feel stupid. All the time I was looking at dumb flowers, he was watching the Pelican. It looks way too big, but it's hard to judge the size of it; this country can make it difficult to tell how big things are. At times, something that is two or three days' travel away will look very close. Other times, a couple of trees on the horizon will seem as big as mountains. Visitor doesn't offer any ideas about this Pelican, so I don't try to decide either, but we both keep our eyes on it until it goes behind a strange cloud, the colour of an open clamshell. And then it disappears completely.

It was good to be soaring again. Time in the glider was a clear, lucid space in his day, one that might give some perspective on the Hopewell effigy. A cross! If there is one shape that is not seen in aboriginal boulder monuments, he thought, it is a bloody cross. And what we've excavated so far is definitely a cross. Today, I'm going to get away from all that, and get away from the airfield too. This glider is tied to airfields as if by an umbilical cord, but today I'm going to cut it loose. Maybe I'll make it back here, or maybe not. Instead I might land on some distant, farmer's field and have to explain myself, and how I plan to get the glider home. And how I'm not a frivolous person and how gliding is such a useful paleontological tool.

His outbound flight plan was to follow the prevailing summer winds that push southeastward across the prairies, passing over the gradual transition from prairie to bushland. Cochrane scanned the now-familiar flight map, and realized he would be flying directly over Hopewell.

The Plexiglas window above him was like a narrow, crystal bubble. Cochrane often wondered if it acted like a weak lens that magnified everything slightly, or whether it was just his heightened awareness. The only sound was the subdued, liquid rush of air over the polished skin of the elegant Polish-built sailplane. He thought of the time he saw an airplane model being tested in a wind tunnel. A friend at university had invited him to see the tunnel in the Engineering Department. The idea seemed childish — grown men playing with model airplanes — until he looked through the tunnel's window. The plane, a scale model of a commercial jet, was festooned with bits of bright-red yarn. He assumed that each piece of yarn would extend straight back towards the rear of the plane but, as he looked closer, he saw that each one had a slightly different tangent as the air spread and looped across the aircraft's wings and fuselage. He was suddenly, and permanently, fascinated. The effect was much like watching smooth water flow over rounded stones; there was so much affinity between surface and medium.

Scanning the land ahead of him, Cochrane spotted a series of small hills and changed course slightly to pass over them. A few cumulus clouds were developing above the hills, a good sign. He positioned the glider so his right wing would pass through the outside edge of where he thought the thermal might be, and waited. Thermalling was always a gamble. You could miss a great thermal by a couple of feet and never know it. Or, you could fly right through the middle of one, circle back, and never find it again. But this time he had hit it, a strong upward surge that bumped and flexed the long, narrow wing. Banking hard right, into the thermal, he set the plane into a tight spiral, and then watched the altimeter.

He had caught the express elevator. This thermal, if he could stay with it, would take him right back to release altitude, maybe even higher.

As he spiralled, Cochrane became aware that he was sharing the thermal with seven white pelicans. These huge birds were strange and pathetic on the ground, and that was how the pelican diorama at the museum had captured them. But Cochrane was not prepared for their striking beauty in the air. Black-tipped wings motionless and fully extended and their long orange beaks knifing through the air, they soared with Olympian detachment. Every movement, down to the last nuance and correction, was shared by the seven, in absolute unison. It was as if they were all connected to a single nervous system. The pelicans were not disturbed by the presence of the glider; they seemed to accept it into their fraternity of rising air. He remembered a lecture the museum's ornithologist had given on the white pelican. The species liked to soar high-up in the air on thermals, the scientist said, but she confessed that no reason could be found for the habit. It had no obvious connection to feeding, courtship, or migration. Something like my gliding, thought Cochrane.

He felt humbled in the company of these great birds. Their beaks were massive and reptilian, and their eyes were immensely sad. Outcasts, dinosaur throwbacks, they were nearing extinction in Canada as their prairie marsh and wetland habitats disappeared. And they could do nothing but soar quietly on oceanic wings until the last of them were gone.

The glider's climb rate was strong and steady. Intuitively, Cochrane had picked just the right position for his spiral. He and the pelicans seemed to be in a different dimension, travelling on some quirk of atmospheric physics.

Finally, the lift began to fade. This thermal had given him two thousand feet of precious altitude, but now it was done. The great warm bubble of air he had floated on was torn, and cooling rapidly. Soon it would extinguish and leave only a residue of cumulus to mark its passing. He spiralled one final time and then straightened the glider out on his original east-southeast course.

When he looked down, the earth below him was partly obscured by thin cloud, almost like a vapour layer. That was odd; he hadn't noticed the layer as he climbed through the thermal. Something just wasn't right; grid roads and wheatfields should be showing through, but neither were visible. Quickly, he checked the compass. It was steady, at ESE. He scanned the horizon for grain elevators —those friendly milestones were almost always in view — but he could see none. He flew straight on, puzzled. The layer below him was even thicker now, and had a strange, milky colour to it. Finally, he reached the ragged edge of the cloud layer and looked down.

The landscape was totally unrecognizable. Familiar wheat and summerfallow patterns were obliterated, grid roads and elevators gone. Huge, ragged tracts of mixed forest replaced the isolated and familiar poplar bluffs. Dark conifers poked up above the tops of the deciduous trees. Long, ragged strips of grassland cut through the forest. Some of the land was not even completely grassed over, and great gashes of raw earth showed through. Off in the distance was a massive, eroded river valley. Cochrane fumbled for a pair of binoculars under the seat, and quickly scanned the horizon; there were no houses, no fields, no roads, nothing but this alien vegetation. The colours of the land were strange and lurid. Great, long piles of bare rock snaked across the landscape, and there were open scars of recent erosion. Cochrane closed his eyes and pinched the bridge of his nose with thumb and forefinger. He drew a deep breath, trying to fight down fear. All the gauges were normal, and the glider was soaring perfectly, right on course. But it was flying in alien air. He looked down again, and panic overtook him. Banking the glider into a hard left-hand turn, he pointed its nose back toward the cloud layer. Thank god it was still there, a tangible link! And the pelicans were still there, circling. He concentrated all his energies toward re-entering the cloud somewhere close to the point where he left it.

The landing was flawless, perfectly balanced on the glider's single landing wheel, but Cochrane never gave it a second thought. After passing over the strange cloud and back to what he had always assumed to be reality, he had carefully chosen a level wheat field for the landing. Now the glider lay in the green sward like a beached albatross. He stayed in the cockpit, sitting quietly, his mind fixed on the incredible spectacle he had just seen. In spite of the shock and an edge of terror, a part of his mind was telling him: this was predictable. You wanted this to happen.

There was no question about what he just flown over. It was a fossil view, one no living person had ever seen. It was the landscape of the late Pleistocene.

Had he piloted the glider through a chronological seam in the air, a rent in the wrinkled curtain of time? Some combination of forces and events had connected an ancient time surface to today's, he thought, and my glider had poked through. This was my home 12,000 years ago, the complex environment I have studied so much, the landscape just after liberation from the glacier, one that was starting literally from scratch. Rapid change and evolution were the orders of that distant day; any living thing that stagnated in that time, even for a moment, was lost for good.

From the time he re-entered the cloud, until he landed, Cochrane was simply numb. In retrospect, it was reassuring to know that he had flown and landed the glider from rote memory and slack muscles. His conscious mind, on the other hand, was utterly consumed by what he had just seen. What it meant, he was not sure, and he had no idea what to do with it.

Dozens of impressions waited to be carefully separated from the fear and shock, and fixed into memory. The grass, the forests, the earth, everything. His recollections of the flight already seemed different from ordinary mental images. He called up scenes from the flight like great still dioramas, to examine their finest detail. The first of those images, from just after passing beyond the opalescent cloud, was overwhelming. The colours of that landscape were bizarre, brush strokes taken from a totally unfamiliar palette. But Cochrane understood their logic; they were the raw colours of protoprairie, of the first postglacial moment. Colours that would change, flowing logically and inevitably down to a fouled and preempted present.

Another memory image slowly crystallized, the last of the series, taken just before his desperate rush back through the cloud-seam, that of rank grassland and unfamiliar shrubs, with forest in the distance. Two human figures stand stark and intrusive on the horizon, possibly a man and a boy. And not far from them, some kind of an encampment. My god, Cochrane thought, not only do I get to see the Pleistocene, but I also get a glimpse of the most shadowy thing of all — the first people of the Americas, the prototypes of the New World.

A breeze caught one wing and lifted it slightly, reminding him that he was still encased in the glider. He had no desire to get out, feeling utterly comfortable in the warm, narrow womb of the cockpit. This was his Plexiglas dream bed, and he was savouring the euphoria of a vision. The ancients would also sort through the images of their visions, then they would choose one for a new identity. I think I would take the white pelican for mine, he decided.

A knock on the Plexiglas cockpit startled him. He couldn't make out who it was in the sun's glare, so he released the cockpit window, undid his harness, and slowly stood up.

"Janet! How did you find me? How did you know I was out here? Jesus, what a flight that was."

He tried to step out of the cockpit but his legs were asleep. Halfway out he collapsed, and Janet reached out to catch him. Each trying to steady the other, they stumbled and both sprawled onto the wheat in a tangle.

"Are you all right?" he said, concerned.

Janet's laugh answered him. It was rippling, impulsive. He realized he had never heard it before.

"Of course I'm all right, I landed on top of you."

She propped herself up on her elbows.

"I had something to show you, but I got to the airfield just as you took off. So, I thought I'd follow the glider in the truck."

She paused, looked around the intimate green room their fall had created in the wheat, and smiled at him. "Looks like it was a good thing I did, too."

Cochrane composed himself. It wouldn't do to describe his experience in a mad rush, and sound like a lunatic. He slid around to face Janet.

"So," Janet said, "how was your flight?"

"Let's hear your news first. No, wait a minute. Let me just ask you one question. Could you see the glider the whole time that I was in the air?"

Janet thought for a minute. "No, I couldn't. I had to make a big detour around Pelican Marsh, so I couldn't watch you all the time. Why do you ask?"

That resolved nothing for Cochrane. He honestly had no idea whether the overflight lasted twenty seconds, or twenty minutes.

"Okay," he said, still wary. "I can sort this out later. So tell me this news of yours."

"We finished excavating the Hopewell monument. Most of it went really easily because the sand was so loose. I had Ron from Drafting come out and make a quick sketch of it. Here." She pulled out a sheet of paper and unfolded it over the flattened wheat stems. Cochrane studied it for a minute, without saying anything. His whole being fought the obvious conclusion.

Janet's voice cut into his stunned silence. "It's crazy, but it looks like some kind of an aircraft."

It's funny how Visitor isn't really interested in our history the way the other adults are. I think he's more concerned with the things that happened before us, and the things that will happen after. He told me about the Others, something none of the adults have spoken of before. The Others were first. First to make the Crossing, first in this country. But they didn't stay. Their homeland was a warm, pleasant country, but other tribes fought with them and they fled. First they moved north, towards the country where our forepeople lived, and stayed there for a couple of generations. But they weren't happy there, and they drifted even farther north, to the lands where winter is the only season. Finally, they crossed the Bridge, and passed through where we are right now. But even then they did not stay, Visitor says, because they hungered for the warmth and remembered landscapes of their original homeland, the one they could never go back to. So they pushed far beyond where we are now, so far, in fact, that they came to a country with no winter at all, and their hunger turned to joy, and now that is where they live, those Others.

Visitor says our forepeople were different, they knew cold and winter well, and they lived not so far from the Bridge. We crossed much later, perhaps many generations later, and that is why we have never seen the Others. Maybe we will though, if we keep going far enough.

Then he told me about the great pulsing of the earth, of times when winter is long and the waters of the oceans are drawn down by thirsty icebergs, and a bridge of land appears in what used to be open ocean, and at the same time the ice walls grow and close the Passage. Then times when summer is more powerful, and the Passage opens, but the seas swell again, and the Bridge disappears. That's why we and the Others had to wait at Old Crow. When the Bridge was open, there was no place to go. Then the Passage finally opened for us to travel down, but the Bridge disappeared, so we were committed. Our People and the Others have lived with that great pulsing, and it has shaped our travels and our lives.

I don't fully understand what Visitor says about the pulsing, so it hasn't settled well in my memory. Maybe I am not meant to understand it yet.

Cochrane and Janet moved respectfully among the stones, as if they were visiting a cemetery. He followed the profile of a long narrow wing; it even had a crude taper to it. Christ. Twelve thousand years would elapse before another tapered wing would be seen. This was his glider they had celebrated with stone, and he could only feel humble. Janet stood near the cockpit, absorbed. In the excitement and confusion of the last several days, their lives had become suddenly and feverishly entwined. Since his flight and the uncovering of the Hopewell effigy they had spent much time together, talking and looking for alternate explanations. The rest of the museum staff were caught up in the ongoing fascination of the budget crisis, and totally ignored the Hopewell find and the sudden, intense collaboration between the paleontologist and the summer student. He had summoned enough courage to ask her an oblique question about her condition, and Janet's answer was straightforward. The pregnancy was the outcome of a brief, very traumatic relationship that was definitely over, and she was determined to keep the baby.

Janet was standing near the effigy's cockpit, lost in thought. The stone effigy really belonged to her; she had measured it, and studied it. He watched her, knowing some of what she felt, being part of a major find, feeling close to a very distant past, feeling that ache of connectedness, and believing very strongly, passionately, in the validity of this past and its people. He was filled with doubt about the reality of his strange flight, but when he finally told her about it, there was a brief moment of disbelief and then she wanted to know every detail. The effigy was her crosswalk to his experience.

Cochrane felt the past and his own present collapsing into each other, like shuffled cards. He walked over next to Janet and sat down, inside the stone cockpit.

They were quiet for a while. Cochrane was the first to break the silence.

"The archaeologists say that effigies were early people's way of codifying important things during periods of rapid change. The rapid change part certainly fits, and so does the important part, but I'm not sure I'm ready to take responsibility for that importance. In fact, I'm just not sure of where I am anymore. Or when I am, I guess is more to the point."

Janet sat slowly down, right close behind him, where the passenger seat would be, and put her arms around his chest. Her touch sent electric tremors through his whole body.

"I don't think you can stop now, John. I know it's all crazy. And risky. But whatever this is, it can be a way of making the past more real. Just our notes and drawings so far are enough to make the world wake up and care about how we got to where we are now. These were different lives, different animals that walked the very same ground we're standing on, and that makes me want to know them."

Cochrane had a momentary flicker of doubt, that her interest might be like that of the Hopewell farmer, anxious to put aside the grim realities of the present. But then her arms tightened around him and he felt the swelling, expectant belly pressing against his back. He didn't want to move, to change anything.

"Okay, I'll carry on," he said softly. "We'll carry on."

She ruffled his hair. No one had done that to him since he was a child.

The next morning he signed both of them out for the day. They met at the airfield to prepare for the flight. Janet would follow on the ground again and both would take notes, which they would compare at the end of the flight.

This is the feeling before the real first solo, Cochrane thought, as he waited for the tow-up. My mouth is dry, my shirt is already damp with perspiration. My biggest fear is not being able to find the opalescent cloud, or not being able to find the seam again. Chet knows that I want to retrace last week's flight as closely as possible, so he's supposed to duplicate the previous tow-up. He thinks I'm just rechecking some thermal activity.

The tow-up seemed interminable, and he fidgeted with the controls. After release, he concentrated on maintaining the exact bearing and altitude from the last flight. The cloud did finally appear. A mere suggestion, at first, it grew thicker as he flew toward it. The same roller-coaster rush came over him as he flew over the far edge. This time he quickly scanned the alternate landscape and divided it into four search quadrats. The most likely one was the southeast, where the river was. That was where the two human figures seemed to be headed when he saw them the first time. He banked the glider towards the northwest, and began a methodical scan of the sector.

The edge of that big river valley was not such a bad place to camp. The adults milled around for the first day or so, until they figured out that we were definitely stopped, but I knew right away that Visitor was not going anywhere for a while. We don't like stopping, Visitor least of all, but now it is different. Big Pelican has something to do with it, I'm sure, and there are Two Man Bison in the area. He showed me their sign, the hoofprints and, here and there, huge piles big enough to put out a campfire.

The moon was new again when Big Pelican returned, and this time it stayed longer. Pelicans are so wary that none of us has ever been close to one, and we don't really know how big they are, but this one is huge. Its body is many spear lengths, and it flies so perfectly the wings never move. We all watched it closely. I could tell some adults were scared, by the way they held their spears, but the great bird wasn't interested in us. It mainly circled above Visitor, who stood on a ridge up above camp. The old guy made quite a sight up there with his stringy legs spread wide apart and shaggy head thrown back, watching. And thinking. He seemed totally without fear, as if he had been expecting Big Pelican.

As soon as Big Pelican left, the adults gathered, to try to make sense of what they had just seen. But it was all just confusion until Visitor got back. He spoke about the honour of seeing Big Pelican, and the need for medicine, to mark that honour. Then he pointed out an open, grassy spot as the place for the monument. We started the hard, boring work hauling rocks and, of course, most of the biggest, strongest adults were busy laying out the plan, and did not haul a single rock. They argued a lot, because this bird was different than any we'd seen before. Visitor didn't talk, he just hauled rocks with us, but slowly. It was as if he'd just had an important conversation with Big Pelican and was busy thinking about it.

Pressure flakes, buffalo pounds. I must, we must, get on with it. I have left my pouch behind. So now, I can travel lighter and faster, leaving behind symbols and collecting only experience. Too fast is the essence of this country, for now. Too fast in movement, too fast in artifice. I know this great thing that I have seen is no bird, but a tool. The taper of its wing matches with the fluted obsidian of my throwing spear. Fast travel and artifice, that's what we are about. And these things we must work through. The buffalo pounds, the tapered wing, the urgency of travel, the confusion of newness with significance. We will study the prototype. Many versions will be called for. This is, after all, the New World.

Visitor is back to tracking those Two Man Bison again. He goes off looking for them by himself, so nobody knows for sure what he's doing. And he leaves way before sunrise, before the rest of us are awake. My guess is that he's getting closer and closer to a herd somewhere nearby. The man can be so totally intent on stalking that he becomes part of the landscape. Blends right in. He'll be a rock one minute, creep forward, and become a patch of grass, then move forward again, and become a tree.

The sun is far along in the sky now, and I have been out most of the day, maybe looking for Visitor, maybe not. Valleys are always interesting to us, and I've been getting to know this one. Its sides are steep, but at the bottom is a wide, flat grassland, and the river loops and winds through it, like a snake. There are big outcrops of rock along the valley side. That's something you don't see much of in this country, big rocks. Maybe the ice wall smashed them all up. The sky overhead is full of those little puffy clouds you see on warm days. I am coming on to a headland where the valley turns sharply, when I see the herd.

Two Man Bison! Visitor was right about the great horns. They are huge animals, way bigger than anything we've seen on the grasslands. Mammoth are bigger, but they're always around the forests, so they get taken down to size by the trees. I duck quickly and sit down for a minute to congratulate myself for outsmarting the Stallions again, and to think things over. The animals are a good distance away from me, grazing along the valley bottom. I'm sure they haven't seen me, and the wind is blowing towards me, so there's not much chance they would catch my scent. What an opportunity; all I have to do is stay out of sight and move quietly. This will be something to tell Visitor.

I make a sight mark on where I should come back to the edge of the valley, then crawl on my belly away from it until I am well out of their line of vision. When I get a long way from the valley edge I stand up again and walk carefully until I pull up even with the sight mark. Then, back on my belly again, and start crawling slowly toward it. I try to become the landscape, like I figure Visitor does; first I am a big, coarse bunchgrass, then a rock, then an old burnt tree stump. Surprise myself too, because these transformations are actually working. As the edge of the valley approaches, I slow way down until I'm like the sun or the moon — they move, but most of the time you can't see them move. The bunchgrass along the valley edge is thin, but if I keep my belly on the ground, it covers me. When I get right up to the edge I am careful not to touch the grasses with any part of my body. Any movement of their tall stems might be seen by the Two Man Bison. I hold my breath as I make the last pull forward to the edge. Gradually, the far side of the valley becomes visible.

There they are. Just two of them would make a mammoth, with muscle rippling all up and down their necks and flanks. They carry their heads low, under the weight of those great horns. They are moving slowly, grazing below a reddish rock ledge that sticks out from the valley side. Every few seconds one of them throws up that big set of horns to sniff the air — wary. I've never seen anything like them.

I'm just so pleased with myself, being so close without them spotting me. I may even be able to stand up and talk at the fire tonight. That will give those Stallions something to think about. I settle in for a long watch when something catches my eye on that rock ledge above the herd. It doesn't move or anything, but it's not quite natural. So I scan the rock ledge again and — I should have known. Flattened right down on the rock, and absolutely still, is Visitor. His legs are braced, and his arms are spread way out in front of him. I think to myself, now that is a funny position to watch from, and then it strikes me, like a lightning flash; he's not there to watch, he's going to jump.

In a few more breaths, the herd will be right underneath him, and Visitor will meet his dream. I try to loosen my muscles, so they won't sense my nervousness, these Superbison. I would never forgive myself if I ruined Visitor's chance. I close my eyes and take a long, slow breath. When I look again, I see the great, silent Pelican wheeling overhead.

Medicine coming together, power in the rock. Now I have come all the way down the heartline to the very centre of this continent, right now, right here, and I am going to jump. Onto the massive, uncontrolled back of the future. My fingers dig into the rock, my vision blurs, and my stomach turns over. My legs are fully sprung and I am ready; if I can make this jump, I will grab the horns of perception.

They sat silently in the cockpit, waiting for the tow-up. Sitting in the stone glider previously had turned out to be a rehearsal for this. Cochrane was aware of his habit of long conversations with himself, and he marvelled at how quickly and completely the longstanding "I" of those interior monologues had shifted to "we." He wondered if her monologues had become plural too. So far, they talked easily when they needed to but, more often, they worked in a mutual silence that to him seemed abuzz with information. They were in one of those right now, sitting inches apart in the glider.

Cochrane's last trip had gone like clockwork, from entering the cloud, to finding the shaggy man at the point where he expected him, to the long, slow circling above him, and the uneventful return. Janet had taken extensive notes and, together with Cochrane's observations, they put together a new, joint flight plan with precise compass bearings, altitude, and elapsed time.

The cable went taut, and the glider lifted off eagerly. They spoke a few times during the tow-up, sticking to mundane things like release point and windspeed, nothing that would suggest the magnitude of the trip ahead. A small kit bag was stowed behind Janet's seat; this was to be a one-way trip. They had laughed and agonized the night before over what to pack for a trip to the Pleistocene, finally settling for two notebooks, pencils, a small pair of binoculars, a litre of water, and windbreakers. Neither had any desire to take a camera.

The now-familiar milky cloud appeared, and when they passed beyond its farthest edge, he fell silent, resisting the urge to be an overzealous tour guide. What if she saw nothing but wheatfields and grid roads? He worked the ailerons and rudder simultaneously to execute a slow 360 degree coordinated turn, all the while sensitive to Janet's breathing near the back of his neck. His own pulse began to pound as he awaited her reaction.

Her first few breaths came quickly and sharply, but then returned to a slow, measured rhythm. He knew then, without asking, that she was witnessing the ragged and alien landscape. He also realized how important it was for him to be present as she, too, felt the euphoria in the cockpit. To be physically close, as every bit of experience was interpreted through the eyes of this quiet and passionate woman.

The low ridge above the proglacial valley now loomed in front of them, and Cochrane was relieved to see that the camp was still occupied. He came in over the camp so that Shaggyman, as they now called him, would see them, and then put the glider into a leisurely circle above the ridge. After twenty minutes of circling, no one had broken away from the camp and moved toward the ridge.

"He's probably out hunting or exploring somewhere," said Cochrane. "We'll follow along the river valley and look for him." She still hadn't said anything, but put her hand on his shoulder. He reached up with his free hand and grasped it tightly. When the glider again came around parallel to the valley, he straightened out his course. The swollen river channel was full of bars and islands, and sunlight glinted off the braided water. They soared in silence for a time. This was the river that had swallowed half the Wisconsonian glacier as it melted, and spit it out into Hudson's Bay. Even in its present diminished, underfit state, the river was imposing, far more so than the modern remnant they were familiar with, a pathetic stream one could nearly jump across, that meandered along the bottom of a massive valley. During the active melting period a few hundred years prior to the time they were gliding through, the river would have been many times bigger yet, carrying off meltwater from eons of ice accumulation.

They both spotted the distant herd at the same time.

"Jesus, what are those things?" He fumbled for the binoculars. "They are huge! I wonder if they could be superbison?" He knew the instant he put the glasses on them. "That's what they are!" He banked a little, so Janet could see past him.

"*Bison latifrons.* The mysterious prince of the Pleistocene. We only speculated, because no one has ever found complete remains. The bloody horns are something like two metres across. The double buffaloes, the Willowbunch giants, and, Jesus, there they are, grazing like a bunch of jersey cows."

The animals seemed to take no notice as the glider came closer.

"I guess anything that big would never sense danger coming from above," Janet speculated.

Just then there was a sudden flurry, and the small herd bolted down the valley at a dead run.

"There's your Shaggyman," Janet shouted, as she handed Cochrane the glasses. "He's on the back of the lead bison!"

Cochrane saw that a human figure was indeed draped over the neck of the bison, hanging on in a desperate embrace. The animal was in complete panic, and charged up the valley slope with the rest of the herd in pursuit. Cochrane and Janet were right above them now, tracking the herd as it reached the lip of the valley and broke onto open ground. The breathless speed of the massive superbison matched that of the delicate glider as they tracked across the landscape.

"How am I going to explain all this to my mother," said Janet.

The superbison showed no signs of slowing down. In fact, it seemed to be settling in for a long run. Shaggyman had worked his way forward and was now sitting upright on the animal's neck. He was grasping the recurved horns, and his wild hair streamed out behind him.

"He looks like Dennis Hopper in *Easy Rider*," said Cochrane. He took the glasses again and scanned the landscape ahead. Then he realized that they were crossing the lobe of a great oxbow bend.

"The river is curving around in front of us." he said. "In a few minutes the herd will be right at the edge of the valley. I sure hope Shaggyman knows what he's doing."

Well, he must have done this before," said Janet. "This can't be the first time."

From their higher vantage point, they could see the sunken valley looming ahead. Its long, steep slope ended in a layer of rock that dropped off to the river level.

"Jesus, I think they're going to go over!" Cochrane said.

They soared on breathlessly, right up to the edge. Suddenly, the invisible thread that had held the herd and the glider together snapped, and the animals plunged down the slope. Then they could see no more, as they passed directly overhead. Cochrane banked the glider sharply to the right, feeling a few seconds of strong lift as they passed over the valley side. As they came around, they caught a glimpse of crumpled bison forms at the foot of the rock ledge. There was no sign of Shaggyman. Now that the excitement was over, they surrendered themselves to the serene quiet of the glider for a few minutes. It flew powerfully and efficiently on the lift of the river valley.

Finally, Cochrane broke the silence. "Now we have that decision to make," he said.

"Do it, John," Janet said emphatically. "We've talked it over a dozen times, and we're both going in on our own free will. If we can't get back, then we'll just learn to live in this country, or rather this time."

"The Pleistocene on Five Dollars a Day. We could buy land real cheap, I bet."

He turned back to face the transparent dome of the cockpit again, and squared his shoulders against the alien horizon. Then, in the most definitive move of his entire life, he banked the glider around again, back towards the treeless prairie in the lobe of the oxbow. Reaching back, he touched her hand briefly.

The terrain of the prairie ahead was flat, thanks to the glacier, and there were no rock outcrops. Cochrane used the flaps to ease the craft back into a slight stall. Altitude and airspeed dropppped quickly, and he began to mentally focus on the single nose wheel built into the fuselage underneath him. Bunchgrass was now rushing by the wingtips, and he felt the turbulence of ground-level air. Then he levelled the glider out again, and finally, he did a last-minute flare, and felt the heavy jolt of the nose wheel touching down. Grass beat noisily against the hollow wings as the craft rushed along the ground. Using the last remnants of wing lift, he kept the glider upright until they finally rolled to a stop. Holocene had entered Pleistocene.

Neither of them said anything. Cochrane knew he would have to inspect the glider, but he was pretty sure it had not sustained any damage on landing. Still he made no move to pop the hatch, wanting to savour a last moment of known and predictable things. In spite of their resolve, his mind schemed an escape: find the Shaggyman, teach him to hold the wing, use the slope of the valley side as a runway, and catch the lift. His reverie was broken as Janet unbuckled her harness and reached over him to pop the cockpit releases. As they climbed out, he could feel the hair on the back of his neck standing straight up.

Their legs wobbled as they started walking towards the edge of the valley. The ground was churned up where the superbison, on their race to oblivion, had passed. When they reached the beginning of the slope, their hearts sank. The hoofprints led straight down over the edge, and no humans or animals were in sight.

"Damn! If he went over the edge, there's no way he could survive," said Cochrane, "but I can't figure out why he would go over."

The slope ended in scattered patches of brush and then the cruel face of the rock ledge itself. Cochrane peered down over the ledge as Janet searched along the slope.

"Here he is!" she shouted, and bent over a crumpled figure lying in a patch of buckbrush off to one side of the buffalo trail.

The shaggyman was lying on his back, almost like he was sleeping. Janet put her fingers to his neck to check for a pulse, and as she did so, his eyes flickered momentarily.

"He's certainly alive, and I don't see any bleeding or broken bones," she said. "What do you think we should do?"

"I'm not sure," said Cochrane. "This is his world, and maybe we should just wait for a bit, to see what happens."

They sat down on the grass beside the brush patch. The broad valley stretched out in front of them, and the Pleistocene slowly reasserted itself. The sound of the wind barely disturbed a profound, regional silence.

The shaggyman stirred again. As they watched him, he slowly opened his eyes. A quick convulsion of fear passed through him as he focussed on Cochrane and Janet for the first time. Then he lay back in his buckbrush bed, and smiled broadly.

My fingers grip the clean bunchgrass, and the crashing of hooves swells louder and louder as the herd comes by underneath me. A powerful waterfall of sound rushes over me, and I hold on desperately as it goes by. I look again. It is like he told it, he is grasping the horns of the lead animal. They have broken out ahead of the rest of the herd now. Their two massive, shaggy heads match. Big Pelican is close above them, steady. Its rigid wings bite cleanly into the sky. Together, they break from the valley up a long coulee, and onto open prairie, still picking up speed. I start running along the edge of the valley. Even though they are on the far side, I try to keep Pelican in sight for as long as I can. The great bird is following Visitor so I follow it. Then I settle down to a slow, regular stride, not at all like Visitor's strange running, but one that I know will carry me a long way. I can think now, try to understand what I have seen, and put it into proper memories. I watched the three of them — Visitor, Two Man Bison, and Big Pelican — as they flew down the valley, into their visions. A big tremor runs through my body; I am the only one who saw this great event. Visitor was in it, was the event, but I am the only witness. So this privilege falls to me, TooYoung. I get to tell the story, and this time I know the adults will listen.

The Cortesian Spud Gun Militia

ALL WEEK THE TINY ISLET OF Mitlenatch called to me, as I taught a writing course on nearby Cortes Island. Seeing an uninhabited islet, splendidly alone in the middle of British Columbia's Georgia Strait and being unable to reach it, is an excellent prescription for fable. During class breaks, I would go outside and stare fixedly at the islet. I had heard stories about Mitlenatch, how its small size, together with its position in the middle of an open stretch of water, meant its climate was totally different from the wet coastal regions that surround it.

Mitlenatch became more and more fabulous to me as the course wore on. In my mind it became an exotic, treeless desert. Next, it morphed into a land populated by strange and wonderful beasts, and bizarre flowers of every description. Then it became a shape-shifter, now appearing close, now far off on the horizon.

In class, I volunteered the information that Mitlenatch was an ecological marvel and that I, an ecologist from the Interior, had never visited it. Finally, one of my students, Maurice, a grizzled Cortesian oyster farmer, agreed to take me there, but only upon one condition.

"Great. What's the condition?" I asked.

"After the visit, you must bear witness to the Presenting of Arms of the Cortesian Spud Gun Militia," Maurice said, gravely.

"Absolutely," I agreed, having no idea what he was talking about.

Maurice's boat was what you call a working boat, an open eighteen-footer with plenty of gas cans, few frills, and a thin, crunchy layer of oyster shuck underfoot. The seats were eminently practical, legless former bar stools bolted onto plastic milk crates. Maurice fired up the big old Mercury outboard and soon we were in open water, sliding laterally up and over long, rolling swells. The water was not at all rough, but the swells put the boat into a rocking-horse motion, highly disturbing to landlubber ecologists. I fixed my attention on Mitlenatch in the distance, trying to ignore the periodic alarms coming from somewhere near my esophagus.

Maurice said something to me, but he was inaudible over the noise of the engine. I moved closer and leaned toward him.

"The native people called the island *Mahkweelaylah*, meaning the closer you get to it, the farther away it appears," Maurice shouted. "Do you want a beer?"

I hastily declined. Looking back to the islet, hoping the fixed point of reference would quiet my stomach, I saw what Maurice was talking about. Sure enough, the islet which at first looked to be only a few minutes away, now appeared quite distant, with a vast stretch of open, very swollen water between it and us. After an interminable, rocking-horse ride, we finally approached the east shore. I realized the trick Mitlenatch plays on people; with no trees on its horizon, no houses, and no other islands near it, the islet gives the eye nothing to calibrate size against. A simple trick of perspective, I told myself.

By now we had rounded the south point, and what I first took to be lumpy black rocks turned out to be a fine herd of massive California sea lions. The air above us was thick with glaucous-winged gulls, harlequin ducks, surf scoters, ravens, and crows. Gawky double-breasted cormorants festooned the rocks, and bonded pairs of oystercatchers picked delicately along the shore. An eagle passed overhead and, as it did so, hundreds of nesting birds swarmed, herding the predator away from their rocky nursery. As Maurice gently steered the boat toward a small bay, we passed a clutch of fat harbour seals.

The incredible biological abundance continued as we stepped ashore. Drifts of pink sea blush, interspersed with yellow monkey flower and blue camas, were strewn artistically across the rocky slopes. Tiger lily, alumroot, saxifrage, saskatoon and Pacific sanicle were all in flower. The lush interweavings of colour were like French Impressionist paintings, but if Claude Monet had seen Mitlenatch, I believe he would have laid his brushes down out of sheer respect.

The magical is also fragile; tiny thirty-six-hectare Mitlenatch and its host of creatures are prone to many human-caused disruptions. As a result, it has provincial park status, and volunteer wardens monitor it closely.

I was reluctant to leave the island, but Maurice reminded me that we had to check his prawn traps, pick up some oysters, and return in time for the Presentation of Arms.

Back at Maurice's snug home, tucked under the cedars of Cortes, we had a delightfully messy feast of fresh oysters, prawns, and beer. Utensils were not offered, or requested. By the time we were finally finished, our respective beards were smeared with garlic butter, prawn juice, and cracker crumbs, and neither one of us cared.

It was time to talk of the Cortesian Spud Gun Militia. Maurice drained one last half-shell, opened another beer for each of us, and settled back to tell the story.

"You've seen those big yachts cruising by to the east of us, eh? Well, they're all headed for Desolation Sound, which is the playground not for the rich, but for the super-rich. The Bill Gates types. Every now and then one of those rich ones gets bored with their private island in the Sound, and starts sniffing around our beloved Island of Cortes. They get the idea they can buy up a big chunk of island property, fence it off, and build a monster mansion, or what we call a starter castle, so they can come up and live in it for two or three weeks every year. Now we Cortesians are pretty much plain folks, nothing fancy. We're fishermen, gardeners, back-to-the-landers, and pensioners, and we aim to keep the island safe and affordable for those sort of people. So the Cortesian Spud Gun Militia is ready at a moment's notice, to man the beachheads as soon as one of those hundred-foot luxury yachts start snooping around our island. And now that you mention it, the time is exactly — eleven twenty-three PM — which means it's time to Present Arms."

We stepped outside into the enfolding quietness of cedar and starlight, and filled our lungs with night air the texture of velvet. Maurice went to the toolshed and returned with an eight-foot spud gun, a real beauty. The combustion chamber was made of five-inch diameter PVC sewerpipe. It was fitted out with a hard-wired Bic barbecue lighter ignition system, a screw-on, gasketed breach, and ergonomic hand grips. The style, construction and features made this spud gun a true classic of the genre.

"Most of the other militia guys have gone with a straight three-inch diameter gun, but the five-inch combustion chamber, stopped down to a three-inch barrel, was my invention," Maurice said proudly. "It packs way more punch."

Maurice deputized me as a militia subaltern, and handed me a large potato he had brought from the kitchen. Following precise instructions, I forced the potato down into the sharpened muzzle, making an airtight, potato-to-PVC seal. Meanwhile, Maurice shook a can of hairspray vigorously. "Paradoxically, the cheapest brand of hairspray makes the most effective propellant," he said, as he sprayed a long blast into the combustion chamber, and quickly screwed the breech back into place.

Hoisting the weapon to his shoulder, bazooka-style, Maurice yelled, "*Present Arms!*" and flicked the Bic. A shockingly elaborate cauliflower of purple and orange flame burst from the muzzle. A split-second later came the wet, potato-sounding explosion, like a popgun on steroids, and a humble Russet No. 2 was flung deeply into the starry and cedar-filled night, in the general direction of Desolation Sound.

Someday, I should like to take the word fabulous back from the Hollywood types who stole it, and return it to its original meaning. Then I could debate whether the ecology of Mitlenatch was more fabulous than the human culture of Cortes, or whether that comparison was even a valid question for debate. Perhaps the important thing, for both sanicles and oyster farmers alike, is to live as close as possible to the edge of fable.

CRYPTOCHITON STELLERI

FROM THE BUCKET, HE KNEW INSTINCTIVELY she was a biologist. There was something timeless, almost paleolithic, about this image of a woman squatting in a tidepool. The white plastic bucket in front of her glared against the jumbled expanse of slick black rock. The Straits beyond were a faded azure. Both the woman's hands were immersed in the tidepool, sorting. Now and then she would bring up an object, break the clinging fronds of seaweed off, rinse it again in the tidepool, and then put it in the bucket.

A drylander, he approached.

"You must be collecting specimens. Can I look?" he said, pointing to the bucket.

"Sure, you can hold them for a moment if you want to." She continued sorting through the pool.

He squatted too. A bizarre variety of creatures breathed patiently in the water-filled bucket. Some were dark and mottled, the colour of seaweed-flecked rock, while others had bold, Aztec patterns. He reached in and gently picked up a crab, then a periwinkle, then a brittle star; each new organism was a marvel of separate design. The woman was revealing the tidepool's hidden phantasmagoria of lifeforms.

"That's a whelk," she said, as he stared at a helically coiled and tapered shell. No precision craftsman, using the finest quality lathe and cutting tools, could have turned anything as perfect.

He sensed in her the kind of anxiety common to naturalists in public; wanting desperately to convey their passion for the subject, yet knowing the organisms and the information would provide only fleeting interest.

"Are you collecting for a research project?" he asked.

"No. I am a marine biologist, but these specimens are for a children's nature class this afternoon. I'll be bringing them back here as soon as the kids are finished looking at them."

He continued dipping into the bucket, holding each organism up to look closely at it. Sensing that he was not looking for a sideshow, she began to name them for him, crustacean after mollusc after arthropod.

The grey-green mass at the bottom of the bucket was visible when he first looked in, but he had passed it over in favour of the more exotic creatures. It was the size and shape of a narrow football split lengthwise, and its humped back was a series of hard, overlapping plates embedded in horny tissue. He grasped it firmly, assuming it was attached, but it came away easily, perhaps unwilling to adhere to the alien surface of the bucket. Turning it over, he began to blush furiously, stunned by the florid, sexual nature of the mollusc in his hands.

"That's *Cryptochiton stelleri*, found in North Pacific waters," she said. "And you're right, the ventral surface certainly does resemble a woman's vagina."

A broad, smooth outer membrane surrounded inner lips that were open, irregular and fleshy; it was as if he were viewing the female organ at its most intimate. Even the orange-peach colour of the flesh was a close match.

"The common name for it is the gumboot chiton. Name doesn't really do it justice, does it?"

He shook his head slowly, not exactly in answer. As he held the chiton, it began to curl in on itself, until its half-moon shape would have mated perfectly against a woman's pelvis. He blushed again and carefully returned the chiton to the bucket.

"Well, I guess I better go," he said lamely, and stood up.

The calm waters of the strait shimmered in the sun. You could see past the frothy clouds, past the Olympic Mountains, all the way to pure imagination. The woman on her haunches washed and sorted. He knew already that she would remain in his own tidepools forever, sorting live things with gentle and knowing hands.

COUNTING FENCE

BUD COURT'S HOUSE WAS IN THE scrub pine country north of Cranbrook. He met me as I drove into his yard, a large bear of a man whose body had already given him several decades of hard work and looked ready for several more. He was a fencing contractor, and I had hired him to build a grazing exclosure for me, as part of a grassland research project. I didn't really have a career, since careers are formal, starchy, and organized affairs. But I had progressed through a series of burgeoning interests, ranging through conscientious objection, Third World development, agronomy, and cowboying. Now, I was in a transitional state, somewhere between range management and ecology, and research into the effects of cattle grazing tickled both of those fancies.

I first met Bud when he brought in his tender, written out in labourious longhand. My project involved fencing out a small, irregular-shaped slough. My notorious inability to estimate acreage was still with me, and I had only a rough idea of the final length of the fence, so I asked for price quotes on a per metre basis. Bud totally ignored that instruction, but once I converted his feet into metric, he turned out to be the low bidder.

Bud's fences, I came to understand, were works of outstanding craftsmanship, known throughout the region. People said he only managed a few years of schooling before his father put him to work, but he had made fencing into a calling. You could always spot a Court fence: five wires straight and true, lowest one high enough to let a calf get back to its mum, deadmen at each corner, all the posts rock-solid, and staples set just right so the wire could give under snowload.

Bud had finished with my fence, and it was time to measure and settle up. We drove to the site in Bud's battered half-ton, bouncing along the Forest Service road. The Rocky Mountain Trench was in its fall finery, aspens starting to turn, a dusting of fresh snow on the mountain tops, and triple-distilled air. The shallow slough Bud had fenced off for me didn't have a name, but one of my colleagues dubbed it Gayton's Folly, since it went dry about three years out of ten. But no matter, I said, since cows will use the area anyway, and I could establish plots inside and outside the fence to monitor the grass over time.

I had brought my hundred-metre measuring tape and pocket calculator with me, to get a precise measurement of the fence. I was determined to hold up my end and pay Bud exactly what he was owed, and not a penny more or less. I explained to Bud how we would measure the complex fence polygon he had created, a hundred metres at a time, until we had the correct distance.

"You can leave that stuff in the truck," Bud said. "I've got my own system, that both you and I can understand." I was sceptical; there was no substitute for good, solid math. Bud reached into the truck box, hauled out a worn leather carpenter's apron, and strapped it on. One of the pouches bulged with fence staples. Then he handed me an empty apron, gesturing I should put it on.

"Ok, this is how it's going to work. There's exactly eight feet between each one of these fenceposts. Now the odd one will be seven-ten or maybe eight-two because of a big rock, but that don't matter because in the end, I build 'em all to eight feet."

He stepped up to the fence and tied his red bandanna around a post.

"I got four hundred staples in this pouch, see. We'll start with this post and walk the line. As we go along, I'm going to hang a staple on the top wire between each post, and I'll count it out as I do. Now you're going to walk behind me and collect that staple, and count it into your empty pouch. Both of us will count quiet, to ourselves, so we don't muck up the other guy's count. When we've gone all the way around and back to this start post, we'll compare the tally, and multiply by eight. If our tallies don't match, we dump the staples out on the tailgate, and count 'em again. And if it still don't work, we count back from four hundred."

I walked humbly behind Bud, collecting one staple at a time. The metallic chink of each staple as it went into my pouch sounded like a cash register. Bud's system honoured the work, and honoured the contract, far more than my measuring tape and calculator would have. I hoped someday I could know my business as well as Bud knew his.

Little Bluestem
and the Geography Of Fascination

It once was a part of a great amber sea, this grass. The sea was drained and ploughed long before the invention of the airplane. Hawks and falcons may carry the memory, but no human has ever seen it from the air. But just to imagine looking down on that tallgrass sea, the grassy ocean that stretched from Winnipeg to Texas, and knowing that *Schizachyrium* was a part, is perhaps enough.

Schizachyrium, it is called. Sky-za-ky-ri-um. Skyzakyrium. It is a word so rarely said, you may put the accent on whichever syllable you like. Not sure why it so took me, really. It could have been the strange and haunting name of this prairie icon, this delicate, brick-red bunchgrass. Or that it is the poster child of a radically different metabolism, and therefore fascinating by its minority, its ethnicity. Should it matter at all, that I found it growing quietly hundreds of kilometres outside its range?

Schizachyrium; some assembly required. It is of course a word constructed from Ancient Greek, but one that takes on meanings of its own. Our nomenclature is based on dead languages because in science we dread connotations, and we abhor the normal evolution of live words. But I wonder. What if the Greek roots of this particular word were so obscure we are forced to invent their meaning? I would develop my own legend about the name *Schizachyrium*, that it doesn't really mean that the seed has a split awn (*schizein*=to split, *achuron*=chaff), but instead refers to the grave and rumpled god Schizachyrio, a lesser Greek deity, one whose particular mojo was Obscure Complexity.

In reality, *Schizachyrium* is little bluestem, a feathery grass that once thrived in the lush, wet summers of southern Manitoba, burgeoned southward across the line into Minnesota, and on to its southern limits in Texas. Westward, it thins out in Saskatchewan, holding to particular saline seeps at the foot of remnant prairie slopes, in dusty places like Big Beaver or Climax.

To find *Schizachyrium* all the way out here in south-eastern British Columbia and, not only that, to find it on a gravelly and beat-up cutslope above the Bull River, certainly makes one mindful of the obscure complexity of ecology. *Schizachyrium* has absolutely no reason for being on the Bull River. It is a prairie plant, showing progressively less enthu-siasm for life the further west it is from its natal Red River Valley, getting sparser and sparser, becoming flat-out rare by the time it reaches the Alberta foothills, and then becoming non-existent, as it gratefully accepts the Rockies as its final barrier. But then voila! reappearing, full of piss and vinegar, on the one gravel cutbank of the lower Bull, and nowhere else.

Now the Bull is one of those mysterious Rockies westslope rivers, a tributary to the Kootenay. To be such a river, it means you started in some high range like the Quinn, way up in the fractalled wilderness of the Rockies' interior. Then you come boiling down your narrow canyon and explode into the gentle valley at the bottom of the Rocky Mountain Trench, like the Ciccorax released from its dungeon. The Bull always looks to me like it is still surprised that the glacier, which once filled the Trench, is gone. It is as if the river was frozen in mid-step while the glacier was morphed out, and trees and grass and people and highways were added in.

During those halcyon days at the end of the Ice Age, the Bull carried probably 5,000 gravel pits worth of river rock, sand, and gravel out of the Rockies. Coming into the Trench at right angles, the Bull ran straight into the great stagnated river of ice, so it sluiced and dumped its unceremonious bedload of Rocky Mountain junk right up against the ice flank. Then, as the dwindling glacier halved, and then halved itself again, the Bull had two choices: either cut right through the triangular mountain of gravel it had built, or sneak around the side of it. The Bull, of course, chose to come right straight down the middle, cutting through its own rubble in order to join the mother Kootenay. Cut down through it a couple of times, as a matter of fact, as the Bull evolved from once-colossal torrent to the underfit but still vigorous river that it is today.

All this is background, of course, to place the rare *Schizachyrium* on a single, steep cutslope the Bull carved, a loose and droughty habitat of Rocky Mountain riverstone and distressed gravel.

Well, not just the Bull River. I must confess Eastham spotted *Schizachyrium* just below the bath houses at Fairmont Hot Springs in 1939. Brink saw it at the same place in 1950. Milroy reported out from near the British Columbia-Montana border town of Grasmere in the summer of 1952, saying he encountered it on the "north side of bush road through S.L. 3 of L. 361 K.D. about midway E-W in S.L. 3." I went to S.L. 3, following old cadastral maps and, as soon as I got close, I knew the population would be gone. Too many cows, roads, logging shows, and alfalfa fields. I tried the old bathhouse site at Fairmont Hot Springs too; the population there had fallen victim to recreational development. A few more sightings remain to be checked: the grounds of the Wycliffe Trap and Skeet Club, and the entrance to Kikomun Creek Park. These sites will either provide me with more points on my map, or else more observations on human impact.

It is tough for a prairie plant to get into British Columbia. One way is over the Crowsnest Pass, which means progressively hitchhiking past Fort MacLeod, up the Crowsnest River, down the Elk River, and into the Rocky Mountain Trench, deciding at that point to either stay put, as *Schizachyrium* did, or venture further west through BC's narrow and labyrinthine valleys.

The other way is to tackle the Rockies in Montana, find a way west through the Bitterroot and the Clark Fork river valleys, then coast northward into BC along the Kootenay, the Pend Orielle, or the Columbia River valleys. An equally challenging route is to brave the cold winters of the Peace River country, slipping around the northern end of the Rockies somewhere near Fort Saint John, and then trickling southward along appropriate river systems.

Or, there is the most prosaic arrival mechanism of all, when a Trench rancher buys some prairie hay from Saskatchewan, to tide his cows through a late spring. Or a local guide-outfitter picks up a good packhorse from Manitoba. These things do happen, and a pile of manure can become a mechanism of contemporary succession.

There are distribution maps for *Schizachyrium*. You might think of them as pathetically inadequate records of the various geographical occurrences of the plant, observed and noted by obscure individuals like Eastham, Brink and Milroy, who knew the species by sight and cared enough to forward their observations. These scattered notations would then be amassed by some aging and reedy botanist, who would

DON GAYTON

turn them into tiny dots on a map. If this botanist possessed any degree of hubris, he or she would draw a sinuous line connecting the outermost dots, thus creating a distribution map. In drawing the map, the botanist might put a question mark next to remote and far-flung dots, casting doubts on their veracity.

A finished plant distribution map represents a huge triple jump from the reality of stateless plants rooted in the ground to an abstracted, incomplete representation along the two dimensions of a political map. Frequently, the map's distribution lines would not extend beyond the boundaries of the government jurisdiction employing the botanist. Nevertheless, I have always loved reading distribution maps, be they of plants, of the northern alligator lizard, or the California bighorn sheep. I could be entertained for hours if I were handed a stack of distribution maps on transparent plastic sheets, all to the same scale. If they were stiff enough, I could shuffle them like cards, and one by one place them over each other, to see if the five-lined skink might confess to some clandestine geographical relationship with the Kirtland's warbler. Or the three-tip sagebrush with the stinkbug, and so on.

With my transparent maps, I could find geographical linkages that hint at evolutionary connectedness, or I could puzzle at the discontinuities where mountain ranges or glaciers or mysterious events have gotten in the way. A Canadian *Schizachyrium* map would, of course, make no sense at all, with its classic disjunct British Columbia distribution. If there was ever a place to put the botanist's accusatory question mark, it would be at Bull River.

Distribution maps could provide me with more than a parlour game, they could even be used as a symbolic language, allowing us to communicate. A bilateral distribution map, showing some boreal population separated from its southern cousins by the Ice Age could be used to warn of upcoming cold weather, for example. Or the strictly maritime distribution of the *Ammophila* grass could be a signal that it's time to go to the beach. Communicating this way would be very difficult, and might appear to be like using ancient Mayan pictographs to describe semiconductors. To do the latter would simply be pointless mental gymnastics, and a terrible waste of energy, whereas communicating in my language of species distribution is to embrace the very lexicon of ecosystems. And who knows, the thoughtful shuffling and display of those mapped cue cards could generate some startling insights into the soft mechanics of nature.

Ecology does have its fascinations.

Two kinds of people study plants like *Schizachyrium*, those who wear lab coats, and those who wear cowboy hats. The former feel most at home in laboratories, the latter are comfortable in the field. Although there is plenty of crossover, these two tribes have a fundamentally different outlook, and each is intensely sceptical of the findings of the other. In Canada, long winters force the tribes to mingle somewhat, but even here that division is strong.

The high priests of the lab-coat tribe are the biochemists, the folks who work at the cellular level, and who refuse to look at a plant until it has been through a Waring blender. The lab-coat biochemists periodically generate spectacular advances that the cowboy-hatted ecologists are forced to acknowledge and deal with. The biochemists generally do not give a damn about the ecologists' fascination with how plants function in nature. They grow their subjects on styrofoam pellets in climate-controlled phytotrons, only to grind them up and extract their chemicals to see how plants work.

The unitary biochemistry of plant photosynthesis was a given in field-plant ecology until the 1960s, when the lab coat boys dropped a new bomb: there was more than one type of photosynthesis. In fact, there were three. They became known by the first products their respective photosynthetic machinery produced — the three-carbon sugar type, the four-carbon sugar type, and the crassulacean acid type. This was precisely the kind of Waring blender-generated information calculated to enrage the cowboys. But it turned out, upon further examination, that these different biochemical groups, at least the first two, fit nicely with one of the cowboys' pet categories — cool-season and warm-season grasses. The biochemical machinery of the four-carbon types functioned better at higher temperatures, and these turned out to be all the warm-season grasses, which typically are not active until late June, but grow well through the hot months of July and August, after the cool-season grasses have already shut down. The cowboys were able to salvage some dignity by adding a corollary from their experience; warm-season grasses do well in hot weather, but they also require reliable moisture in late summer, in order to complete flowering and reproduction.

One of those field ecologists was Jan Looman, a reserved and scholarly Dutchman, who probably never wore a cowboy hat in his life, but must suffer the metaphor. Working first at the federal agricultural research stations at Lethbridge, Alberta, and then at Swift Current, Saskatchewan, he was strongly committed to the field observation of native plants. On days when he could not get away from the research station, he could usually be found in the herbarium, looking at pressed plants. Looman's primary interest was in plant geography, and the reasons behind why prairie plants, like *Schizachyrium*, were found in some places, but not in others. Humans are rarely content with randomness as an explanation, and the urge to understand and classify was particularly strong in Jan Looman, who had a classical European training in ecology. Looman was looking for regional keys to explain plant distribution. Soils could explain some local distribution patterns, but he concluded that soils were too variable to be the primary driver of distribution. Looman also eliminated altitude as a factor. Even though many classical plant geography studies explained plant distribution by changes in elevation, the Canadian prairies are basically a tabletop, with minimal elevation change. And temperature, he concluded, could not be the primary factor either; there were just too many places across the prairies that reached forty degrees centigrade in the summer and then dropped to minus forty in the winter.

Precipitation was a more obvious driver of prairie plant distribution, Looman hypothesized, as it varied dramatically across the prairies. On a west-to-east axis, precipitation is high in the foothills of the Rockies, decreases rapidly as one moves eastward, hitting a low point somewhere around Swift Current, but then increases slowly towards the Manitoba border, and reaches high levels again around Winnipeg. The south-to-north pattern is similar. The OneFour area, on the Alberta-Saskatchewan-Montana border, is cactus country, but there is a steady increase in precipitation as you track directly northward into aspen parkland and, finally, to boreal forest. But Looman knew there was more to the story than just precipitation amount. The seasonal life cycle of a plant had to fit the distribution of precipitation through the growing season. So, he began to divide the prairies into zones of distinct spring and summer rainfall patterns, eventually developing eight different areas. Then he painstak-ingly reviewed the distribution of dozens of typical grassland species, to see if they corresponded to his climatic areas.

The results of Looman's cross-matching were disap-pointing; all species wilfully crossed and recrossed his climatic boundaries, except for one. *Schizachyrium*'s contiguous range fit very nicely with a climatic area he called the Moosomin, a narrow belt which ran parallel to the Manitoba-North Dakota border, and then looped upward into southeastern Saskatchewan. The Moosomin area had moderate levels of rainfall in spring, but high levels during its warm summers. Cool-season grasses generally flower in the wet month of June, but *Schizachyrium* flowers in August, and adequate moisture during flowering is a necessity for any plant. The result of Dr. Looman's effort was a small, highly qualified, but valuable synthesis of biochemistry, maps, climate and field observation — *Schizachyrium* prefers areas of adequate spring moisture, abundant summer moisture, and warm summer temperatures.

Looman's hypothesis was a broad regional one, and made no attempt to explain the localized and disjunct populations of *Schizachyrium*, like the one at Bull River. These are left for us to puzzle over.

There are many different kinds of time, and the one that bedevils plant geographers most is successional time. *Schizachyrium* might be at Bull River for reasons as myste-rious as the galaxies, or as mundane as a prairie hay bale, or as the advance guard of some future invasion of the plant into British Columbia. Or, it may be a tattered remnant of an ancient continental distribution. Canada went through a climatic episode six to eight thousand years ago, known as the Hypsithermal, when the climate was warmer than it is today. Isolated populations of *Schizachyrium* in Ontario and Quebec, as well as the Bull River community, may actually be the remains of a more-widespread Hypsithermal tallgrass distribution.

Plants move. The rapid and widespread invasion of Eurasian weeds is testimony to that. But beyond this rapid, human-induced movement of alien species, there is a much slower movement of native grassland species within their own realms and rhythms. This is the successional time that we know nothing about. If these plants are, in fact, moving, why are they moving? Does their movement represent an expansion or a contraction? Are some species moving more rapidly than others? How really, does nature work?

Sky Zachary Um. That was how one botanist spelled it out for me, when I was still struggling with the pronunciation. My first thought was, this could be the name of the first-born child of some New Age couple, rather than the name of the god of Obscure Complexity, or just plain split awn. The reputedly dead name is very much alive, multiplying into interesting new layers of meaning.

The Bull River bluestem is the westernmost outlier, a tiny bay left from a now drained sea. Linguists often seek far-flung émigré populations to study earlier versions of a language. Like the Gaelic spoken in the Canadian Maritimes, the Bull River population may contain rich patterns and rhythms of an earlier time.

I am still not sure why the *Schizachyrium* of Bull River has so taken me. Perhaps as we are both western outliers, it of a ploughed sea, me of origins less obvious, we have a bond. We shall stick together, and advocate for our rights as question marks on the map.

The Burden of Horn

As soon as he entered the dense stand of alder and birch at the mouth of the Tashoti, seventeen years of familiarity rose up and enveloped him, like the smell of rotting leaves. Seventeen of these falls right up underneath the Yukon border, seventeen separate months of vividness punctuated by eleven-month stretches of memory and desire. He chuckled to himself as he saw a blazed alder. Jimmy Ignace, the guide that first introduced him to the Tashoti Valley, had marked it, one of a series of false blazes to lead strangers away from the real trail, a narrow track that threaded through a boggy tangle of alder and birch.

Jimmy had quit the guiding business years ago, but still came to the valley to hunt on his own, so that made two who knew this valley. And eight years previous, a cagey and determined hunter from Fort Nelson had found his way in, and the small Tashoti club was reluctantly expanded to three. Occasionally a group of hunters would stumble over the south ridge from the Duniza, but inevitably, they would misunderstand the unique game movements in the valley, and soon leave. The solitude of this valley was precious to him. It was hard and unchanging, like gemstone.

Frosts had already come, and there was a light skiff of crusty snow that would make tracking easier. He stopped to adjust his heavy pack, the first of two he would take into his base camp. Hunting was more serious now since he had switched to the bow. He had to get closer, and the terms were a little more even. Last fall had been a turning point though, a break in the cycle of seventeen; he had buried an arrow deep into the shoulder of a male brown bear, and then tracked it for three days without ever finding it. Even now, a year later, the bear incident was an unhealed wound, and he was careful around the memory.

A geological technician, his knowledge of the North came from stints in the assay labs of the Hercules, Opax, and Reliant mines. He made a few investments and, when it came time, he moved down south to Trail, and bought a house just big enough for one. He had grown to like industrial towns. Housing was usually cheap, and at least one restaurant would stay open all night to serve shiftworkers. He consulted occasionally, and did some politics. Large chunks of time passed, particularly in the months leading up to the fall hunt. With his body parked in a lawn chair on the tiny back porch, his mind went over the gentle contours of the Tashoti. From there, he could walk those lichen-stained ridges and look down on the valley's contained peacefulness, storing up his concentration for the real trip.

To the inexperienced southerner, the valley seemed odd, with trees, shrubs, and grass not occupying their customary places. The meandering river seemed to get smaller in the downstream reaches, as if its waters drained away through some unseen cleft. The climate was harsh — winter could start any time in August — but the landscape itself was gentle, almost feminine. Streams were slow-moving, with plenty of willow flats and oxbows. Rounded valleys followed rounded hills, broken here and there by modest escarpments that spoke of ancient tilting and faulting. The heathlands of the ridgetops were timeless, where even a mastodont would not have looked out of place. The steep, fractured mountains of his home in the South seemed new and raw by comparison.

Even though he loved the valley now, his first few trips with Jimmy had been daunting. He remembered being frankly nervous about pushing so far beyond everything he knew. Odd thoughts popped into his head on those early trips. What if they couldn't get out? How long could they survive here? Even if he could get out physically, would his mind refuse to leave, choosing instead to maroon itself there? But the same terrain that had seemed so hostile on those first trips was almost intimate now, even though the rivers all drained northward, toward the Arctic Ocean. The Tashoti now meshed perfectly with his recurring landscape dreams, of shimmering oases, tangled labyrinths, and secret trails.

Emerging two hours later from the dense forest at the head of the valley, he set the first pack down on dry, level ground next to an old firepit, one that he and Jimmy had built in the early eighties. This would be base camp. From here he could travel lightly on day trips to all corners of the valley. Slinging a rope into a tree, he hoisted his heavy pack high above the ground, and then turned immediately back to get the second one.

As he walked, lightly now, he began to think of last year's bear. Bears are poor bleeders and unpredictable when wounded, but he had been absolutely confident of his knowledge of the valley, and of his tracking skills. He had told no one of the incident, not even Jimmy. It had been a massive personal failure, a jagged break in the cycle of seventeen, a violation of the sacred trust between himself and the animal. This time he planned to hunt only sheep, which bled well and could be counted on to retreat to predictable ground.

Two weeks later, he was on top of a boulder outcrop on the north ridge of the valley, watching a Dall sheep. He had learned the craft of lengthy and patient stillness, perfecting it by posing for life drawing classes back in Trail. He hadn't taken anything yet, other than a whitetail for meat in camp, but that was okay; the Tashoti landscape was sustaining him well, and he had supplies for many more days, even weeks. He had chosen this stand on the outcrop carefully, and the wind was blowing toward him.

Through the binoculars, he could see the animal's massive, annulated horns. His eye automatically traced the geometry: horn tip extends upward beyond a straight line drawn through the centre of the nostril and the lowest, hindmost portion of the horn base. That was how the Regulations described the exaltation of full curl. He watched the animal as it browsed carefully, choosing first sprigs of blueberry and then only the tenderest green leaves from a small bunchgrass. After an hour, the ram was so close he could see its nostrils flare as it breathed.

His life then, was finally reduced to a component of the oldest and most compelling of equations, one that combined a valley, an ungulate, a human. Earlier than commerce, earlier than agriculture, it was perhaps the only equation involving humans that ever balanced, the only one that preserved all the values and valences. With fierce concentration, he noted everything about the ram: where it stepped, what it browsed, what kinds of noises caused it to look up, the surprising rain of pellets when it shat. But mostly he watched the eyes, honing the binoculars in on those expressionless, deep-green pools. The moment of total assimilation approached, when the burden of horn shifted to his own shoulders. This was the moment when he had failed the bear, a failure that would never happen again.

The ram stopped grazing, and raised its massive head. He followed its gaze with the binoculars, but could see nothing unusual in the graceful sweep of the valley below. Watching, listening, and even smelling, he tried to detect what it was the ram was responding to, but nothing materialized. He had a perfectly good shot, but decided to wait. Dropping this ram could come later, much later, as a footnote. The animal hadn't budged for several minutes. If it were watching some predator or another hunter, he too would have seen it by now. The ram had become like a totem on the rocky and windswept ridge. Then, finally, it dawned — the ram was admiring the landscape. It was looking at the valley itself.

Raising up and drawing the bow in a slow, fluid, and almost mesmeric movement, he aimed and shot a symbolic miss, planting the arrow straight through the centre of a dwarf willow, just under the ram's nose.

CURIOUS RARITY

RARITY IS A CURIOUS THING, AND rarity can get you into trouble. As a grassland ecologist, I hear a lot about rare species, because one-third of British Columbia's species-at-risk live, mate, burrow, or pupate on our grasslands. But, of course, you never see them, since they are rare. Or other people see them, but I don't. I either miss their location by a hundred metres or their appearance by three days, or else I'm scheduled for carpet cleaning or a tax audit on the one rainy, moonless night between the second and fourth of June, when temperatures hover between eight and ten degrees Celsius, and the planets have the correct alignment, when some red-listed creepy-crawly can be seen slithering or flitting about in carnal lust on a particular stretch of rural backroad, exactly 12.9 kilometres south-southwest of an unmarked intersection, known only to the illuminati. Or worse yet, I am supposed to meet all those exacting directions, ambient temperature, and timing require-ments not to just-miss *seeing* something, but to just-miss *hearing* a faint croak or chirp that purportedly issues from the throat of some endangered creature.

I have a desperate and inexplicable need to see endangered species in their own habitat, so desperate, in fact, that I once drove 1600 kilometres to meet a guy who promised he could show me the pygmy horned lizard of southern Saskatchewan. So, naturally, when I do stumble onto some listed species (and the key word here is stumble since I have never found a listed species when I actually went out looking for one), it is a big deal for me. Such an event actually happened, or so I thought, on a humble and rather ordinary piece of grassland known as the Granton, east of the town of Grand Forks. The Granton is an unlikely place for any kind of rarity, since, as far as I can tell, it is a piece of land that has been used and abused by all and sundry since the late Pleistocene. There are roads and powerlines and transmission lines and pipelines and ATV trails and mine adits and unauthorized trash dumps and way too many deer, cows, elk, and wild sheep. As a result, the Granton is a virtual laboratory, a botanical garden of noxious weeds. You are far more likely to find a rear fender for a 1957 Chevrolet on the Granton than you are a rare plant. But I walk the Granton anyway, and its humble delights do shine through for me, despite the carnage.

I was exploring the far-eastern edge of the Granton that fateful day, along a small ephemeral stream. As the stream's watercourse reaches a slope break, there is an alluvial fan of sorts, where shrubs seemed to prosper. Many of the saskatoons and mock oranges were head high and more. As I wandered through this curious gallery, one of the shrubs caught my sleeve with a viciously sharp thorn, a good two inches long. There were hawthorns in the area, and that was my first thought. But with its dusky, smooth-margined leaves, this was no hawthorn. I took out a pocketknife and carefully cut a sample to take home for identification.

I started with the BC flora — no luck — and expanded from there. The flora of Alberta identified my heavily armed shrub as a *Shepherdia*, but not the usual *canadensis*; this was *Shepherdia argentea*, or silver buffaloberry, and it rang some long-forgotten prairie bells for me. According to the books, its sole, known location in BC was right smack on the Alberta border, somewhere near Crowsnest Pass. I looked further, and it showed up on the BC Conservation Data Centre's endangered species list. I was totally excited. Now I could earn some credibility as a naturalist, by announcing to the world this important discovery, and a monumental range extension of a thousand kilometres at least. My palms began to sweat. Career possibilities loomed. Front page on the BC Naturalist newsletter. A permanent niche in the University Herbarium. Lucrative contracts with the Discovery Channel. The lecture circuit. If I could work a political angle to buffaloberry, I might even get on the Jon Stewart show.

But first, I would tell the benighted locals about this marvellous rarity growing right in their own backyard, that same Granton that was a combination playground, dump, exercise facility, and tragedy of the commons. As it happened, a meeting of the Granton management committee was imminent.

Now the Granton management committee was a curious animal in its own right. A heterogeneous collection of hard-core hunters, third-generation ranchers, intransigent guide-outfitters, power-hungry naturalists, cranky local historians, and bored civil servants, the committee met twice a year to indulge in verbal sparring, sectoral partisanship, and total management stasis. They were living, collective proof that the perfect is the enemy of the good. More than once, after attending their lengthy committee wrangles, I thought about erecting a plaque with bronze letters that stated "on this date, absolutely nothing happened here".

The committee meeting was a perfect venue to announce my historic find. As the meeting opened, the chair called for new agenda items, and I asked for time to announce the historic discovery of a rare shrub on the Granton. The chairman was reluctant, since it would cut into their valuable bickering time, but he grudgingly allowed me a small time slot after the coffee break. The meeting droned on in its usual dysfunctional manner. Each sectoral representative would play out his or her role, airing historical grievances, bashing the other sectors, bashing government, and announcing that all other interests except his or her own interests were responsible for the sorry state of the Granton. It was like watching a Greek Tragedy; everyone played a pre-determined role, the script never changed, and no one could avoid the inevitable gut-wrenching and totally predictable catastrophe.

Finally the committee broke for coffee and homemade cookies and, in true Canadian fashion, everyone was jovial. Al, the rancher representative, came over and suggested we go outside for a few moments, to get some fresh air.

"So, you found a rare shrub on the Granton, eh?" Al asked. "You bet I did," I responded, proudly. "Just east of Stubbs Creek, on that alluvial fan."

Al was silent for a moment. Right away I knew something was up, since Al was rarely silent.

"Well, Don, I don't know how to break this to you, but me and some guys from the Ministry of Environment planted those shrubs in the 1970s, as a wildlife browse enhancement project. It was an experimental trial, and we planted eight different species. We didn't plant them in rows, because the ground was too stony. So we just shoved the plants in wherever we could. Most of them died except the buffaloberry, and it just kind of took over."

My career as the famous intrepid naturalist-explorer collapsed like a house of cards. Interviews, lecture tours, tenure, all lay buried in the smoking ruins.

I must have visibly slumped down, because Al reached over and patted me on the shoulder. "Hey," he said, "look on the bright side. At least now you won't make an ass of yourself in front of the committee."

That incident happened many years ago. Now, whenever I pass by the Granton, I stop to walk it, and visit the buffalo-berry patch, the architect of my ecological humbling. I have fully absorbed that little life lesson, but now I speculate on the larger meaning of this Canadian native plant, naturalized and thriving — and reproducing — in its little niche in the Granton. As an ecologist, I honestly don't know whether to eradicate it, or encourage it.

It is theoretically possible, and the buffaloberry suggests it, that we could collectively choose a rare native species, research it, cultivate it, multiply it, and reintroduce it back into suitable native habitat, to the point that it would no longer be rare. Would we then lose interest in this newly-common species? Is there a value to these organisms that extends beyond their few-ness?

The contemporary ecological thinker Frederick Turner says that we have three responsibilities to nature: we need to protect existing ecosystems, we need to restore damaged ecosystems, and we need to create new ecosystems. As I walk the troubled Granton, I know we are failing miserably at our first two duties. Our obsession with suburban growth and development virtually guarantees the ecological demise of native valley grasslands. Those that are not directly eviscerated by housing, roads, and retail succumb to the suburban halo effect of soil disturbance and alien weed invasion.

The third duty is the controversial one, and it turns on the curious ecological concept of "nativeness". A species can be native to a single valley, or native to a continent. It is a question of scale. For me there is a clear distinction between the native North American buffaloberry and its nefarious cousin the Russian olive, introduced from western Asia. As I walk the troubled Granton, the silver-leaved buffaloberry prompts me to confront my worst ecological nightmare, Turner's third duty. Instead of passively standing by and watching wave after wave of introduced alien species break over our native grasslands, bickering about whose fault it is, and seeing the whole biome collapse under the weight of management stasis, suburbanization, and climate change, we might listen to nature through the quiet voice of the Granton buffaloberry, which says: touch me, albeit carefully. Engage me. Get to know me by working with me.

A SCHOONER IN MEMORY

I SAT BESIDE MY FATHER ON a driftwood log, and felt the tension of family history begin to give way to the clarity of the landscape. Behind us, a dense and boreal forest came right down to the narrow shingle beach. In front lay peaceful Argyle Sound, sparkling in the summer sun and dotted with islands, where Acadians hid during the brutal expulsion of 1755. Among the wrack at the tide line was a smashed lobster pot and a great curved chunk of wood, its graceful arc plainly of nautical origin. In the halcyon days of Nova Scotia shipbuilding, "knees" like this one were cut from the flaring trunks of old-growth spruce.

We had come to find our ancestor, Thomas, who was born in Ireland. When he was eleven years old, Thomas' parents sold him into indenture to a Nova Scotia shipowner. The reasons for this transaction are not known, but one can surmise too many children and not enough food. That was in 1805. Thomas' life thereafter was tied to ships, first fishing off the coast of Newfoundland, then working in the Halifax dockyards, and finally as master of a schooner based in Argyle Sound, on Nova Scotia's South Shore. His ship plied the Maritime and New England coasts until he died in 1858. His was a life in place, the known elements of which are confined to less than a paragraph.

Our trip to find this Thomas began in Halifax. After an exhausting flight across the country, I arrived at the airport late in the afternoon. Since there was time to kill — Dad wasn't due in until the next morning — I started walking to the airport hotel, a few kilometres away. A busy freeway overpass loomed in front of me, and I realized it had no sidewalk. For me, overpasses are among the most inhospitable structures on the planet, and I felt an old, and slightly rancid, alienation as I walked across this one. In my pedestrian, hitchhiking youth, this overpass would have been a flagrant denial of my rights. Now, I found it simply unpleasant, and hurried across.

The anonymous hotel lay curled in the concrete embrace of a highway cloverleaf. Right after checking in, I went outside for a run, to rid myself of the accumulated dross of three separate airports, and to get a foretaste of the Nova Scotia landscapes we would see. The famous fogs of Halifax dictated that its airport was fifty kilometres out of town, and I realized that the whole complex of airport, interchange, and hotel were just a small enclave surrounded by forest. The road I ran on angled inland and pavement quickly gave way to gravel. There were no houses and the road was dead straight and lonesome, a road built strictly for exploiting resources. The forest on either side of me was more engaging — a mix of second-growth white spruce, tamarack, and the odd white pine. The tallest trees barely reached thirty feet, and the spruces had heavy, clumped tops. There were pockets where the trees were only a few feet high and widely scattered, and in those areas, understory took over. Saskatoon shrubs were all in blossom, but they were no doubt called something different here. Exotic, white, branching lichens reached all the way up to the shrub layer, and the ground was patterned into humps and depressions. The tamaracks, or what I, as a westerner, am pleased to call larches, heralded oncoming spring with incomparably green sprays of needles. Passing a boggy spot, I saw the classic, unfolding fiddlehead ferns, like the necks of green violins. At a roadcut, I stopped to dig my fingers for the first time into the yielding red clay of my ancestral Atlantic Canada.

After running for forty-five minutes, slowing occasionally to look at plants, I finally stopped at the crest of a hill. The odd, sub-boreal forest stretched away indefinitely to the west, and a low ceiling of braided cloud rolled overhead. What a first sight this must have been for Thomas, all this unclaimed expanse, for an eleven-year-old born to a country as land-poor as Ireland.

Turning back, I mulled over my reasons for being here. Neither Dad nor I had ever been to Nova Scotia, but we had talked about a "roots trip" there for probably twenty years, and now it was a reality. I reminded myself that genealogy is a clever trap, waiting to snare the writer into thinking the material is inherently interesting and important. Dad and I might have gained more from picking some town in Iowa or Manitoba, and researching a historical family chosen at random. Genealogy represented a kind of patriarchal, deterministic view, and was most often called upon to show some splendidly early arrival date or a connection to the rich and famous. On balance though, genealogy could be my crack in the present, my chance to practice history, and a rare opportunity to examine place. Place, as the intersection of local people and local landscape, that seductive entity that I crave so much.

Dad arrived the next morning. Somehow he could get from California to Nova Scotia in a few hours; from British Columbia it had taken me all day. We hugged warmly, but he was preoccupied; his suitcase had not arrived with him. The people at the airline desk assured him it would be on the next flight and if he would leave the suitcase's key with them, they would clear it through customs and send it on by cab to us in Halifax. I hadn't seen my father in several years, and I watched his grave and massive presence as he talked with the airline people. The weather-beaten skin of his neck was the colour of old, dark wood, and his close-cropped beard alternated brown and silver. We left, but Dad was worried about his pajamas, which were in the suitcase. I granted him that mundane worry. At seventy-five he was entitled. I myself had reached the age where I was beginning to accept our similarities.

We splurged on a full-size rental car, rationalizing that both of us were six-feet-four, and that father-son tours of ancestral Nova Scotia come only once a lifetime. We drove in state down to Halifax harbour, where we knew the young Thomas Gayton had helped repair the British gunboats, *Shannon* and *Chesapeake*, during the War of 1812. I remarked how curious it was that Thomas aided England, but his great and great great grandsons — my New England-raised father and grandfather — harboured the traditional Yankee dislike for the British, whom they both often referred to as "the bloody lobsterbacks".

Dad's suitcase finally arrived, minus its key, and we drove south down the coast, passing Lunenburg, then Shelburne. Before we checked into our hotel in Yarmouth, we stopped at a hardware store and bought a key blank and a file, to reproduce the childishly simple suitcase key that had gone astray. Here were two more family similarities: we both frequented hardware stores, and both were more comfortable when hand tools were available. As Dad worked on filing the key, I fiddled with the suitcase, idly spinning the tumblers on a combination lock that apparently provided an additional level of security. Dad soon had both the key locks open, but was stunned when the veteran leather suitcase remained shut.

"Did you fool with the combination lock?" he asked, accusingly.

"Well, yes, but don't you know the combination?"

He shook his head slowly. "It's your grandfather's suitcase, and I've never used the combination lock. I've always simply left it unlocked and used the key locks instead."

The pajamas again became theoretical. I busied myself with the combination lock, turning the tumblers with my ear pressed against them, hoping for some telltale click.

Dad was examining the side of the suitcase. "That's it, Black Horse!" he said excitedly, and pointed to the letters ACO printed in small letters on the side.

"What on earth do ACO and Black Horse mean?" I said.

Dad was busy counting on his fingers: "Never mind, try 347."

I stared at him blankly.

"Just try it."

I dialed in the numbers, and the suitcase popped open. I looked at Dad with amazement.

He smiled, and explained. "It's a mnemonic, you see. Dad wanted a way to remember combinations, so he dreamed this one up years ago. You find a ten-letter word or a phrase that has no letters repeated, and you assign a number to each letter. With Black Horse, B stands for zero, L for one, A for two, and so on. Then you write the letter equivalent to the combination right near the lock somewhere. No one else has any idea what it means, and all you have to remember is Black Horse."

He took out his pajamas triumphantly.

Genealogy is indeed a grievous trap, I thought. Here was the grandfather, Donald the First, who created alphanumeric mnemonics and built pendulum clocks from scratch; my father, Donald the Second, who can arrive at pi from a dozen mathematical pathways; and me, Donald the Third, horrified yet fascinated, who stands to inherit this mnemonic suitcase full of sticky and complicated obsessions. Donald, Donald, Donald. We named our first child Ivan, trying to put an emphatic end to this blood-and-fathers nonsense, but there are obvious traces, as that son builds guitars with fret placements honed to the third decimal place. That night I fell asleep wondering what other family traits might be woven all the way forward from Thomas.

After his stint in the Halifax shipyards, young Thomas was sent to the South Shore community of Argyle, between Yarmouth and Cape Sable, to work as a sailor on a ship belonging to Isaac Spinney. Thomas married Spinney's daughter, Anne, took up 200 acres of land somewhere along the Tusket River, and sailed for the rest of his life, becoming the master of at least one ship of fifty-ton capacity, the small schooner, *Armenia*. His wife bore eight children. One of them was lost at sea.

This Thomas we had come to find was a minor participant in perhaps the finest hour of Canadian entrepreneurship, the great clipper-ship trading era. Between 1786 and 1920, some 4,000 wooden ships of over 500 tons draft were built in the Canadian Maritimes, and they sailed the seven seas, moving fish, lumber, gypsum, salt, molasses, and a hundred other commodities. The port of Yarmouth, at one time, had the second-largest fleet registry in Canada, just behind Halifax, and the ships of Nova Scotia's South Shore competed head-to-head with ships from Boston and Liverpool. Nova Scotia produced the greatest designer of the clipper-ship era, Donald Mckay, as well as its greatest sailor, Joshua Slocum.

Thomas skippered a two-masted, coastal schooner. The schooner was a New World innovation, born along North America's eastern seaboard, where crews were scarce and coastlines serrated. The schooner's fore-and-aft sails could be raised and lowered right from the deck with a much smaller crew than the traditional square-rigged ships required, and could also tack more easily and go farther "into the wind". The sons and nephews of Thomas gravitated to the trans-Atlantic trade, which was dominated by the bigger, square-rigged barques and brigantines.

Nova Scotia ships were built as a community enterprise. Two or three families, in places like Meteghan or Port Greville or Barrington would pool labour and capital, set up a shipyard, and begin hauling logs from the forests behind. Meanwhile, a tabletop scale model of the ship's hull was prepared, sculpted, and re-sculpted, based on tradition and the ship's intended use. Ships destined to carry heavy-ore cargoes, for instance, required broader beams and sturdier construction. But with each craft, there always some leaven of innovation.

Once the model was completed to everyone's satisfaction, dimensions were scaled up to full size, and work began in earnest. Sawyers cut tamarack, spruce, pine, oak, and fir planks, each for a particular application. The critical spruce knees were also cut. These tough, right-angled slabs were used to reinforce the critical joints between the deck and the hull. The keel would be laid, and a small steam plant would be set up to bend the hull planks to the right curvature. Metal fittings, rope, and canvas would be ordered from Halifax. The "ways", a complex track that would carry the completed ship on its only terrestrial journey, from the yard into the water, were also constructed.

It is sobering to realize that the vast quantities of information, technology, and skill required to design, build, and launch a seaworthy schooner, to sail it along poorly marked coasts and unpredictable seas, and to run it as a multinational business, all resided in these tiny, isolated communities of Nova Scotia's South Shore.

Thomas Gayton died in 1858, leaving few marks on the landscape and none on a sea that forbids them. He was not alone in his invisibility; of the 238 people claiming occupation in the 1861 census of the Argyle District, thirty-four were mariners, and thirty-eight were fishermen, all notable by their absence from terrestrial record. A few left memoirs, as did Captain Benjamin Doane of nearby Barrington, but most did not. Lives such as these can be expanded slightly by inferential research, but far more substantially by a kind of place-centred imagination. The true biographer of Thomas and his kind would have to be a novelist.

The next morning, Dad and I had a long, leisurely breakfast at a restaurant overlooking Yarmouth harbour. It was pleasant to finally be beyond the bitter arguments about the Vietnam War that had poisoned our relationship for so long. Yet it was painful at the same time. The warmth we felt now could have been in place for the last two decades, if we had been able to come to terms. Looking back, I realized his judgment of my conscientious objection was framed by World War II. A mere twenty years separated that honourable war from the ethical and political swamp that was Vietnam. It was too soon for him, too big a gulf for an old man to bridge.

After eating, we lingered on, sipping coffee and watching the ocean-going ferry arrive on its overnight run from Portland, Maine. I asked Dad to go over again the familiar ground of his childhood in the small deepwater port of Tiverton, Rhode Island. He grew up surrounded by venerable maritime tradition, spending much of his youth either on the docks or at his uncle's sail loft, taking in the dying sights and smells of the clipper-ship era. He pulled a mechanical pencil from the pocket of his Pendleton shirt and began sketching out a map of his Tiverton neighbourhood on the paper placemat. I watched with pleasure as the map progressed. Bold, ruler-straight lines, precise arcs and labels in Roman capital all flowed from his confident hand. He truly did see the world through the medium of geometry. I noticed another similarity: both of us favour mechanical pencils and they often rest comfortably in our hands, even when not in use.

By the time Dad left Tiverton, most of those ships were either beached and abandoned, or converted to pleasure craft for wealthy Bostonians. My father's Tiverton experience linked him directly to the Nova Scotia clipper ships; I on the other hand, grew up a drylander and didn't know a mainsail from a marlinspike. But I was sure I could feel the impetus of our ancestral experience, like one feels an onshore wind.

After breakfast, we drove to the Yarmouth County Archives, situated in an elegant old stone church. We had phoned in advance, and the Archivist met us with stacks of sources. For the next several hours we fossicked through genealogies, land titles, censuses, records of shipping, maps, and diaries, each of us coming away with a raft of notes. One of our objectives was to find Thomas' grave, and the archivist suggested we try the Kemptville cemetery, as she had a record of a Gayton buried there. This was odd, since everything we had read associated the family with Argyle, on the coast. Kemptville was several kilometres inland. How little is written down about the lives of ordinary people, unless they write it themselves.

We folded ourselves into the big Buick rental again, and drove toward Kemptville. I soon discovered that, in this part of the Maritimes, there are several different routes leading to the same place, none of them very direct. I also learned that one must be quite specific about the community you are travelling to. As for our destination, we had the choice of Kemptville Corner, East Kemptville, or North Kemptville. The nearby Pubnicos offered the choice of West, Middle West, Lower West, East, Middle East, and plain Pubnico; then there was Argyle Head, Central Argyle, and Lower Argyle. These were communities, all right, but not in the sense that you could tell when you were at their centre. Some would have gas stations or churchs; others were simply collections of widely-spaced houses and small farms.

Kemptville Corner lay in rolling terrain and Acadian scrub forest. The cemetery yielded the grave of one Havey Gayton who died in 1866 at age one, and clouds of black-flies, but no Thomas or Anne. The surnames of Nickerson, Crowell, Spinney, Ryder, and Goodman abounded though, and we knew from our research that these people were connected by marriage to Thomas and his descendants. I stopped at a country store and asked about other cemeteries in the immediate area, and the teenage girl at the counter drew us an excellent map showing the locations of two others. We scouted both of those, to no avail, and decided to try the Argyle area next.

Argyle Sound is a long, open bay that cuts deeply into the Nova Scotia coastline, ending at Argyle Head. The other Argyles were ranged further down the sound. We started with the big cemetery at Argyle Head. Again, we found contemporaries of Thomas and Anne, but not those two. Next, we tried the cemetery at Central Argyle, with no luck. To be so concerned with finding graves was silly on the face of it, since they would give us no more information than we already had, yet somehow it was important. Thomas was unique in our ancestry as the only one who came to a place as a young man and stayed resident there until he died. His grave would celebrate that fact.

We got back in the car and continued down the sound. Even though we hadn't found the grave yet, we knew we were in Thomas' home territory. Dense second-growth tamarack, white spruce, and alder came right down to the shore. A few of the houses looked ancestral, but there were others from every era right up to the present. How many groups had stormed or slunk onto this storied and shingly coast, I wondered: Vikings, MicMacs, Acadians, Planters, Loyalists, freed slaves, Novascotiamen, draft dodgers (from several wars), rumrunners, American tourists.

Time was running short, but we decided to stop a few moments at a beach, to sit on a driftwood log, and bask in the sunshine. It was then that I saw the two washed-up maritime symbols, the ship knee and the lobster pot, one signifying art and the other, possibly rape.

An examination of family roots ultimately becomes an examination of landscape, and as we sat on the driftwood log, I made a comparison between the imagined landscape I had once created for Thomas as I read our genealogy, and the real one in front of me. I had envisioned a broader band of open coastal vegetation, with windswept trees and beach grass. Of course I imagined the upright, two-story white clapboard houses with long windows facing the sea, of which there were a few, but my imagination had made no room for the ordinary bungalows, the designer beach homes, and the comfortable old farmhouses that were also scattered along the Argyle road. My imagined Argyle also came complete with compass directions, which turned out to be quite correct, as was my sense of the salt-laden air.

This small sound spawned fifty-six ocean-going ships, built and launched between 1800 and 1895. Now it was a quiet backwater. Even Yarmouth, once a key port in the international shipping trade, now had only a few fishing boats. The big ocean ferry only docked there briefly; it was based in Boston.

We got back into the car and resumed our search, both somewhat skeptical of ever finding the graves. We knew Thomas and Anne lived in the Argyles for some time, but that was all. They could have moved to a different community toward the end of their lives, or become indigent, unable to afford headstones. Jackson Ricker's *Historical Sketches of Glenwood and the Argyles*, one of our sources, spoke ominously of abandoned graveyards and, for all we knew, Thomas could be resting under second-growth forest.

The next cemetery, at Lower Argyle, was a small, treeless plot tucked between two farmhouses. Some of the headstones were from the 1700s — how different from the Western-Canadian graveyards, which celebrate barely a hundred years of immigrant history. By now, we had established a cemetery drill; Dad took the right, I took the left, and we slowly worked our way along the rows, checking each headstone. Some of the older ones were almost undecipherable. It was as if the letters were wounds in the stone that had healed over the decades. Just as the injured body carries an image of itself that is a blueprint for healing, these old stones were compelled to return to their original, mute, smooth surfaces.

Dad let out a shout and I knew immediately that he had found the graves. The day brightened, going from humdrum back to adventure again. It was actually a single granite, four-sided family memorial, with bronze plaques attached. One plaque had an anchor on it, and read:

Thomas Gayton
A Native of Ireland
Died October 10, 1858
Aged 64 Years
At Rest

The next side was Anne's, reading:

Anne
Beloved Wife of Thomas Gayton
Died May 3 1857
Aged 64 Years

The third side read:

Jeremiah
Youngest Son of Thomas and Anne Gayton
Died At Sea
April 7, 1880
Aged 49 Years

So, this was the tiny bit of tangible ancestry we had come so far for. We used an adjacent gravestone as a camera rest and took photographs of ourselves next to the memorial, each vying, as always, for the highest ground so as to appear tallest. We nudged and jostled and mugged for the camera, trying on the piercing, seaward gazes each thought might be worthy of our maritime ancestors. Even though we came to it from very different directions, it was a fine moment.

We had gleaned a bit of cryptic information on Jeremiah Gayton from Ricker's book: "Mr. Jeremiah Gayton of Lower Argyle who had been away from home for twenty years and was returning home as one of the crew of the barque *Clydesdale*, fell from aloft and was instantly killed." I am not sure what tack the biographer/novelist would take to expand on Jeremiah. Perhaps it would be the nearly unbearable pathos of random chance — after twenty years away, accidental death within sight of home. Or the lifelong sailor's revulsion at the prospect of being beached in domesticity. Or possibly the carnage of rum.

We looked further into the little graveyard and found the markers of two other sons of Thomas and Anne, plus a grand-nephew James, who died at sea at age twenty-six. Of this James, Ricker's genealogy read: "James Gayton, son of James, of Argyle, died at sea in 1878, being drowned on board the schooner *Moero*, himself the captain, on a voyage from Yarmouth, N.S. to St. Kitts, West Indies. In a heavy gale of wind the vessel was thrown on her beam ends, dismasted and waterlogged. Only two of the crew survived." We looked for another nephew, Isaac Gayton, whom Ricker had listed as the captain of the four-masted brigantine the *Gypsum Empress*, but he was not to be found.

Driving on beyond the cemetery, we saw the Lower Argyle dock, which was crowded with broad, squat lobster boats. We got out and wandered slowly along the dock, feeling a bit self-conscious in tourist clothes. This was not a tourist dock. A short, powerful man in T-shirt and baseball cap said hello and we stopped to chat. He said the three-week lobster season was about half over and the catch had been good so far. To my ear, untrained in East Coast speech, he could pass for an Irishman with a faded accent. He introduced himself as Nathan

Goodman, and he recognized our surname, even though the last of the Argyle Gaytons had either departed or died more than a century ago. Nova Scotians, I was beginning to realize, have long memories. We compared notes, and concluded that the Gaytons and the Goodmans were probably distant relatives, and enjoyed that brief moment without further family entanglements. After saying goodbye, Dad said that was enough for one day, and we drove slowly back to the hotel.

After Dad went to bed, I borrowed his long, black raincoat and walked the night streets of Yarmouth. So, I had finally captured Argyle, this place of personal and historical and imagined dimensions, a balance point on my family heartline, one that my grandfather first told me about when I was a child. Argyle was given to me then as a kind of unblemished Anglo-Saxon verity, which I subsequently rejected for a couple of decades, but which now presented itself as a real place, a backwater of mildly turbulent, mildly romantic history, where my great-great-great-grandfather chose, or perhaps was told, to live and die.

A great welter of impressions awaited sorting and reflection. Now I had the flesh and blood of Argyle, the stony beach and subdued forest, and a place for Thomas. I could see him there on a Sunday afternoon, on an infrequent home stay. Church and meal are over and there is the pleasant hum and rhythm of children. He leaves the house and moves slowly down the path to the dock and the schooner, to check on some inconsequential matter. His black suit absorbs the summer sunshine, and unaccustomed warmth spreads pleasantly across his back and shoulders. The shingle rock crunches underfoot as he steps onto the empty beach, now midway on the path between schooner and home. The water of Argyle Sound sparkles, the breeze has dropped to mere cat's paws, and the earth is dreaming, suspended in a long afternoon nap. Destiny or random economics had casually given him, Thomas, this place, this Argyle, which he had no choice but to passionately embrace. He must do everything, to bend himself into relation with this place. Thomas, with his mandates, indentures, and memories of Ireland forever in the way, would find that difficult. The land of Argyle, for its part, did nothing, save to embrace him at the end of his life. His finished work of person-in-place, of Thomas-of-Argyle, would not be for him to appreciate, but for his itinerant great-great-great-grandson to see and envy.

When I travel, I don't seem to need much sleep, and nervous energy accumulates. Walking at night has always been a way to drain off some of that energy, and that night I walked for hours, along the huddled streets and lanes of Yarmouth. Dad's black raincoat reminded me of a photograph I had once seen of writer Loren Eiseley, another insomniac, wearing a similar coat as he walked his own night streets.

The memory of our visit to the dock bothered me, and I turned the scene over and over as I walked. A walk down a picturesque dock crowded with lobster boats on a sunny Nova Scotia afternoon is not normal cause for concern. I had no idea of the condition of the lobster fishery, but my gut reaction was that virtually every resource extraction that we do — from logging to fishing to farming — was in some kind of trouble, and this one would be no exception. The docks and boats and river drives and lumber camps and farm fields that we have invested with nostalgic romanticism are now all suspect. Is the lobster fishery sustainable in the long term? Are we simply equitably dividing up a steadily diminishing remainder until the last one is gone? Is the lobster simply the next animal on the food chain, somewhere below the already pillaged cod? Did my ancestors set a pattern of selfish resource extraction that we carry on, but on a much grander scale? In his memoir *Following the Sea*, Benjamin Doane, a Nova Scotia contemporary of Thomas, describes a telling encounter with an albatross during a whaling expedition:

> Not only for the purposes of food, however, were gooneys [albatrosses] killed, but often merely to gratify that savage instinct which sometimes possesses men to kill for the sake of killing and to gloat upon scenes of suffering. That tendency in me received one day a check, the influence of which has never left me. It was when the sharks were thick about the carcase of a whale which we had alongside, and I was chopping at them with the spade. A large gooney scaled down to pick up a sliver that lay drifting in the sleek water. A sudden thoughtless impulse made me strike at him, and the keen edge of the spade gave him a glancing blow upon the neck. He trailed away, mortally wounded, his snowy breast reddening with blood, his reproachful eyes upon me as they glazed in death.

In Doane's mind, there was a clear separation between his random and purposeless killing of an albatross and his systematic and purposeful slaughter of whales. Could he have any inkling of where his profession of whaling was headed? Perhaps even more than the western cowboy or the old-time logger, the whaler has traditionally been the ultimate romantic male profession. Yet now, with most of the world's whale populations collapsing or worse, whalers are virtual pariahs, operating in a kind of moral shadowland between ignorance of ecology and contempt for it.

Ruthless extraction of resources is done exclusively by males, often in very intimate, almost tribal situations, of which Doane's whaling crew was a classic example. The biological horror of what they did — kill huge mammals for a few barrels of oil — was vested with romance and diffused over a tightly bonded group of men. Recruits in these male exploitation guilds were often very young (as Benjamin Doane was) and any moral revulsions about the nature of their work are quickly overridden by their intense desire to become accepted as part of the guild.

Still, I am not sure that I can indict Thomas and his contemporaries. They came to Nova Scotia with rudimentary technologies, incredible persistence, and flashes of brilliance. Their forefathers had brutally evicted the Acadians (it would not surprise me to find the farmland that Thomas bought had once belonged to an Acadian), and they had a very limited understanding of the complex terrestrial and marine ecosystems they imposed themselves on. These people were no more or less far-sighted then we are, plus they had to inure themselves to maritime death tolls that broke over them, like the waves of an endless storm. Their saving graces were perhaps the scale and capacity of their works, neither of which were very large. If I indict Thomas, I must also indict myself. We know more, but we also destroy more.

Thomas and Anne Gayton endured, and had eight children. Their firstborn, John, became a sailor like his father, and married Abigail Smith from nearby Barrington. John and Abigail in turn produced eight children, as well as adopting a boy named Manassah Spinney. As a young woman, this Abigail, my great-great-grandmother, started a journal on New Years' day of 1840, and she penned the last entry — in the same book — in 1896. Abigail was a tough woman. Her constant ally was the Baptist Church, and her implacable enemy was the sea, which kept her an agonized single parent for most of her married life. As her five sons grew, she formed a powerful resolution to keep them away from seafaring. Again, using Benjamin Doane as interlocutor, we get a sense of the Maritime mother's lot as the young son prepares to leave home on a three-year whaling voyage:

> At home, mother sat knitting and though she said little, I knew that her chief thoughts and all her hopes and fears were for me. Three of her sons had gone away to sea, never to return in life. Now I, her youngest was about to go on a long and dangerous voyage, and she was old, and feared she would never see me again.

Abigail was more outspoken than Benjamin Doane's mother. Anyone who keeps a journal in the same book for fifty-six years has some measure of determination, and Abigail finally won her battle with the sea. In the spring of 1862, their lives more than half over, John, Abigail, their children, and a number of other families chartered a vessel to take them to St. John, New Brunswick, thence up the St. John River to Hartland, and then overland to a place in the forest they christened Knowlesville, in honour of the Baptist minister who led them there. Abigail knew the soils of Lower Argyle, as an alternative to the sea, were just thick enough to go broke on. The deeper soils of their new home in New Brunswick were somewhat more productive, and after a brutal decade of clearing land, stumping, and building fences, they had a farm.

Abigail was a passionate Baptist. I think her ultimate triumph, even greater than that of vanquishing the sea, would have been to have her menfolk throw themselves down in front of another male, the minister, and say "I believe". From her journal, it is obvious she was not successful in this. Subsequent Gayton menfolk seem to have carried that skeptical tradition forward.

Dad and I checked out of our motel the next morning, and we drove through Lower Argyle once more, just to fix the place in memory. I wanted to see more of the South Shore, so after leaving Lower Argyle we stayed off the highway, following the coast road through the Pubnicos, Woods Harbour, Shag Harbour, Doctor's Cove, and Barrington, where Abigail and Benjamin Doane grew up.

Getting back onto the highway at Shelburne, I began to look more critically at the forests around me. This was obviously not the same forest that produced thousands of wooden ships. Nor was it the same forest in which every oak over twenty inches in diameter was marked with a broad arrow and was the property of the British Navy. In fact, I saw no oaks at all. This was not the same forest in which the old-timers recall never felling a hemlock of less than twenty-four inches diameter on the butt. This was not the same forest that produced trees big enough for the masts of a bluenoser or a Novascotiaman. I found out later that the forests looked stunted and boreal not by nature, but because of overharvesting and excessive slash burning.

We detoured off the highway to Lunenburg, the Canadian equivalent of Mecca, home of the schooner, *Bluenose*. My American father knew of the *Bluenose*, but couldn't understand all the hoopla. I showed him our dime and explained that it was the fastest schooner ever built and that it was a kind of Canadian Liberty Bell, the only difference being we probably wouldn't go to war over it. The ship was graceful and beautiful, even with its sails furled and moored as it was next to a parking lot. Sailboats can verge on the biological; I see them as part organism.

I knew the ship was actually the *Bluenose II*, a modern replica, the original having been destroyed in a flagrant case of national negligence. Pursuing this connection between landscape and local industry, I asked the interpretive guide where the masts for the new ship came from. The fellow replied, with misplaced patriotic pride, that they were made from Douglas fir that came all the way from British Columbia. I was beginning to get the picture.

Back on the highway, Dad and I talked about the generations that followed Thomas. John and Abigail's first son, Ebenezer Crowell Gayton, my great-grandfather, left the hardscrabble New Brunswick farm as soon as he could for upstate New York. Evidently Knowlesville soils weren't thick enough to hold Ebenezer, and that was the case with many of his neighbours as well. A forester colleague of mine, who had once worked around Knowlesville, told me that in the middle of mature forests, he would occasionally stumble onto old furrows from abandoned farm fields.

Ebenezer went to work in the brand-new petroleum industry (so our lamps could be lit by dead plants instead of live whales), and later on became the fire chief in the small town of Gowanda. Having arrived to the New World in steerage, so to speak, we were doing all right. But there was a tendency to scatter; as with Argyle, no Gaytons now remain in Knowlesville.

Among the family odds and ends I have is a copy of Ebenezer's 1894 US citizenship certificate, which demands that he "renounce and abjure all allegiance and fidelity to every Foreign Prince, Potentate, State or Sovereignty, and particularly to the Queen of the Kingdom of Great Britain", of whom he was then a subject. When I became a Canadian in the early 1970s, I was asked to swear the reverse oath, but I confess to crossing my fingers behind my back when it came to the part about allegiance to the Queen.

Families were getting smaller now; Donald Vince Gayton, the First, was one of only five children fathered by Ebenezer. Donald the First moved from New York to California as soon as he was able. He and his first son, Donald the Second, pursued a hostile, but oddly binary relationship, living in various locations up and down the US west coast, bestowing on the present first son, the third and last Donald, all the geographical and national ambiguity that has carried forward since Thomas.

Periodically, I build fascinations, and another one, now completed, has slid down its ways to sail my mental waters — the link between the evolution of forest landscapes and historical shipbuilding on Nova Scotia's South Shore. To have that link firmly in mind would seem to me to be very valuable. Place and landscape and vegetation have obvious influence on history only occasionally, but to know of these instances can give us the feeling, whether it is illusion or not, that we are actually rooted to the earth, and even have a chance at sustainability.

Back in Halifax, my father and I said our goodbyes, and winged our separate ways across four time zones, each to his own home. When I arrived, I rooted around in a closet until I found an old cedar cigar box I had saved from childhood. This was my talisman box, containing objects that were fiercely important to me at one time: arrowheads, rusted square nails, old foreign coins, agates from trips to the desert, wisps of a shed snakeskin, a petrified shark's tooth dredged from one of old Ebenezer's oil wells. Among them was Thomas' old pocket compass, given to me by my grandfather at the height of my talismanic age, probably twelve or so.

The small compass was made in France, and its case had the particular rich, burnished colour unique to old brass. The rose was badly oxidized and the glass was not removable, so I spent an evening injecting various solvents through a pinhole opening in the side of the casing, trying to loosen the rust. By inserting a fine needle wrapped with thread, I was able to clean off the cardinal points, but not the degrees. Symbolic talismans such as an old compass are not so compelling to me now as they once were, and I cleaned it now more from a sense of historical duty. If I were to choose a current talisman, it would be that wooden ship's knee, that aged and graceful meeting of spruce and local artifice, half-buried on the beach at Lower Argyle.

THE FRACTURE OF GOOD ORDER

FORTY YEARS OUT OF HIGH SCHOOL was an abstract notion, right up to the moment I entered the decorated community hall and saw all those faces. Graduating in 1964 and spinning far out of the orbit of Franklin High School in Seattle, and even the United States, I was suddenly seeing those eighteen-year-old faces — including mine — after a forty-year interval.

The first waves of reunion recognition were those of my fellow football players. I was surprised at how intimate and durable those bonds were, after lying dormant those many years. I had been an interior lineman, so the faces I knew best were the other unglamorous guards, tackles, and centres. No matter how well you performed as an interior lineman, either on offense or defense, you would not get written up in the school newspaper, and the cheerleaders never remembered your name. But we had aged well, and were comfortable with our anonymity. As we gleefully punched and sized up each other's waistlines, I mentally began to reassemble our offensive line. I think if I had yelled out a play number, these affable gentlemen would have instinctively gone into 3-point stances.

I had arrived in Seattle a bit early for the reunion, so I toured the area around the school. The football field and encircling track, which I remembered as a vast plain of effort, pain, and occasional glory, now seemed tiny. Nearby Dag's Drive-In, home of the nineteen-cent burger as well as many after-game fistfights, was gone. The Beanery, a local store that served me as well as my parents when they went to Franklin, was also gone, a victim of racial troubles in the late sixties. But neighbourhood life had moved on. Empire Way was now Martin Luther King Drive, and Franklin's many-splintered neighbourhood had added Vietnamese and Somalians to its ethnic mix.

Looking beyond the football players, the next set of faces I recognized were the beatniks. Writers, artists, intellectuals. The long-dormant bonds with this group were equally strong. In highschool I was a loner, but what social time I did have at Franklin was all with these two disparate groups — the jocks and the beatniks — with nothing in between. So I was conflicted. I didn't join the athletic Lettermen's club, since it meant taking an oath about smoking and drinking. I didn't talk about books in the locker room, or football with the beatniks.

I experienced a mild reunion euphoria as I drifted through the room, listening to Top 40 rock and roll from 1963 and 1964, and smiling at half-remembered faces. Then I spotted Jef, the most durable and hardcore of the beatnik crowd, and we danced outrageously to the music of Chubby Checker.

It turned out a remarkable number of my classmates still lived in Seattle, and saw each other periodically. Since I was a strange face, some people were curious. A typical conversation would begin like this: "Oh, so you're Don Gayton. What have you been doing all this time?" "Well, I was a conscientious objector," I would reply. "I moved to Canada and became an ecologist." To which the typical response was: "Gee, I'd love to talk more about that, but I'm double-parked." Or, "Excuse me, I'm just going to nip over to the bar and get a refill." Or, "I can't hear a thing you're saying, over all this racket."

After a few of these encounters I got on a roll, and started approaching the most Republican-looking types I could find, to introduce myself and tell my story before they had a chance to get away. It was great sport for a while, until I spotted the Dearly Departed display, with grad pictures of those class-mates no longer with us. One car accident. One suicide. Five killed in Vietnam.

On my long drive home, I thought about those fresh, young faces, envisioning them as soldiers, caught in a war they knew nothing about. Politics aside, did my courage and my convictions match theirs? Was I truly morally opposed to war, or was I just a coward? Could I put conscientious objection, war resistance and the Peace Corps on some kind of moral balance beam, and compare it to the sacrifice of the soldier? How could I oppose a war without dishonouring the soldier? Do I have the right to refuse certain wars, and embrace others? Damn Johnson and Nixon for forcing such heavy choices on our young minds.

As soon as men go to war, a series of inevitabilities, of absolutes, get locked in. Self-preservation and loyalty to your fellow soldier are two of those absolutes, and they override everything. Facing death, and experiencing the death of comrades, are also absolutes. And, by their very nature, these absolutes tend to polarize citizens into unquestioning support or full-on hatred.

As I made my way homeward through the Snoqualmie Pass and down through my old haunts in the Columbia Basin, I settled in to thinking about that conflict. The Vietnam War was not about Vietnam; it was about China. One of the great tragedies of this war and there are many, is that sixty thousand of my contemporaries died for the sake of the "domino theory," which stated that if Vietnam fell to the

Chinese communist plague, then all of Asia would fall. Now, fifty years later, America is economically in bed with China, borrowing its money and lusting after its cheap consumer goods.

I thought about the Catholic priest, Daniel Berrigan, who broke into a Draft Board office and poured sheep's blood on the files, apologizing as he did so for the fracture of good order. I thought about Major Gordon Livingston, a doctor serving in Vietnam, who wrote the famous Blackhorse Prayer:

God, our Heavenly Father, hear our prayer. We acknowledge our shortcomings and ask thy help in being better soldiers for thee. Grant us, O Lord, those things we need to do the work more effectively. Give us this day a gun that will fire ten thousand rounds a second, a napalm that will burn for a week. Help us to bring death and destruction wherever we go, for we do it in thy name and therefore it is meet and just. We thank thee for this war, fully mindful that, while it is not the best of all wars, it is better than no war at all. We remember that Christ said "I come not to send peace, but a sword," and we pledge ourselves in all our works to be like Him. Forget not the least of thy children as they hide from us in the jungles; bring them under our merciful hand that we may end their suffering. In all things, O God, assist us, for we do our noble work in the knowledge that only with thy help can we avoid the catastrophe of peace that threatens us ever. All of which we ask in the name of thy son, George Patton. Amen.

He made copies of this prayer and handed it out to guests at a Change of Command ceremony honouring Col. George S. Patton III. Some of the journalists present assumed that the document was the unit's official prayer. Major Livingston was not treated kindly, but because he was a West Point graduate, a court-martial would have been a public relations nightmare, so he was merely dismissed from the Army.

Reflecting back on the high school reunion, one encounter made a lasting impression, and gave me some peace. Midway through the evening, one of my old football comrades pulled me aside into a quiet corner. I knew he had done a tour as a soldier in Vietnam. He said, "Gayton, I did the right thing, and so did you."

Pupating in Texas

BEFORE HE MOVED TO NELSON, RAYMOND Furtan, CPA, had never even considered monarchs. They had been completely absent from his life. He could remember none from his childhood, and certainly none from his career as a successful Houston accountant. All that changed though, when Raymond's doctor, concerned about his longstanding and mysterious metabolic disorder, recommended that he move to a more unpolluted rural environment.

Accordingly, Raymond and his wife, Sylvia, sat down with maps, pollution indices, geomagnetic atlases, ozone layer reports, and fallout patterns to determine where they should live. The nexus of these diverse indicators pointed to Nelson, British Columbia, a place they had never heard of, in a country just barely within their awareness.

Raymond closed most of his client accounts and Sylvia put their luxury condo up for sale. They had no children, and few connections to the community, so the move was surprisingly easy. Three months later, on a fine summer day, Raymond stood in the backyard of their newly purchased home on the North Shore, a sunny and secluded area outside of Nelson. He felt a little awkward, wearing the casual jeans and workshirt that Sylvia had bought for him in town. Looking down, he saw that a large butterfly had lit on the back of his hand. He raised his hand slowly to get a better look realizing, as he did so, that this was the first time he had looked closely at a butterfly. It was nearly four inches across, and its four wings were a riot of rich orange, yellow, black and white. It seemed not at all afraid of him. Raymond felt a slight pang of regret about living half his life without being aware of these gorgeous creatures.

Days later, while he read in the backyard, three more butterflies appeared as though out of nowhere. They seemed excited and milled about on the back of his hand, like dogs waiting to be fed. Raymond became a little concerned, since he had not seen anyone else in the neighbourhood who attracted butterflies, and none had landed on Sylvia. Either Nelsonites were very secretive about their relationships with these insects, or else he was somehow special.

The next day, he waited until Sylvia left to paint before he returned to the backyard. He thought it prudent to investigate this phenomenon a bit more before he told her about it. Raymond shared everything with Sylvia. They were deeply in love, and when his illness had rendered him impotent several years previous, they had found other ways to express their affection. Sylvia had become an accomplished landscape painter, and she had been taking daily forays to the countryside around their new home, scouting locations and doing preliminary sketches. He could surprise her with his new-found butterfly-attracting talent, and he was sure she would want to do paintings of them. But first he had to come to terms with his bizarre and unusual skill.

He went outside clad in just a bathing suit, and lay down on the chaise lounge they had brought from the house in Houston. It was only a few minutes before he saw them spiralling down toward him, like gaily-coloured scraps of paper floating against the blue sky. There were a dozen or more. He shuddered in fascination, knowing this was no coincidence. Some secret thing about his body connected him to these butterflies. He could feel the slight breezes against the pale skin of his chest as each one landed. As he watched them, their startlingly beautiful wings opened and closed in erratic, pulsing motions, as if they were part of some complex breathing apparatus. He racked his brains, trying to think of the names of butterflies, any name. He could describe in detail seven or eight distinct forms of leveraged buyout, but could not come up with the name of a single butterfly. Raymond forced himself to lie back in the chaise lounge, and surrender himself to this curious event. It was as if meeting with these creatures was a destiny that patiently waited for him as he pupated for years in his air-conditioned life in Houston.

Rousing himself, Raymond dressed quickly and drove to the library in town, anxious to gather more detail on his new friends. With the obligatory Dewey decimal number in hand, Raymond was about to scan a long line of books when a picture book lying open on the shelf caught his attention. There it was, a lovely full-page colour illustration of his butterfly. The monarch, it was called, the largest of North American butter-flies. *Danaus plexippus* was its scientific name, and he silently mouthed those exotic words until they were committed to memory. He read further:

"The monarch is one of the few migratory butterflies. In a complex and poorly understood migration that takes three generations to complete, the monarchs return every fall from far-flung locations across western North America to the same wintering locations in Mexico."

Raymond shivered slightly, even though the library was quite warm. Were it not for his doctor, he would still be sealed in Houston while the invisible legions of monarchs passed overhead. Why had they never been attracted to him there? he wondered, and then chuckled to himself. The answer was obvious, his life in Houston was conducted in a series of sealed, climate-controlled containers: the condo, the BMW, his high-rise office, the corporate boardrooms. The butterflies never knew he existed.

He returned to the book and read on:

"The monarch feeds exclusively on the toxic sap of the milkweed plant, a dazzling metabolic accomplishment. In fact, it seems that the monarch requires the milkweed toxin, as a measure of protection for itself against predators."

Raymond's mind reeled. That was it. The monarchs were after the toxins produced by his own metabolic disorder, toxins that somehow mimicked those of the milkweed. They were cleansing him, purging the poisons from his system, perhaps even shouldering the burden of his disorder. He put the book back on the shelf and slowly walked out of the crowded library, sensing a new, more-physical Raymond Furtan, whose walk was now more loose and rhythmic, and whose soul was no longer defined by CPA. At the door he turned around, wondering if anyone had noticed the new Raymond.

Sylvia was not back yet when he arrived home, meaning that she had found a location to her liking and had stopped to paint. Raymond stripped completely naked, and lay down in the chaise lounge in their secluded backyard. Again the invisible signal went out, and again he saw the tiny point in the sky above him, a point that soon broke into many points, and then into hundreds, fluttering and spiralling gaily on the summer air. This time he opened himself to the monarchs, and they gently covered him in a living blanket.

Time slowed down for Raymond, and flickered in shades of yellow and orange and black. Images from the butterfly book floated through his mind. There was the cottony fluff of the milkweed seed, as it broke from the parent pod and floated off into pregnant air. And the stately oyamel tree, highly prized by the monarchs and found in only a few places in Mexico, festooned like a maypole with thousands of butterflies. Then he saw images of Sylvia and himself, following the migration, drifting on the winds, Sylvia and Raymond searching out the milkweed and the oyamel, him watching, Sylvia painting, and then both of them making love, and then moving again, following the continental imperatives of the monarch. Sylvia would do paintings of the butterfly, the milkweed, and the oyamel to sell, Raymond would use his actuarial skills to create a fund to save monarch habitat, and their lives would pulse and breathe, like the wings of the resting monarch . . .

Raymond's reverie was interrupted by a definite stirring between his legs, something he hadn't felt for years. Shocked and embarrassed, he opened his eyes, only to see the pulsating curtains of yellow and orange and black. He closed them again, and welcomed the blissful sensation of this long-dormant animal, this endangered species, as it swelled and rolled across his belly.

Gradually, Raymond became aware of another presence beside him, a presence just beyond the monarchs and his prodigal manhood. He turned his head slowly to one side and, through vision blurred by monarch wings, he saw Sylvia, standing quietly and watching. He reached out and, after gently dislodging the monarchs from his hand, found hers and squeezed it tightly. Sylvia responded, carefully brushed the butterflies from his face, and kissed him passionately. Raymond's whole body rose to meet her and the kiss dissolved into a mounting swirl of yellow and orange and black, milkweed and oyamel, male and female, until there was a massive and silent detonation, and he felt a warm stickiness spread across his belly.

Sylvia removed the handmade sweater she was wearing, and dipped her fingers into the warm pool on his belly. She traced the wetness around each of her nipples, and then spiralled outward over her splendid milky curvatures, until the entire terrain was covered. Gaggles of monarchs followed her hand obediently, and soon she was clothed again, this time in a pulsating, erotic lingerie of yellow and orange and black.

A Pine To Ponder

Trees do speak of local place, and none more so than the ponderosa pine. A tree native to southern British Columbia, and native to northern Mexico. A definer of landscapes from the Cascade-Sierra spine eastward, all the way to the Hundredth Meridian. Favouring the dry, rocky, and fire-prone places, ponderosa hosts exotic woodpeckers, provides thermal cover for wintering elk, and offers itself as maypole for dancing butterflies. It mingles with sagebrush and bunch-grass at low elevation, and consorts uneasily with Douglas fir on the high. Rock faces and cliffs form frequent backdrops for the ponderosa pine. It grows in places heartrendingly beautiful to look upon, but tough to make a living in. I have known this tree since before I can remember; its sticky pitch endures on my clothes, my hands. The tree is resinous, and resonant.

We share a common geography, this curious ponderosa and I. We are both Westerners, and we both carry all the paradoxical baggage that title implies.

"Three-needled pine," the book says, but often there are only two in a bundle, and occasionally five. Often as long as my hand, the bright-green needles are grouped in radial explosions around twisted, dark branches. The longest needles were favoured by First Nations women for weaving their elegant small baskets.

Sometimes the wood of a ponderosa's main trunk will grow in a bizarre, corkscrew spiral, always counter-clockwise, but since the bark of a corkscrew tree is like any other, the spiral wood is hidden until the tree comes down. Competing theories on the cause of spiralling do exist, but none have been able to fully explain why certain trees do that. Corkscrew ponderosas are often found on the very toughest of growing sites. If Douglas fir commonly did this, scientists would have explained it already, but ponderosa pine's commercial value is low enough that it can keep some of its secrets.

Ponderosa is a tactile, sensory tree. Children and adults alike indulge in its vanilla smell, its remarkable puzzle bark, its big, prickly cones, its sticky resin. John Muir called it "silver pine", because of the way light refracts off the waxy needles. He described light coming off a ponderosa as "beaten to the finest dust and shed off in myriads of minute sparkles that seem to radiate from the very heart of the tree." He also firmly believed that no tree gave forth finer music to the winds.

The Pend Oreille river runs through a steep, east-west valley near Trail, BC, and its south-facing slopes are clothed in ponderosa pine. In the days before all the dams went in, asthmatics would summer in the Pend Oreille, for rest and a forest cure. Noonday sun heated ponderosas on the high slopes, causing them to release their airborne cargo of volatile oils, vanillins, and terpenes. Then in late afternoon the freighted air would cool dramatically and settle to the valley bottom, where visitors gratefully breathed it in for the cure.

One of the great research scholars of the ponderosa pine, Harold Weaver, had his own tactile sense of the tree. He would walk his forest plots barefoot, to heighten his awareness of the grand forest cycle of tree growth, litter fall, fire, and decay.

The Syilx people of the Okanagan have known the tree as s'at'qlp, for centuries. Lewis and Clark first noted the species in 1809, but it was David Douglas who struck its curiously appropriate name, *Pinus ponderosa*, the ponderous pine, the reflective pine. Regional names vary, as they should: bull pine, pino real, pitchpine. In some areas, the juveniles are known as blackjacks, and the veterans, yellowbellies.

More than once I've walked through a dry forest and unexpectedly, like stumbling into a church, entered a glade of ponderosa veterans. Some historical event foreordains these glades — perhaps a pocket of beetle kill or an intense jackpot fire that left an initial opening. Then chance offers back-to-back wet summers, and a corps of new trees start on their way to eventual and overwhelming dominance. The glade's veteran yellowbellies form a rough circle and invite you to sit, on their finely woven carpet of needles. The massive bulk of their trunks are untrammeled by limbs to twice head height. The bark colours, ranging from brick red to a rich yellow, are tinged here and there with black scorch from old fires. Plangent summer sunlight shatters high in the canopy and is becalmed by the needles on its way to earth. The dry, mountain air of the glade is laced with vanilla, and the tobacco-leaf smell of *Ceanothus*, a shrub consort to the ponderosa. These glades are council groves, for sober statesmanship. A place to reflect, to ponder the enduring mystery of our relationship to nature.

As they twist and contort into old age, ponderosa's broad, flat upper branches provide roosting and nesting platforms for a host of raptors. When they metamorphose into standing dead snags, a host of cavity-nesting birds, many of them red-listed, move in. Like poor Thidwick's horns in the Dr. Seuss story, these ponderosa veterans become highly desirable, zero-vacancy, wildlife condominiums.

I've had the privilege of consorting with ponderosa pine throughout its range in British Columbia — Lillooet, Cache Creek, Okanagan Falls, Wasa, and all the dry points in between. I know the pine from the eastslopes of Washington and Oregon, and from the mountains of California, Montana, Idaho, and New Mexico. From childhood camping trips and research tours and long-distance drives and solitary rambles. In each place, the tree looks totally at home on the landscape, and it makes me feel at home, too.

The far-flung distribution map of ponderosa pine has curious empty circles within it. If you worked out the geometric centre of the ponderosa's range, it would land within the biggest empty circle, the Great Basin Desert, where there are no pines. Washington's Columbia Basin and California's Imperial Valley are smaller empty circles. These zones are so dry they even challenge the renowned drought tolerance of the ponderosa.

One of the largest contiguous tracts of ponderosa distribution is in northern Mexico's Sierra Madre, which I have yet to visit. I love looking at species distribution maps, for armchair travel and for presence, but absence is equally interesting.

When I travel north from the British Columbia town of Cranbrook, heading up the Rocky Mountain Trench along Highway 93, I can track ponderosa along the valley up to Columbia Lake. The Trench keeps going north for another several hundred kilometres, but here is where ponderosa drops out. However, if I turn west out of the Trench, climb a couple hundred metres in elevation and enter the lonely splendour of the Findlay Basin, there sits a vigorous and totally isolated stand of ponderosa pine. Why it is there I don't yet know, but thinking about species distribution limits is good practice. It engages the tough questions of botany, ecology, succession, climate, and climate change.

The primal dynamic of the ponderosa pine landscape is fire. There are other disturbance processes, of course — like the pine beetle. But fire, and the lack of it, are dominant. Ponderosa is defined by fire.

The individual ponderosa is programmed to resist fire. As the tree matures, the bark thickens rapidly, and by the time it has reached veteran status of 150 years or more, the compressed maze of insulating puzzle plates, each with a thin air space in between, fully protect the precious underlying cambium. These vets also tend to drop their lower limbs, reducing the opportunity for ground fires to creep up into the tree's canopy. But even if fire does get up into the tree, over two-thirds of the green needles must be killed before the tree finally gives up.

Individual trees withstand fire, but as a community, ponderosa relies on fire. Like most tree species, the ponderosa produces thousands of germinants, in order that a few may survive. Young ponderosas, up to about Christmas-tree size, are easily killed by fire but, due to the wildly random nature of fire events, a few, scattered juveniles will always escape, and grow into boilerplated adults. Open, fire-maintained stands produce big pines, in spite of the harsh sites they often grow in.

Ponderosa has an alter ego, in the form of two-needled lodgepole, the dark cousin. Lodgepole has no resistance to fire, in fact goes up like a Roman candle at the merest spark. Lodgepole embraces fire, is immolated by it but, in return, quickly recolonizes the burnt, ashy moonscapes left by hot wildfires.

All forests produce fuel, on a continuous basis. Needles and twigs fall, bark flakes off, branches drop, whole trees die. In wet, coastal forests, those fuels are broken down into non-flammable humus by an energetic army of fungi, beetles, ants, and the like. In ponderosa forests the rate of biological breakdown is quite slow; there just isn't enough moisture for the fungi and microbes and bugs to turn wood quickly into non-flammable humus. Fuel stays as fuel, still available for burning decades after it has fallen. So the paradox of fire in dry forests is this: the more frequently it burns, the less damage it does.

Dendrochronology, First Nations accounts, archival photographs, and explorer's journals have contributed to an understanding of what pre-fire suppression ponderosa forests looked like, and how often they burned. There was little fuel accumulation. Forests were a patchwork, with a dominant theme of open stands of large, well-spaced trees and a diverse understory of shrubs, herbs, and grasses. There was abundant "edge", which nature so dearly loves. Periodic ground-oriented fires performed the vital functions of thinning and fuel consumption.

Our disruption of the historical fire regime has had profound consequences for ponderosa pine forests. Overdense stands stagger under the weight of too many trees, too much fuel, and a depauperate understory. It is now common to see a large veteran with a lethal mound of accumulated needles and bark around its base. These are trees that have had the adapt-ability and wisdom to survive for two or three centuries, and our management over the last few decades has marked them for almost certain death, in the next wildfire.

Somewhere, in some windowless government office, sits a computer that monitors the number and location of lightning strikes. The data it produces shows that there aren't enough strikes in the dry, interior West to produce a fire-maintained ecosystem; First Nations prescribed burning, together with lightning, produced the frequent fire regimes of the pre-suppression era. From this conjunction of historical forces the ponderosa pine evolved, as well as a ponderosa ecosystem.

So, a ponderosa glade is a good place in which to ponder the question, where does nature leave off, and the human enterprise begin? How do I define the "natural state" of an ecosystem that depends on human intervention for its health? And how do I justify intervention in nature at all, since so much of what we do now is intrusive and catastrophic — not marriage, but rape? What about the preservationist's sacred duty, to lock up as much nature as possible, and throw away the key? Can something as random and primeval as fire be brought back into our overdeveloped and hardwired and carbon-conscious society? Yet how can I possibly sacrifice this tree, this icon of Western wilderness, this friend to cowboy, Indian, naturalist, poet, painter, and seeker of solitude?

It is a corkscrew paradox, wrapped in puzzle bark.

Resisterville

Southeastern British Columbia contains an irregular piece of geography that holds a curious fascination for Americans. It is conventionally referred to as "the West Kootenays", but that term is imprecise, since it includes places like Trail and Creston, both of which are outside this quirky little universe I refer to. Rather the area is a U-shape, with one leg being the north end of Kootenay Lake and the little communities of Argenta, Meadow Creek, and Kaslo. The other leg is the winding and hippie-bucolic Slocan Valley and its communities of Vallican, Winlaw, and New Denver. The bottom of the U is the West Arm of the Kootenay River. Nelson, which revels in a kind of permanent 1960s time warp, is the nexus and nerve centre of this U.

In the 1950s, long before the Vietnam war started, disaffected Quakers from Southern California, searching for a more satisfying existence, made their way north. They settled along the steep shores of the pristine North Arm of Kootenay Lake. Then, in the middle and late 1960s, the Slocan Valley became a destination for draft dodgers. Information about this obscure valley made its way to places like Sacramento and Minneapolis by way of various support groups — the Fellowship of Reconciliation, the Quakers, Students for A Democratic Society, and others. This strange and remarkable geographical connection was partly due to the sense of solidarity and trust in the anti-war community at the time.

If some lonely American twenty-year-old 1A fugitive-to-be wandered into a Quaker meeting and asked where he should go in Canada, and the answer was the Slocan Valley, that's where he went, no questions asked. Other than where it was and how to get there.

For draft dodgers, the Slocan had two strong selling points. The first was cheap land, since the antiwar activity of the 1960s was partly political protest, and partly a back-to-the-land movement. The valley's second selling point was the Doukhobors. A religious sect that had been persecuted in their home country of Russia, the Doukhobors enlisted the support of the great novelist Leo Tolstoy to emigrate *en masse* to Canada. Arriving in the early 1900s, the Doukhobors settled mainly in Saskatchewan, but a large number of them subsequently moved on to the Slocan Valley and nearby Castlegar. The Doukhobors embodied the very lifestyle that hippies and draft dodgers dreamed of: pacifism, small-scale agriculture, self reliance, and a tradition of communal living. The Doukhobors and the draft dodgers never interacted extensively, except during peace marches, but they made comfortable neighbours.

So, the draft dodgers settled into the Slocan, adding their quota of quirks to an already quirky valley. For the more affluent, the Volkswagen van was the favoured mode of transportation, to be followed by the Toyota Tercel. The rest hitchhiked. For housing, they built yurts, geodesic domes, or funky, Hobbit-like cottages tucked in under the cedar trees. For work, they started organic gardens and orchards, worked in local sawmills, or built furniture. Some supplemented their income with small marijuana plantations. A few were fortunate to have inheritances or stipends, and didn't have to scrabble for a living in the permanently anemic

Slocan economy. At first, these new immigrants made only infrequent and reluctant trips to the bustling megalopolis of Nelson, which had parking metres, several stoplights, and nearly ten thousand people. But the pull of the Organic Food Co-op, the movie theatre, the town's famously hardcore coffee shops, and the occasional real job was strong. So some fell into Nelson's orbit, but retained their valley roots.

I happened to be walking Nelson's downtown Baker Street with a friend when some tourists stopped us and asked directions to the Slocan Valley. I turned to my friend, who lived in the valley. He stroked his long beard, looked down at his handmade sandals, and finally replied, "The Slocan Valley is really more of a concept than it is a place," and then walked on.

My arrival in Nelson was more or less accidental, because of a forestry job. It was only later that I realized how ironically appropriate the choice of location actually was. As I got to know people in the area, a few self-identified themselves as ex-Americans; others did so unconsciously, by untamable accents. But most, curiously, chose to blend in. This was completely counter to the usual "American Abroad" stereotype. Here was an area with the highest per-capita concentration of draft dodgers and ex-Americans, living in a country that goes out of its way to encourage ethnic and national origin identification, and yet these people remained a virtually invisible demographic. Not so other local groups; in the true Canadian multicultural spirit, Nelson boasts an Italian Club, a Francophone society, a German fraternity, and so on. These various ethnic groups vie with each other for the best float in the summer parade. But the Americans, uncharacteristically, melted right into the general population, and the draft dodgers, in particular, chose to remain almost completely anonymous.

I guess I had more or less done the same. My experience of living abroad had honed my linguistic ear, and assimilation into Canadian ways and speech patterns was straightforward. US West Coast accents are not strong to begin with, so only the keenest students of accents could identify my American origins.

The US invasion of Iraq in 2002 shook the anonymous complacency that I and many of my ex-American, war-resister colleagues had slipped into. As if suddenly re-living a long-forgotten bad dream, we heard the same bellicose and simplistic statements from President Bush and his aides, and we saw the same grainy footage of air strikes, troop mobilizations, and body bags. The long shadow of Vietnam lay over Iraq. It was a sick, miasmic feeling.

At this juncture another American arrived in Nelson. Isaac Romano was several years younger than the Vietnam generation, but was fully immersed in peace issues. He made a proposal to create a small sculpture in one of the city parks that would be a monument to draft dodgers and to the Canadians that helped them. City Council, no doubt busy with other things, agreed to the proposal. That was the beginning of a fascinating media spiral. No one knows how, but the item found its way from City Council minutes to the right-wing news networks in the US, which seized upon it as proof of Canada's subversive nature. Hate mail began to arrive. Vietnam veteran groups wrote to the Nelson City Council, threatening a boycott of all American tourism to Nelson. The mayor instantly reversed his position, saying that he had no intention of allowing such a memorial on city property. But the cat was out of the bag, and the American media had discovered Nelson. The *New York Times* sent a journalist, who dubbed Nelson "Resisterville". In classic fashion, once one media outlet does a story, it suddenly becomes news for every other outlet. The *Los Angeles Times* then sent their guy to Nelson, and in turn, the *LA Times* article caused the *Vancouver Sun* to send their guy to do a story.

Isaac didn't back off. Sensing the growing interest in the war-resistance issue, he and his colleagues shifted their focus from the memorial to holding a reunion for Vietnam-era draft dodgers as well as Vietnam veterans. True to form, the Doukhobors lent their support, and the "Our Way Home" event was held in a Doukhobor meeting hall in Castlegar, near Nelson, in the summer of 2006. At first I was dubious about attending; the ongoing media interest could easily turn the event into a superficial circus. But curiosity got the best of me, and I went.

As we filed into a large room, I scanned for familiar faces amongst the forty of us and saw a few locals, but most were from away. I realized that if I were ever to acknowledge a peer group, this would have to be it. Mostly, they were Americans who had moved permanently to Canada, and there were others who had stayed for a time but had gone back after President Jimmy Carter's 1977 amnesty. There were a few deserters, some who had spent time in military jails, a few that were imprisoned as civilians for refusing the draft, a few Vietnam veterans, and a few local peace activists. There were also wives of draft dodgers and — I was surprised by this — a few American women who had come to Canada on their own because of the War. I was struck by how old, and also how young these people were. Like most of us, I see aging in the faces and bodies of other people but less so in myself. The exoskeleton might be sixty, but the self-image was still cast in the age of tie-dye and war protests. But I had to acknowledge that for sixty-year-olds, most were in pretty good shape. Perhaps dissent slows the aging process.

The standard round of introductions quickly broke through into a profoundly meaningful experience when one of the first to speak, a woman, began pouring her heart out. She cried quietly for a moment, composed herself, and then finished a painful account of the loss of her father. She had left Minnesota for Canada during the Vietnam War, and her father had disowned her. Years later she returned home — uninvited — to see her father on his deathbed. She was hoping against hope for some kind of reconciliation. The hospital room encounter lasted less than one minute. His only, and last, words to her were: "Don't ever darken my door."

The woman's story acted as a kind of cathartic, the lancing of a communal boil. The speakers following skipped the usual superficialities and spoke also of pain, isolation, and moral anguish. There was no self-glorification here; even those whose force of commitment landed them in prison spoke plainly and without ego. Each story was intensely personal, and yet it almost seemed like we were talking in third person, dissecting the experiences of someone else.

In the two hours that it took for everyone to tell their stories, the scattered flotsam of anti-war experiences merged into a long-delayed, spiritual convalescence, and a collective vindication of our solitary convictions. A fascinating dynamic was created by the two Vietnam vets that attended. From opposite banks of an uncrossable Rubicon, we recognized that our respective levels of personal commitment and sacrifice were somehow on par with each other.

I am profoundly suspicious of group processes, particularly the temporary and false intimacy that workshops and conferences can sometimes generate. But this opening up and reaching out was absolutely genuine. Fortunately, the facilitator was smart enough to recognize the enormity of these personal stories, and scrapped his agenda, which had allocated fifteen minutes for the introduction process. This was our moment.

I spoke of my own situation, of how the complex serendipity of the Conscientious Objection appeal process and the Draft Lottery meant I was not forced to go to Canada as a draft dodger, but how political conviction and anger led my wife and me to choose Canada voluntarily, as draft and Vietnam war rejectors. I spoke of losing my relationship with my father, far less crushing than what the Minnesota woman had dealt with, but very painful nonetheless. I spoke of my commitment to Canada's ideals as the peacekeeper nation, and my concern over the rapid erosion of that honourable role. And finally I spoke of the odd, but somehow logical, personal transition I had made, from war resister to rural extension agent to ecologist. And, I was proud to say, I was still swimming upstream, and still facing west.

Photo by Ivan Gayton

DON GAYTON is the author of five books of non-fiction: *The Wheatgrass Mechanism*, *Landscapes of the Interior*, *Kokanee*, *Interwoven Wild* and *Okanagan Odyssey*. His writing has garnered several awards, including the US National Outdoor Book Award, the Canadian Science Writer's award and two shortlistings for the British Columbia Book Awards. He was the Roderick Haig-Brown Writer in Residence at the University of Victoria in 2009. He lives in Summerland, BC, where he works as an ecologist. Gayton is married, with six children.